CW00498180

# TO THE BITTER END

## NICKY SHEARSBY

SRL Publishing Ltd

SRL Publishing Ltd
London
www.srlpublishing.co.uk

First published worldwide by SRL Publishing in 2022

Copyright © NICKY SHEARSBY 2022

The author has reserved the right to be identified as the author of this work
which has been asserted by them in accordance with the Copyright, Designs,
and Patents Act 1988.

ISBN: 978-1915073-02-0

1 3 5 7 9 10 8 6 4 2

This book is sold subject to the condition that it shall not, by way of trade or
otherwise, be reproduced or transmitted in any form or by any means,
electronic, mechanical, photocopying or otherwise, without the prior
permission of the publishers.

SRL Publishing and Pen Nib logo are registered trademarks owned by SRL
Publishing Ltd.

This book is a work of fiction. Names, characters, places, and incidents are
either a product of the author's imagination or are used fictitiously. Any
resemblance to actual people, living or dead, events or locales, is entirely
coincidental.

A CIP catalogue record for this book is available from the British Library

SRL Publishing is a Climate Positive publisher removing more carbon
emissions than it emits.

*How far would you go to protect the people you love? Would you be prepared to change who you are, in order to serve justice on those you felt deserved it? Be careful what you wish for. You may find yourself taking things*
*to the bitter end.*

*Also by Nicky Shearsby*

THE FLANIGAN FILES

#1 Beyond the Veil

GREEN MONSTER DUOLOGY

#2 Black Widow
#1 Green Monsters

# Chapter 1

It had been a day like all the rest. Another humdrum mid-week working day whereby nothing significant had happened that would make me believe for one moment that I might remember it at all. I drove home after an incredibly intense gym workout, singing along to songs on the radio I barely remembered the words to, not caring that I probably sounded utterly out of tune and slightly erratic. I tapped the steering wheel in time to the beat and performed loudly within the confines of my car, noticing nothing of how I must have looked to any passer-by, nodding my head with the music, the sight of me a probable source of amusement for all.

Although my usual daily routine consisted of eight tedious hours that banded together to form my working day, my mind was permanently elsewhere these days. My thoughts were set firmly on a future unconfirmed by even the most psychic of positive thinkers. It was a future I had convinced myself could be achievable if I focused enough, simply committing my mind and body to the potential outcome it may just afford me.

Motocross was a sport that had given me something I hadn't expected to experience over the last couple of years. I felt alive when I was out on the track because I was completely and utterly free to be the person I enjoyed being when I was amid an adrenaline-fueled race. It was exhilarating, and as time passed and I became better at it, motocross became the one thing I found myself thinking consistently about. The mere notion that I could swap my humdrum existence for something far better kept me motivated to the point where I was pushing my body beyond the limitations of normal acceptance.

I ignored health warnings from everyone around me, including medics and personal trainers, because as far as I was concerned, my success would be the one thing that would make all my hard work worthwhile. I was pushing my body hard and did not for a single moment allow myself to believe that this elusive future could be anything other than well within my grasp.

Looking back, it seems almost surreal to think how quickly time escapes us, and the confident nineteen-year-old I had been at that point now seems a distant memory that I have almost forgotten. Some people say that life is made up of milestones, collections of memories that take us back to the times when we were most happy. For me, it was the simple feeling of exhilaration moments before a race began. It reflected a time when I had no commitments, no worries, and no fear of a future uncertain. I loved motocross. With no responsibilities and absolutely no regard for anything other than being alive, it is a time in my life that I will always reserve a special place.

I was oblivious to the drive home that night, focused only on how I could get my body into the best physical shape of my life. I knew I needed to concentrate hard over the upcoming winter months to ready myself for what I hoped would be the season to see me sign with Honda and begin earning a professional living as a fully insured motocross sportsman. More to the point, it meant I could quit my nine-to-five job for good and finally live the life I'd been dreaming of for so long. Don't get me wrong, I didn't entirely dislike my job. I was actually quite good at what I did. My hard-working ethics ensured that my boss, Andrew, expressed fairness towards me that meant if I needed time off for any reason, he was happy to extend me the courtesy.

I was a young lad, lucky to have a job at all at that point and grateful simply to be earning a wage. But I had unwittingly found myself working as a trainee electrical engineer for a back street firm on a tiny industrial estate on the outskirts of Milborough town, where I lived in the Midlands. Despite having left school at sixteen with little in the way of any actual education, mine wasn't a job I aspired to do for the rest of my life. I was determined, focused, seemingly invincible, and to be quite honest, genuinely happy to be pushing towards an amazingly bright future I'd created in my head. I honestly felt I could make anything happen, simply unable to allow myself to consider any other outcome. I smiled when I thought about how proud Rebecca would be of my forthcoming achievements, knowing that all the training I'd devoted my time to was about to pay off. I was excited and eager to dream of a future unknown, and I knew that I could make anything happen if I worked hard enough.

I was still feeling the buzz of my heightened sense of awareness as I settled down in front of the television with a large plate of chicken salad balancing on my knee. I flicked channels with half-interested intention as I tried to avoid unsavoury glances from my dog, Bella. She had been out for her walk and already had a belly full of leftover chicken that I'd mixed with her dog biscuits.

'Lie down, please.' I gave Bella a single nod as she continued to stare at me with her huge brown eyes that attempted to throw me into submission. She grumbled, licked her lips, and begrudgingly laid her head on my foot with a thud.

I ate my meal in relative peace, tidied away my plate,

took a well-needed shower, and cleaned the kitchen to a semi-satisfactory state that I hoped would pass as acceptable to any potential visitor. It was getting quite late by this time, so when I heard a knock at the front door, I was a little unnerved and irritated to have been disturbed. Bella instantly ran to the window, barking her usual warnings to any passing stranger that she was in no mood for anyone's company at such a late hour. Despite her aggressive-looking German Sheppard appearance, her soft and gentle nature meant she would have been no actual match for any serious would-be intruder.

I smiled at the thought as I took her gently by the collar and guided her into the kitchen, closing the door behind me and trying to ignore her tiny whimpers and attempts to reaffirm my attention. It's funny to think how quickly an elevated mood can alter because in the few seconds it took to walk the length of the hallway and unlock the front door, my calm exhilaration had shifted to one of uncertainty and fear.

I opened the door to the sight of my next-door neighbour standing somewhat uneasily inside my unlit porch. Her slipper-covered feet were soaking up the damp October air as she pulled her dressing gown firmly around her body in an attempt to avoid shivering in the cold.

'Hi, Jen. Is everything okay?' I asked. She had a look on her face that immediately caused an uneasy sensation to develop in my stomach. She actually looked as if she was apprehensive about something yet didn't quite know how to express it.

'Oh, Craig, thank God,' she sounded relieved to see me standing in front of her as if fearing I might not be home at all. 'Grace has just called. She asked if I could get you to drive straight over to the flat now. I'm sorry it's so late.'

I shared a house with some friends from the motocross club, and as we couldn't afford a telephone of our own at that time; if anyone needed to contact us, they would simply call next door. Jen was a good neighbour, and the arrangement had always suited us well. It was something she never usually minded. Having little in the way of any family herself, she was often glad of the distraction. Yet I now felt slightly guilty that my poor neighbour, an already ageing woman herself, had probably been forced out of her bed at this hour, purely to contact me. And urgently, it seemed.

'Why would Grace call so late?' I glanced at the clock in the hallway, noting it had just turned ten-thirty and wondering what could have been so important that poor old Jen had been disturbed because of it. I hadn't spoken to either of the girls that day. I would usually drive around to their flat after work to say hi, but today I'd wanted to fit in a session at the gym and subsequently hadn't allowed enough time to do both. My attention was now firmly caught by the notion that something terrible had happened to two of my closest friends and my chicken salad threatened to make a fresh appearance. 'Did she tell you what was wrong?' Something didn't feel right, and Jen noticed the look of confusion on my face as she smoothed a hair out of her own.

'No, I'm afraid she wouldn't tell me what the problem was over the phone, Craig. She just said she'd explain everything to you when you get over there.' It was evident by the look on her face that Jen had sensed something in Grace's tone, and it worried me. Grace would rarely need to call the house anyway and would only do so if something required my urgent attention. Something had happened, and it must have been serious, judging by the expression on my neighbour's face. A knot began to form in my stomach as I stood in my hallway that night, slightly unsure how to react to a message that I wasn't even certain signified anything consequential at all. Yet I couldn't help wondering if there was indeed nothing for me to worry about, why had Grace not simply passed Jen a message or called at a more reasonable hour and prevented the panic that was rising in the back of my throat?

'Is Rebecca okay? Did Grace mention anything to you about Rebecca?' I had no idea what I expected to hear, and I could not understand why my brain was going into overdrive. Jen shook her head. It was clear she genuinely didn't know much at all. In a daze, I grabbed my car keys from the shelf in the hallway and left Bella whining softly in the kitchen behind me. I didn't even give myself time to check that she was okay before I slammed the front door shut. 'Thanks, Jen,' I called back nervously.

'Drive carefully,' I heard her mutter as I clambered hastily into my car.

Thoughts I could not control raced through my mind as seemingly every set of traffic lights between Somerton Village and Milborough attempted to slow my progress, mocking my rising fear with their infuriating red tinge. What had been so vital that Grace had felt the need to launch me into this uneasy state? Surely she would have known how I would react to such a none descript message? I thought about Bella for a moment, guilty that I had left in such a hurry, yet knowing she would be fine in the kitchen with her water bowl and bed for comfort. I was glad that I had already taken her out to do her business. She was a good dog. She would be okay for a couple of hours.

\*\*\*

As busy as our lives had become in recent years, I always made an effort to call in on my friends after work on the days when I wasn't at the gym. I would often share a meal with them and take a shower at their flat to save time when I got home, so the fact that I hadn't spoken to either of the girls tonight only added to my increasing anxiety levels. As they began working away more often with their modelling work, the little time we were able to spend together became incredibly precious to the three of us. Subsequently, we treasured any opportunity we had to catch up with each other's lives. It didn't matter where in the world Rebecca was at any given time or how obscure the time differences were because she would always call me to say hello. I would often receive a phone call at four in the morning from some exotic location. The long-distance charges must have cost her a fortune.

Those country roads seemed to stretch on forever that night, and by the time I had finally arrived at the girls flat, my nerves were already in tatters to the point I considered the idea of throwing up. I parked carelessly on the curb outside, my hands shaking slightly even though I still had no idea why I had been summoned in such a hurry. The girl's cars were parked on the driveway, and at first glance, everything appeared completely normal. I scrambled to unlock the buildings main door, unable to stop the tremble in my hands and missing the lock twice before I actually managed to get the key into the hole. As I raced up the stairs taking two at a time, I simply could have had no idea what I was about to witness.

Grace met me in the doorway as I attempted to barge unceremoniously into the flat, oblivious at that moment to everything around me, including her. She placed a trembling hand on my arm to stop me. I hadn't even registered that her face was pure white. It was as if she had experienced a terrifying ordeal that she had absolutely no idea how to process.

'Grace?' I asked, seeing a painful look behind her eyes that I couldn't have possibly understood right then. 'What's happened? Are you okay?' Grace shook her head as the alarming look in her eyes told its own story. Her cheeks had an ashen grey tinge, and she was biting her bottom lip with an absent abandonment I couldn't quite fathom. 'Grace? Talk to me. For God's sake, what's happened?'

I placed my own hands onto her shoulders in some random attempt to make sense of this extraordinary situation I had found myself in, panic steadily threatening to tip me over the proverbial edge at any moment. She shook her head yet offered no immediate answer. It genuinely seemed that she didn't know how to deal with my presence once I was actually standing in front of her. I pulled my arm free and pushed by her, unsure as to what I was about to find and terrified by her unusual silence. As I swung open the door into the living room, the sight that met me quite literally stopped me dead in my tracks and is one I will never forget.

\*\*\*

I couldn't exactly see her face initially, and yet I immediately noticed how Rebecca was curled up against the far edge of the sofa. Her knees were tucked under her chin, trembling like a child forced to endure one of the worst nightmares anyone could imagine. Her hair was damp as if she had just stepped out of the shower, glued to the side of her face and covering her eyes so that I was unable to see her correctly. She was sobbing uncontrollably, her body trembling and shaking, nothing but a towel wrapped around her goose-bumped body. I stepped a couple of feet towards her and quietly called her name. I could not understand anything of what I was witnessing and wondering what the hell had happened to make her behave in this way.

Rebecca flinched, and for a moment, I genuinely thought she had failed to recognise me. She would not even look at me. She was like a feral animal, terrified and anxious, desperate to be left alone to process events unknown to the rest of the world. It was at complete odds with the person Rebecca usually was. Nothing ever bothered her. Not ever, and if for any reason something did happen to upset her, I was always the first person she turned to when something was wrong. And my God, this felt wrong. This felt very wrong indeed.

'Rebecca?' I simply could not understand what was going on, my words escaping my mouth like a whispered strangle that didn't sound like my voice at all. I was barely able to comprehend the sound of my own words or the appalling image of the person sitting in front of me. Slowly she turned her tear-stained face in my direction, careful to keep her chin pressed towards her chest so she could avoid eye contact with me altogether. I stared at her for a moment, wondering why she was hesitant to look at me until the realisation of what I was witnessing began to sink in. I took in a sharp breath and staggered backwards, accidentally knocking Grace sideways, who was now standing trembling behind me. I spun around to look at her, desperate for an explanation that wasn't immediately forthcoming.

I could not believe what I was seeing. Rebecca's face was swollen, covered in a mixture of dried blood and smudged makeup that made her features look slightly inhuman and out of proportion. Her top lip was three times its natural size, and her left eye had an angry purple tinge, almost entirely closed shut due to the sheer amount of swelling surrounding it. For a moment, I hardly recognised her. Tears were running freely down both cheeks, and she was clutching her arms so tightly across her chest she had caused her skin to turn white where she had deliberately pressed her nails into her own flesh.

I turned again to Grace, who mirrored the same look of total shock on her face as my own. 'Jesus Christ, Grace, what the hell happened?' I somehow managed to ask the question, yet my terrified voice was unable to comprehend anything I was beholding, my confusion and anger growing with each ticking second of the clock on the wall. When Grace opened her mouth to speak, I froze, dreading the words that were about to emerge from her lips. 'Someone had better start talking and fast.' I tried to keep my tone as calm as I could muster the strength, desperate for this silence to end and relieve me of this excruciating suspense that was building like an impending bomb explosion. I glanced between the two girls, frantic to know what had happened and terrified of what I was about to hear.

Grace took a breath. 'I came home and found them both in here, Craig.' She was choking back tears and shock of her own. She pointed to the rug at her feet that looked as if someone had battled with it and the rug had lost.

'Found who?' I couldn't help yelling at Grace as I jerked my head sharply towards her, accidentally making Rebecca flinch again in the process. By this time, my heart was seriously pounding, threatening to burst a vessel at any moment. Rebecca hadn't spoken a single word since my arrival, and I desperately needed to know what the hell was going on. She looked up at me then, and for a brief moment, I spotted a distinct look of terror in her eyes. She knew. She knew exactly what I would do when I discovered what had happened here tonight. Grace leaned in and hugged me. Hard. I threw my arms around her, hoping I could ease her pain, even for a moment. She looked so fragile, so frightened. 'Will someone please tell me what the hell is going on?'

'Ryan and Justin.' Grace spat those names as if they were acid that burned her.

'What about them?' As I yelled the words, Rebecca involuntarily cried out and cowered further towards the edge of her sofa as if the very thought of those men were enough to send her into a fresh panic. 'Please don't tell me they did this to her?' I instinctively moved forward to comfort her, but she pulled away from me sharply. It was as if she didn't want me anywhere near her, tears still falling from her unrecognisable features that only added to her somewhat swollen appearance.

I slumped onto the arm of the sofa and automatically leaned over to gently touch her hand. I only wanted to let her know that I was here and that she was safe, but she let out a tiny cry of fear and curled up even tighter into the corner of the chair, pulling her knees into her face so that I couldn't see it. She had never acted that way towards me before, not ever. I felt physically sick.

'They were in here when I came home.' Grace was sobbing now, uncontrollably, like a small child reliving a nightmare. She was standing in the middle of the room trembling, with seemingly no idea at all of what she should actually be doing. 'They had Rebecca on the floor. They were holding her down. Oh, Craig, it was horrible.' Rebecca became uncontrollable as her sobs began to engulf the room, the sound of her friend's words cutting into her as if she had just been stabbed in the heart. I sat perched on the arm of that sofa like a helpless child trying to understand what I was hearing, painful words hitting me in the chest like a rogue missile at the sudden implementation of what had happened.

'I beg your pardon?' I wasn't even sure the voice I was hearing was my own. How could it have been Ryan and Justin who had done this to Rebecca? Surely I had heard wrong. I felt a lump rise in the back of my throat and, for a moment, considered the idea of vomiting. The realisation of what had been done to my best friend was suddenly undeniable, and I took a deep breath that my lungs didn't seem able to deal with. I got to my feet in an attempt to steady my now jelly-like legs, struggling to maintain any composure whatsoever. Every beat of my heart felt as if an express train was hitting me in the chest over and over; every vein in my body pulsating and threatened to burst open at any moment. I could barely keep myself upright. Jesus Christ, no. What the hell had they done? The question itself seemed ridiculous even as it formed in my mind because I already knew exactly what they had done.

'Tell me exactly what happened.' I had to literally force myself to speak. The mere idea of actually knowing the whole story was simply unacceptable to my brain.

'They ran when they saw me.' Grace tried to offer some kind of explanation that even she couldn't understand. 'Ryan pushed me over on his way out of the door.' She was clutching her arm, and although at the time I hadn't given it much thought, it was actually quite severely bruised. 'Bastard,' she spat as I placed my hand over hers.

I forced myself to look at Rebecca properly then as if it were the first time I was able to see her, my eyes needing to take in the scene in its entirety yet my brain unwilling to accept what I knew had happened here tonight. I had never seen anything like it in my entire life, and to be quite honest, I genuinely had no idea what to do. They had made a complete mess of her. My head was spinning. I couldn't think, I couldn't breathe, and I simply couldn't take in what I was observing. She looked so vulnerable, so fragile. So far removed from the happy, carefree girl she had been when we had first met. I remembered that day well.

We had been merely six years old, just kids looking for friendship in the most unlikely of places. She had the cheekiest smile I had ever seen. It was the first thing that had struck me about her and something I had always loved. She was always laughing, with a natural bounce in her persona that made everyone around her feel somehow happy and alive. She was one of the most vibrant people I had ever known, yet looking at her now, I couldn't imagine anything even remotely able to put a smile back on her face.

12

She had this incredible infectious energy that lit up a room. It's strange to explain it adequately without sounding clichéd, but even as a child, her manner and attitude were far beyond her years. She always made the best out of any situation, never letting anything get her down for long. If I were to describe Rebecca in a single sentence, it would be to say that she always lived life to the fullest. She would often say that life is for living, and anyone who had the good fortune to be in her company would quickly become infected with her unfeigned lust for life. It was an attribute that was to grow as she did, but looking at her now, sitting frozen to the spot, half-naked and shaking like a small, terrified child, I had no idea how to comfort her or make this pain go away. I couldn't take it in. At that moment, I felt my entire life come crashing down around me. How the hell could I fix this?

# Chapter 2

Within the time it took me to realise what had happened to Rebecca, my day had successfully changed from enthusiasm for my own future to total shock and devastation for my best friend's suffering. As I stood in the middle of the girl's lounge room that night, a clock ticking in my ear and a distinct aroma of Rebecca's perfume catching my senses, I knew without hesitation precisely what needed to be done for me to fix this.

'Where are you going?' Grace spun round to face me as I headed towards the door, a knowing look on my face that would have been plain for anyone to see, yet one I didn't fully understand myself right then. She attempted to grab my jacket but misjudged her timing, managing to break a nail as she caught the edge of my belt in her haste. We looked at each other for a brief moment, our worlds colliding in agony. Grace knew exactly where I was going, and we both knew there wasn't a damned thing she could have done to stop me.

'Where the hell do you think?' I frantically pulled my car keys from my pocket, not even caring that I had managed to tear the lining of my trousers in the process. If I had to stop and evaluate the situation, I would probably have been unsure of my exact intentions. However, I knew I was more than ready, if needed, to literally kill the bastards that had done this to Rebecca. I visualised standing in front of them, strangling them with my bare hands and enjoying every moment of it. How dare they think they could get away with what they had done to her tonight?

Did they seriously believe they could escape justice with no repercussions from me whatsoever? Anger building in my gut, I was beyond furious, and no words from Grace would have been able to calm me at that point even had she attempted to do so.

'Don't you dare-' Grace tried to step in front of me, to prevent me from doing something that, in her opinion, would be completely and utterly stupid.

'Get out of my way.'

'No-'

'Craig. Please.' The words escaped Rebecca's mouth as if simply saying my name was a task too exhausting for her to undertake, emerging as a tiny whimper that hurt my ears. 'Don't do it. Please.' I could tell she was trying as hard as she could to hold back her tears, a desperate longing in her plea that I was entirely unprepared for. It floored me. I stopped short of yanking the front door off its hinges, my hand pulsating with fury as I stood holding onto the handle as if my life depended on it, Grace standing between me and my impending revenge mission.

For a moment, I didn't quite know what to do for the best. I knew without a shred of doubt that I could not let this go, and yet I probably should not have been surprised that it was Rebecca's words that had actually prevented me from leaving the flat and most likely, if I'm honest, causing even more chaos in the process. She always seemed to know exactly how to diffuse my anguish, although tonight, I seriously did not know if it would be enough.

Rebecca's words and terrified tone were more than I could stand. I turned around and shakily walked the few feet across the carpet towards her, desperate to take away the pain I knew in my heart I could never actually do. I couldn't believe how unsteady my legs felt. The look on her face was soul-destroying. The way her bottom lip quivered, displaying only a glimpse of the agony she must have been experiencing right then, both mentally and physically.

I stopped short of placing my hand against her arm for fear of the reaction I might receive if I did. My mind trembled with the image of what they had done to her. I wanted to scream. I wanted to hold her tight and tell her that no one would ever again be able to hurt her as long as I had breath in my body. But instead, I stood in front of her like a small boy, unsure what to do for the best or how I could possibly make any of this better at all.

'Have you called the police?' I could barely control my voice as I asked the question that had been aimed towards Grace yet seemed to float out into the room's void. I was not able to take my eyes off Rebecca for a second.

'Yes, of course, I did.' I could sense Grace was irritated by the fact that I even had to ask. She was pacing up and down, although I could not bring myself to look in her direction. I did not want to see the confirmation in Grace's eyes that the events she had just revealed to me were actually real. 'They should be on their way, actually.' I heard her slide down onto one of Rebecca's oversized beanbags on the floor. Obviously, she was as unsure of what she was actually meant to be doing as I was.

I slumped onto the carpet in front of Rebecca, desperate to tell her that everything would be okay, yet knew in my heart that none of this was okay at all. 'Hey, Bex.' I was unable to keep my voice steady as I clumsily attempted to try and calm my friend. To let her know that I had it all under control, despite the fact I knew I was convincing no one. 'What happened?' The question itself sounded stupid before it had even left my lips. As if I needed to ask. I knew exactly what had happened. It was obvious. It took all the strength I had not to break down in front of her there and then. The mere thought of her suffering like that was more than my mind could conclude. She had started to rock gently back and forth, still clutching her arms to her body as if she were afraid her insides would fall out if she didn't. Neither myself nor Grace could get any sense out of her, our efforts to calm her going unheeded for quite some time. All we could do was helplessly sit and listen to her heart-breaking sobs as she struggled to steady her own breath or comprehend the events of the evening. Rebecca was locked inside her own memories, the terrifying ordeal of the last couple of hours too much for any of us to cope with.

***

Rebecca's boyfriend had never been the type of person you would want to be in the company of for long, but even I couldn't have suspected he might actually be capable of something like this. Looking back, I guess I knew the signs had always been there. He had a manner about him I could never quite put my finger on. There was always something in his tone, a silent arrogance that had never sat well with me. It was no secret that we didn't like each other, and Justin was no better, being the type of person who would gladly hang on to every word Ryan said. He was a typical bullies henchman, obviously wanting to come across to any would-be onlooker as untouchable and important. Left to his own devices, Justin might not have been so bad, I guess, had he not become involved with the drugs that Ryan callously pushed onto innocent people for his own gain. For that reason alone, I hated him as much as I hated Ryan.

Ryan only ever came to the flat to see Rebecca when he wanted money, sex, or both, and I would always make damned sure that if he turned up whilst I was there, I would make a hasty retreat and leave. I avoided being in his presence if I didn't have to and genuinely had no idea what Rebecca actually saw in him. I had known for quite some time that he was insanely jealous of the relationship I had with Rebecca, and this only fuelled the hatred he had for me.

However, it was lucky for me that she didn't give a damn about what other people thought. She had always made it clear that she would never jeopardise the friendship we shared, not for him or anyone else. We had grown up together, and if he didn't like it, it was simply too bad. I admired Rebecca for that. Now though, as I contemplated what he had potentially done to her tonight, I wondered about all those times when I had previously left her alone with him, and it made me feel sick to my stomach. Maybe I should have tried harder to get her to see him for what he really was? Yet how on earth could I have known that he would turn on her in this way?

It may have been because we had no one else in our lives, but Rebecca and I had grown incredibly close over the course of a few short years. Cuddling up together on the sofa was normal for us, and Rebecca's legs and arms were usually draped around mine somehow as if we only shared one body between us. It must have looked rather comical to outsiders because I swear most people couldn't often tell where Rebecca ended and I began. Yet, I never once stopped to consider what any of that might look like to those around us. We were always messing around together, tickling each other and play fighting like children who had no cares in the world to concern ourselves with. It was a commonplace and innocent thing for us to do.

We were both naturally flirty and teased each other unobtrusively whenever we had the chance. Yet it never entered our heads to become anything more to each other than the very best friends we already were. We were closer than any brother and sister could have been, and I loved the dynamics of our relationship. It was the way I wanted it to always remain. I was extremely protective of her and could not understand how she had dated someone like Ryan. I could never quite think for the life of me what she saw in him.

I don't know why, but I have always felt more comfortable in the company of females than men. I guess that is how I came to be surrounded by the women I classed as friends. The guys I hung around with tended to spend most of their time talking about themselves and how they could impress potential conquests, their egos far more prominent than anything they possessed in their trousers. I would often watch my male friends chatting up girls in bars with tales of a life that was not their own. It was impressive at just how far they would go to make themselves look better than they actually were, and despite being male myself, I could not believe the lies that poured openly out of their mouths simply to increase their chances of having sex.

There had never been any inhibitions between us, and I had lost count of how many times Rebecca had emerged from the bathroom totally naked while I had been obliviously watching some random rubbish on the television. We were so comfortable around each other that there had never been any sexual tension between us at all. Everything we did felt completely normal to us, and for the most part, we could do and say pretty much whatever we liked in front of each other without embarrassment or fear of repercussion.

I am the first to admit that we flirted on occasion. Actually, we flirted most of the time if I'm being completely candid. It was just the way we were. Our friends would often tease us about the so-called sexual tension they assumed they could see between us. Yet, I had never experienced that at all. It never once crossed my mind to take our relationship beyond the friendship I had come to depend on.

To me, we were simply perfect exactly the way we were. I had my own life, Rebecca had hers, and somewhere in the middle, we came together to enjoy one of the most precious relationships that I had ever known up to that point in my life. As far as I was concerned, Rebecca was my sister, my best friend, and the one person I always knew would be there for me in life, no matter what might happen along the way. It felt good for Rebecca to need me, and deep down, I genuinely needed Rebecca to need me. I couldn't imagine not having that undeniable connection to her because it was the only way I was ever going to survive this thing called life. Without her, I honestly felt that I would be alone. Now, however, it felt as if I had totally let her down. There was no way I could allow my brain to consider any other notion.

*** 

By the time the police had finally arrived, Grace had twice more prevented me from leaving the flat, the only thing on my mind being pure and unadulterated revenge. The thought of those two alone with Rebecca made me sicker than I had ever felt in my life, and although the details had not yet been directly disclosed, it didn't take a genius to work out what they had done to her. 'Don't you dare,' Grace warned, noting the look of cold calculation on my face as I glanced towards the door on more than one occasion. 'The last thing any of us want is you up on an assault charge.'

'Oh, I don't want to assault them, Grace,' I spat towards her, not caring how bitter my tone sounded or how angry I came across. 'I want to kill the bastards.' And I honestly meant it. I meant it more than I had realised until I uttered the words aloud. Until that point in my life, my thoughts on hatred had been somewhat neutral because I was far too busy enjoying my time on this earth to worry about such a strong and extreme emotion. People and their so-called viewpoints hardly bothered me. I had never taken the time to consider too much about how other people think outside my own group of friends because my friends were my world, and it didn't matter about what anyone else thought. I was always perfectly happy to admit, however, that there were indeed specific individuals that I didn't exactly like, Ryan being just one of them, but hate is a powerful word and one that I never really fully considered. Until now, that was. Now I was entirely consumed by the concept.

Without warning, my brain was overtaken by an insane desire to commit murder, fuelled by a need for vengeance that seemed to emerge from nowhere. I was not even ashamed of my thinking. I simply could not consider a thing beyond my own desperate need to punch the living daylights out of them both until there was nothing left of them apart from pulverised lumps of flesh that bore no resemblance to the people they once were.

It's hard to explain the feelings that engulf you when you find yourself faced with the devastating results of a vicious attack that has been aimed directly at someone you care deeply about. I am sure that anyone faced with these circumstances would react exactly the same way I did because you can never express how much anger you feel until it actually happens to you. And I have certainly learned that you can never judge a situation until you have seen things from a different point of view. I had promised Rebecca that I would always protect her, and I had failed. I would not fail to make things up to her. That much I did know.

***

Police are always professional in their approach, methodical and calculated, pretty much like my thinking seemed to be right then, but when two police officers entered the flat, the terror that arose in my gut at what they might say and how they would make Rebecca feel was more than I could stand. A young female officer took a seat on the opposite side of the sofa, being careful to give Rebecca the space she knew she needed, a look of sympathy in her manner that appeared as calm as her training had taught her to act.

'Hello there, sweetheart,' she said, taking out her radio and placing it carefully onto the coffee table in front of her, sliding several discarded magazines to one side. 'My name is WPC Manning. We're here to have a chat with you about what's happened here tonight. Is that okay with you?' Although it was obvious to everyone in the room what had happened, it was a formality that the police needed to go through to piece together the evening's actual events. They needed to record what had happened to Rebecca in the tiniest of detail for them to build a picture of the situation. I didn't know what I dreaded the most. Hearing the traumatised words that might come out of Rebecca's mouth or that she may not even be able to speak to them at all.

'Who called us?' It was the male police officers turn to speak as he glanced in turn towards myself and Grace. He had settled himself opposite his colleague in an old armchair that Rebecca had refused to throw out, no matter how much I protested.

'I did,' Grace offered, staring wildly at some random plastic keyring she was now holding in her hand and seemingly unable to acknowledge her own predicament. Rebecca glanced at me briefly, fresh tears welling in her eyes.

'It's okay, miss,' the female officer spoke again to Rebecca, her gentle manner not able to diffuse the situation we had unwittingly found ourselves entwined in. 'But we do need you to tell us in your own time exactly what happened. There really is no rush.' She attempted a weak smile but obviously noticed the pain that Rebecca was in because she looked away for a moment as if something had caught her attention.

When Rebecca spoke, her words came out as little more than broken sobs, and it took everything I had inside me to remain still. My brain was screaming at me to climb into my car and kick the very life out of them both. I wanted to kill them, and that is not a metaphor. How could any human being ever do this to another and feel nothing whatsoever about doing it? Without warning, Rebecca reached out and grabbed my hand. I couldn't tell if it were her way of trying to prevent me from leaving the flat or because she was terrified of how her own words would sound, but knowing she needed me right then was enough to make me stay precisely where I was.

'I was taking a shower,' she began, her throat creating involuntary hiccups as she slowly attempted to form the scene that had led to the sorry state she had found herself now in. 'I could hear someone in the flat and assumed it would either be Grace or Craig.' She nodded towards me, and the police officers scribbled notes in small, black books that I wanted to grab from their hands and tear into pieces. 'Because they both have keys,' she added as if to confirm that none of us would be ridiculous enough to break in. 'I called out, but no one answered, so I got out of the shower and came in here. I could see them both going through my drawers and cupboards, throwing things all over the place and making a total bloody mess in the process.' I glanced around, noticing that the flat was indeed in a terrible state with items strewn around the floor. I had only just realised.

'Who was this?' the male officer asked.

'Her ex and his mate,' I was barely able to control my reaction. I didn't even care if the police could sense my desire for revenge.

'Do these men have names?'

'Ryan Miller and Justin Anderson.' I felt my throat tighten as the words erupted from my lips. Rebecca flinched, and I squeezed her hand gently.

Rebecca was gestured to continue, and I sat statuesque as she explained how the evening had played out in forced detail. 'They demanded money, and when I told them to get out, they got angry with me.' Rebecca stopped, obviously terrified of having to say anything further.

'It's okay,' the female officer spoke calmly. 'Take your time.'

'They noticed I was only wearing a towel.' Rebecca closed her eyes. The swelling in her left eye was now so pronounced that I saw her flinch in pain.

'Justin grabbed me around the throat and ripped off my towel. He thought it was funny. That's when Ryan punched me in the face, and I fell to the floor. Justin was grabbing-' she paused for a moment. 'My breasts.' I automatically glanced down, noticing angry bruising above Rebecca's breasts that her towel was failing to cover. I closed my eyes as she continued. 'I could feel him pushing his fingers between my legs. I tried to stop him, I really did, but he was laughing at me as he held my arms down. I couldn't move. That's when Ryan pushed his tongue down my throat. I could feel him opening my legs-'

'Did he rape you, Rebecca?' The police female asked, poised for a response.

Rebecca shook her head. 'I don't think so. I don't think he had the time.' She glanced towards Grace, her embarrassment and confusion plain for everyone to see.

'I came home and caught them in here with her,' Grace muttered, unable to keep her own words calm as she recalled that horrific moment. 'They ran out when they saw me.' The police officers nodded and prompted Grace to explain exactly what she had witnessed. I didn't know if I could stand hearing much more of this. At one point, I felt as if I was actually going to be sick. The ordeal had left Rebecca a complete shell of the person she usually was. It took every single ounce of strength I had not to grab the first sharp object I could lay my hands on and run screaming from the flat in pursuit of revenge; the police officers witnesses to my actions.

When a police doctor arrived, Rebecca was forced to endure the humiliating ordeal of an internal examination. There was no doubt that she had been sexually assaulted, and she was asked if she wanted to press charges. After saying she did and taking as much detail as they could, the police left us all to calm her down, her burden too much for any of us to comprehend.

Although Grace had arrived home before they had actually raped her, both men had managed to thrust their fingers and other items inside Rebecca, leaving her bleeding, torn and in a devastating amount of pain. It took me over an hour to persuade her to go to bed so she could rest. The sounds that occasionally erupted from her mouth made me feel powerless and weak. Eventually, though, I managed to get her settled into bed, where she clung to me until exhaustion became too much for her and she fell asleep.

# Chapter 3

No one ever really understood the relationship that Rebecca and I shared. Those around us assumed we obviously must have been more than just friends because we had always been so open with each other. They simply could not understand how it could have possibly been anything other than a sexual thing we had going on. But it wasn't actually like that for us. Born two days apart, we were more like brother and sister than best friends.

In fact, despite the forty-eight-hour age gap, we were actually more like twins than anything else. We even seemed to sense when the other was feeling low or needed to talk about something important. No matter what problems we had between us or how often those little things in life niggled us, we could always speak openly to each other about anything.

Rebecca never judged or formed unnecessary opinions, and she always seemed to have a solution to every situation. It was actually quite refreshing to be in her company if I'm honest. She had helped me through many difficult times with my own family when I was a kid, and because of her kindness and genuine nature, I had always been more than happy to reciprocate. I felt safe when I was with her, yet even I could not have had any idea how important she would become to me throughout the course of our relationship. When we were together, nothing else in life seemed to matter. It was a good feeling, yet one I fully understood would not have been truly appreciated by other people. Ours was an undeniably unusual setup, and not many people could have understood how the dynamics worked.

She was always so confident and had everything in her life mapped out in the tiniest of details. She had a plan to be running her own modelling agency by the time she was thirty, earning her money sitting on the opposite side of the modelling fence instead of being the one in front of the camera. As a glamour model, she would often prance around the flat in nothing but a thong, joking that she would only need to get her tits out for another few years before being able to earn money whilst keeping her clothes on. She simply had no inhibitions at all and did not see nudity as something to be ashamed of. I guess, because of that, I too didn't overly concern myself with the appearance of naked flesh, Rebecca's especially.

Yet, at that time, she had no idea I had been secretly worrying about how her lifestyle would eventually affect our long-term relationship. For someone so young, she already appeared to have everything she had ever dreamed of and, compared to hers, my own life looked somewhat bleak. I had no real education to speak of, no meaningful qualifications, and my only genuine prospect was a motocross career that I was working too hard to achieve. I desperately wanted to make her as proud of me as I was of her, although I felt I was falling short of the mark.

As happy as Rebecca was to see me whenever we were forced to spend time apart, something deep inside was beginning to eat away at me. It was something I couldn't shake, yet I hadn't felt able to talk to her about it until seeing her so vulnerable tonight made me question my own insecurities. For a while, I had been worrying that we were drifting apart. We led such different lives. She enjoyed a jet-set lifestyle consisting of endless parties, airport lounges, and lavish hotel rooms that her modelling career had provided. They had become a staple part of her life, and I knew she loved her job so much. I worked at a small engineering factory on an industrial estate on the outskirts of Milborough and rented the spare room of someone else's house. Our lives were worlds apart.

I stroked her hair as she slept, listening to her breathing and glad she had been given a short respite from tonight's ordeal. It was then that I realised it actually didn't matter at all at how different our lives were. We needed each other. It was as simple as that, and there was only one thing on my mind right then that made any sense to me at all. It was the only thing, in fact, that I could allow myself to think about. Revenge. And how I could extract it to find justice for Rebecca.

*** 

I found Grace curled up on the sofa, quietly crying into a cushion that was now stained with tears and makeup. Although Rebecca had been the one subjected to tonight's ordeal, Grace appeared equally fragile and terrified, and my heart went out to her. I lightly touched her hair and she lifted her head, grabbing my hand in response and clutching onto my fingers as if she needed my presence to simply breathe. We sat together in silence for a while. Neither of us knew what to say to each other, and raw anger bubbled inside me like a volcano destined to erupt at any moment. I had never felt so helpless in my life, and I could offer no words of comfort to either girl that would have made the tiniest bit of difference anyway.

Neither of us could comprehend the events that had taken place here tonight. A few hours earlier, my day had seemed so different. I felt almost guilty. I had driven home from the gym feeling on top of the world, dreaming of how I wanted my life to be and making plans for my own future, whilst Rebecca was enduring an attack that I could never have comprehended in my wildest nightmares. Every time I allowed my mind to wander, images swam around my head and with every fresh vision that unwittingly came to me, I simply wanted to commit murder. Grace obviously knew how I was feeling and clung to me tightly, her fingers digging into my skin at the mere thought of me leaving her alone. I'm sure she knew that left to my own devices, I would probably have slipped out of the flat undetected, ready to exact my necessary vengeance on them both without remorse.

'Why would they do that to her, Craig?' Grace lifted her head and wiped a hand over her cheek. 'Why would Ryan do that to his own girlfriend?'

I shook my head. I had no idea how anyone could possibly hurt a woman in that way, or, come to think of it, anyone at all, be it female or male. However, the one thing that I did know for sure was that Rebecca would want nothing more to do with Ryan now. I should have been pleased about that concept, and yet I couldn't help contemplating what a disgusting way it had been to end a relationship, all the same. I dared not dwell too long on that thought, and I couldn't bring myself to imagine what Rebecca was currently making of that knowledge herself. I had always known that Ryan wasn't a good person, but even I didn't believe he could possibly be capable of something as horrendous as that. It was another nail in the coffin of incidents that had recently occurred with Ryan and Justin at the centre, and I couldn't help feeling that tonight's attack had happened because of some trouble I had coincidentally previously triggered.

'I think it might have something to do with what

happened with Lisa and that drugs couple.' I didn't want to believe this was possible, but it seemed to fit with the way events had been going recently.

'Do you think? They wouldn't take it out on Bex, though, would they, surely?' Grace had a look of concern on her face that matched my own.

'Who knows what goes through their head.' Obviously nothing good, I surmised. 'But I don't think it is a coincidence that just two weeks after my car was trashed, this happens tonight.'

'Yeah, but Bex had nothing to do with any of that-'

'Come on, Grace. Bex is my best friend, and Ryan hates my guts. What better way to get back at me than to hurt her?'

'No. No way. I don't buy it-'

'I don't think they came here intending to rape her, Grace.' The mere thought of that did not sit right in my head. 'Bex said they were looking for money.' Grace stared at me, the truth slowly sinking in. 'It's obvious, isn't it? They thought she would be able to compensate for the drug money I lost them.'

Grace sat upright, an understanding hitting her that I might actually be right. 'Oh, shit-'

'Shit, indeed.' I got to my feet, a sudden discomfort growing in my belly that I needed to try and shake off before it overwhelmed me completely. 'If I hadn't found out that Justin had given Lisa LCD that night in the club, I wouldn't have discovered that Ryan was even pushing drugs at all.' I thought for a moment about poor Lisa. She was usually such a quiet girl. A good friend of Grace's, I knew something had been way off with her that night. She was acting totally out of character, and it didn't take me long to figure out that drugs were to blame. 'And I certainly wouldn't have been able to shop that couple whose house they were using as a drug-dealing base because I wouldn't have known about any of it.'

'Yeah, but they had kids in the house, Craig, you did the right thing by telling the police-'

'I know I did, but Ryan and Justin wouldn't have seen it like that, would they?' I reeled at the thought of their despicable drug dealings. There was no way I could stand by and watch innocent kids get mixed up with drugs, so without hesitating, I had called the police on them. As far as I was concerned, it was the right thing to do and the only way to protect those innocent children from exposure to substances that could potentially kill them. I never found out how they discovered it was me who had tipped off the police, but Ryan and Justin knew I had instigated the raid, and it kick-started a series of events that had no doubt led to tonight's attack. I couldn't get the thought out of my head.

'Who do you think keyed my car along the entire length on both sides? Who do you think slashed my tyres and poured brake fluid over the goddamned paintwork?' I recalled Bella barking on the very night my car had been vandalised. It was two o'clock in the morning. I should have paid more attention, but I was tired, and I had incorrectly assumed that Bella was just playing up, so ignored her completely.

'Why didn't you tell the police about any of that stuff tonight?' Grace was biting her nails. I hated it when she did that because she only did it when she was nervous.

'Would it have made any difference? Besides, I'll deal with it myself, Grace.' We looked at each other for a moment, the concept that I was not about to let this go, something I knew she wouldn't understand even if I tried to explain.

Although the attack on my car had caused some inconvenience, it hadn't actually worried me beyond the aggravation of claiming on my car insurance. Without the back up of their other acquaintances, Ryan and Justin were nothing more than a pair of sniffling cowards, and I knew I could handle myself well if I ever needed to go up against either of them physically. I never in a million years thought they would step up their violent behaviour, and I had never considered the notion they would actually involve the girls. It was me they had the issue with, not them.

'Do you want a drink?' Grace asked when the silence between us became unbearable, and her nail-biting became too much even for her. I shook my head. No liquid would have been able to soothe my racing mind at that moment. Grace disappeared into the kitchen, the sound of tea making doing nothing whatsoever for my fragile state of mind. I stared at the blank television screen, unable to move a muscle, my reflection inside its glass rim as dark and distressing as the very images that flashed through my mind.

I sat and allowed my thoughts to paint pictures inside the television confines, where I was happily making those bastards suffer. My mind raced with terrible ideas that consumed me. I could hear Rebecca crying out occasionally in her sleep, and my need to protect my friends grew painfully intense. I rose slowly to my feet and went in to check on her. I was thankful she was asleep, yet the bruises on her face, neck, and arms were raw, screaming angrily at me from across the room.

I could barely bring myself to look at her without feeling my stomach churn. I swallowed hard and lowered myself carefully onto the bed, watching as she slept. Was she dreaming? Was the pain of this night blissfully keeping its distance? I looked away, and as a tear fell onto my cheek, I felt a hand stroke my own. I glanced up to see Rebecca looking at me as if she didn't know what to say, and yet that single look from her told me everything I needed to know. She squeezed my hand and began to sob then, harsher and with more suffering than I had ever heard. I was utterly powerless to help as her full strength and independence fled her body in that one single moment.

\*\*\*

I did not leave the girls' flat again for three days, going home only to check that the guys I lived with were feeding Bella properly and to take her out for a walk because I knew they probably wouldn't. And only when I was absolutely sure Grace and Rebecca were both safely locked inside. Even then, I did not trust the new bolts that I had fitted to the inside of their front door, and I must have recklessly broken every speed limit from Milborough to Somerton Village, and back again, so I could get back to them quickly. I cried off work, abandoned my training and spent every waking moment experiencing a fit of intense anger that burned me.

It was a terrible time for us all, and I was desperate to serve some cold justice to both Ryan and Justin. I wanted to stand in front of them and watch as their bullyboy tactics disappeared beneath the full blows of my fists. I wanted them to feel the pain they had inflicted on Rebecca, to suffer as she had done. The only thing preventing me from committing my own acts of violence were the girls. They wanted police justice, and although I was not exactly happy about the concept, I was willing to go along with their plan. For now, at least.

\*\*\*

Rebecca was a different person now, eating food only when we made it for her and answering questions only when we asked them. She did not engage well in conversations and spent the majority of her time curled up like an infant on the sofa, sitting in her dressing gown and socks with her hair tied back in a ponytail that she couldn't be bothered to wash.

When she stood to go to the toilet or to take a shower, she tried her best to hide the pain she was in, but Grace and I could see all too clearly exactly what she was going through.

'Just let the police do their job,' Grace whispered as we both stood in the kitchen watching Rebecca staring at the television in the next room.

'I need to do something Grace, before I go mad.' I picked up a hot mug of coffee from the countertop, ready to take it to Rebecca. 'I'm not letting them get away with this.'

'No-one's asking you to-'

'Then, for Christ's sake, don't,' I snapped back. This last week had broken us all, and I was in no mood for reasoning.

'The police know what they are doing Craig,' Grace looked at me as if she genuinely believed the police would come through for Rebecca. 'The evidence was plain to see. Even they can't ignore that.' But that was just the thing. It was 1988. Rapes rarely stood up in court, even with evidence screaming at all who looked at it. A girl could be accused of asking for it if her skirt was too short, or if she looked at a man in that way. I was scared. I was scared for all of us.

A knock on the door temporarily broke my pattern of thought, and when another of Rebecca's closest friends walked into the flat, her face echoed my own pain. Jade ran across the living room and hugged me. I knew what she was thinking even before she spoke. 'Is it true that Justin was involved?' She almost whispered. I am sure it was so Rebecca wouldn't overhear, but I think she heard anyway. I nodded, and Jade took in a sharp breath, squeezing her eyes shut with the mere thoughts of the concept. 'Jesus Christ,' she breathed. 'I'm so sorry.'

'Why the hell is it your fault?' I didn't mean to sound so irritated. This whole thing was becoming way too much for me to cope with.

'Because he's my ex. And because I would never have

dreamed that he could have-' Jade placed a hand across her mouth as if even she did not want to think about what Justin had done. I could only imagine the thoughts that must have gone through her mind when she had learned of Rebecca's fate. It was hardly her fault that she had previously chosen to date a scumbag. I was just glad he was now indeed her ex-boyfriend and not her current one. She had some sense, at least. Jade turned towards Rebecca and crossed the room slowly, sitting down next to her friend as if she had no words to express how sorry she felt. They looked at each other for a moment before flinging their arms around each other.

\*\*\*

Grace turned down several modelling jobs so that Rebecca would not have to be left alone in the flat, explaining to the agency that she had personal issues to deal with. They seemed to accept her needs without question, making me thankful that there were still a few understanding people left in the world. When I had no choice but to return to work after making up my own weak excuses for almost two weeks, I would race back to the flat during every lunch break simply to ensure everything was okay.

We lived like this for weeks, walking on eggshells around each other and not knowing what to say or do that would make any of it easier to deal with. It was hard to absorb the fact that our typical, open and often oblivious sexual attitudes towards each other was now gone. None of us indulged in any conversation where sex was a topic, and the atmosphere quickly became strained and cold.

It felt like an eternity waiting for the police to actually begin proceedings. And yet, within just over a month, Rebecca had received the letter we had been waiting for. She was to attend an informal hearing to decide if a case could be made against her attackers. During this hearing, it would be determined if they had enough evidence for a trial and try to get a conviction.

Both girls had made me promise that under no circumstances would I try to find either Ryan or Justin. They knew the seriousness of this situation and did not want the worry of an assault charge on top of everything else. They knew what I was like and what I was capable of if provoked. It was unbearable, but I promised them that I would stay away. The only thing that kept me going was the thought of police justice. Anything else was simply unacceptable.

# Chapter 4

On the morning of the hearing, Rebecca emerged from her bedroom far more fragile than I have ever seen her. She slowly pulled on her jeans and tied back her hair, not bothering with any makeup for fear of drawing unwarranted attention to herself in court. She did not speak to either of us at all, her nerves physically causing her hands to shake as she pulled on her boots. She looked so pale, so frightened. I wished there was something, anything, that I could do to tell her that everything would be okay, yet I knew somewhere deep down that today might not go how we all hoped, and that wasn't something I wanted to share with the girls. It was a sickening possibility that I tried not to think about. I placed my hand over hers and calmly helped tie her laces. 'It's going to be okay,' I tried to reassure her gently, but my words went completely unnoticed as if I hadn't spoken at all.

We drove to the courthouse in silence and sat in a small room that felt oppressive and smelled of coffee and old wood that had witnessed many a tale too unbearable to think about. I thought for a moment that I might actually suffocate in this place as I glanced around at strangers who were meant to be dealing with Rebecca's case. We had been gathered to listen to the evidence collected, yet something in the back of my mind niggled at me that we would not achieve the outcome we were hoping for. To make matters worse, Ryan and Justin were both sitting calmly on the opposite side of the room as if nothing in the world could touch them.

I could not take my eyes off either of them. I wanted them to see the hatred I had for them, and I wanted them to understand that I was not about to let this go, no matter what. Ryan was sitting cross-legged, leaning back in his seat and occasionally yawning as if he found this whole thing extremely boring. Justin was equally preoccupied with some poster on the wall that I wanted to ram down the back of his throat. I tried and failed to ignore Rebecca's body as it involuntarily trembled next to mine, her shallow breath and pounding heart sending my brain into overdrive. I held her hand, and every now and again, Grace would send a tiny smile my way, just to let me know that she was there for me, too.

We listened to Rebecca's solicitor present her evidence to the panel, the details of that fateful night slicing into our hearts with fresh enthusiasm as if someone had carelessly torn open a bleeding wound with a blunt knife. Photographs were shown, police reports were recapped, and when the defence solicitor got to his feet and cleared his throat, I wanted to throttle the life out of him, too. 'It would appear to me that this case has no merit on which to stand any ground.'

He had a patronising tone to his voice that unnerved me, and upon hearing his words, I involuntarily stiffened in my seat. Rebecca grabbed my hand and squeezed. It was the first she had taken any notice of her surroundings that day, holding onto my hand as if she were literally unable to see anything around her and needed reassurance that I was still actually there.

'My clients are acquaintances of the *apparent* victim.' I wanted to know exactly why he had felt the need to emphasise the word, apparent. It seemed as if, as far as he was concerned, Rebecca's ordeal simply did not happen in the way it had been presented to the court. 'And,' he continued, 'it is my actual understanding that one of the accused is, in fact, an ex-boyfriend of the so-called victim.' He paused for effect, almost looking as if he wanted to laugh as he glanced around the room at the faces before him. Obviously, he wanted to share his opinion of this matter with everyone present, as if people in relationships can't possibly accuse each other of rape.

The fact he had also referred to Rebecca as a so-called victim implied he didn't believe a single word that was being said. 'In fact-' I am sure I heard him suppress a snigger under his breath. It made my nostrils flare, and my throat tighten. 'The only "key witness" to this apparent attack is in actual fact having a sexual relationship with Miss Taylor herself.' He finalised his statement by placing the folder he was holding onto the desk in front of him with a thud. I attempted to get to my feet, but Rebecca dug her nails into my arm. It actually hurt.

'What is the point of your statement, please?' Rebecca's solicitor got to her feet as if in response to my thoughts.

'My point is that my client, Mr Ryan Miller, actually instigated a break up with Miss Rebecca Taylor just one week before the alleged attack. In fact, the break up caused your client such upset that she became extremely bitter and angry towards my client, openly displaying her rejection by lashing out in the only way she knew how.'

'That's a complete lie.' I got to my feet and yelled. I couldn't help myself. Those bastards were making up a pack of lies, and I was damned sure they wouldn't get away with it.

'There will be order here,' someone called in my direction, and Rebecca pulled me back onto the chair. She glared at me and shook her head, but it was too late. I had already been tipped way over the edge.

Ryan and Justin's solicitor glared at me as if I was some

smudge of dirt that needed wiping away quickly so that it wouldn't leave a stain. 'If I may continue,' he said as he retrieved his papers from the desk. He had a smug look that I wanted to wipe from his ugly face. He held out a hand towards Justin. 'My second client, Mr Justin Anderson, also happens to be an ex-boyfriend of one of Miss Taylor's female friends. I put it to the court that it does not take a genius to work out how easy it would be for a group of scorned young women to get together and invent a story, purely in revenge at having recently lost their boyfriends.'

He slammed his papers onto the desk again, sending a clear message to the room that he found this entire hearing downright laughable. 'I put it to the panel that this whole thing is an elaborate and disgusting ploy to get back at my clients for having been dumped.' He paused again and looked straight at me as if he wanted to see the look on my face as he spoke. 'As the key witness is having a sexual relationship with Miss Taylor, we cannot take her evidence as admissible in this hearing. I am under the impression that the entire accusation has been manufactured by these young women who feel scorned by men who no longer wish to have any type of relationship with them.'

'Excuse me.' Rebecca's solicitor rose to her feet, knocking over her chair in haste that made a dirty mark on the wall behind her. 'If this attack has been made up, as you so clearly assume, how on earth do you account for the physical bruising on my client's body?' She, too, slammed a file down onto the desk. This was turning into a farce. If the situation had not been so serious, I might have actually laughed.

Ryan and Justin's solicitor shook his head. 'Oh my dear,' he continued in his now overbearing and patronising tone. 'I have no doubt that an attack of some description did indeed occur, but it was certainly not committed by my clients. No semen was found from either one of my clients on or inside the victim's body, and no actual evidence to support your theory other than a statement made by your client's so-called girlfriend.' He emphasised the word girlfriend to reiterate that the whole thing was nothing more than one huge joke. I was sure a few people in the panel actually hid sneers behind their hands.

'Let's not forget for one moment,' he added as he raised a fat index finger into the air, 'that your client is, in actual fact, a glamour model who takes her clothes off for anyone who wants to have a look.' I saw red.

'What the hell kind of bullshit is this?' I screamed, clambering to my feet and ready to jump over the table to Ryan, Justin, and their aggravating solicitor. I was prepared to take them all on. Rebecca and Grace scrambled to their feet in response to my outburst and grabbed my arms simultaneously as security guards were called in to restrain me. I simply could not believe what I was hearing. Who the hell did that guy think he was speaking about Rebecca in that way? Someone grabbed my arm firmly, but I held up my hands in defeat, and they let me go. I knew that if they forced me out of this room right then, I would not be able to support Rebecca. She certainly did not need my dramas adding further insult to her own anguish.

Once the room was brought under control and my temper was temporarily calmed, the hearing was allowed to continue. Statements and information were thrown between both solicitors and the judge for a further two hours, but in the end, it was concluded that there simply was not enough evidence to bring the case to court, and the whole thing was thrown out.

In the 1980s, victims of rape and sexual attacks often did not get the chance to bring their attackers to court. In Rebecca's case, the fact that she took her clothes off in front of the camera and made a living out of it, and had previously been in a relationship with Ryan, made it appear to the panel that she was not trustworthy. Add the fact that she also was having a casual relationship with Grace, she didn't stand a chance. At that time, less than one per cent of all sex attackers were actually bought to justice, and it made me sick.

I genuinely felt sorry for Grace at that moment. She was openly gay and had always been happy to express who she truly was and how she felt. It was refreshing, actually. She didn't trust men, and after what had happened to Rebecca, I could fully understand why. For the last year or so, she had been having a somewhat relaxed sexual relationship with Rebecca, and to be honest, I did not believe it was anyone's business but their own what they chose to do behind closed doors.

I did not even know that Ryan actually knew about any of that stuff and hated what he must have said about Rebecca behind her back. He was probably jealous that she had chosen a woman over him, and yet they did not exactly broadcast their personal lives to the world. They were already several months into their relationship before they even got round to telling me about any of it. It might have begun because of their closeness, their shared career or something else entirely, yet both girls had always been very open with each other. I truly felt this only made Rebecca's attack all that more unbearable for Grace.

As the verdict was read out, I felt Rebecca slide away from me, and I only just managed to catch her before she hit the floor. I glared at Ryan and Justin, who were smugly grinning and shaking hands with the slimy pig that had represented them. I have to admit, I had never felt anger like the anger I felt building in me when I saw the look of satisfaction on their faces that day. I actually felt sick with the idea of what I wanted to do to them. Every inch of me ached for revenge. If I had not been so busy holding Rebecca upright, I probably would not have been responsible for my actions that day.

\*\*\*

We drove back to the flat in total silence. Weeks of anxiety and suffering with Rebecca waking in the middle of the night crying out randomly seemed to have been all for nothing. She was so quiet during the drive back to the flat. She stared blankly out of the window during the entire journey, and I couldn't help noticing that the usual sparkle in her eyes was now completely gone. It was as if someone had turned off her internal life force, and Grace and I both knew this had broken her spirit. How could someone do such a disgusting thing to another human being and not even feel one ounce of remorse for their actions? It was a thought I simply could not perceive. As I helped Rebecca out of the car, my hand brushed over her painfully thin shoulder, and for a moment, I wondered if we would ever get her back to how she once was.

I watched the girls as they walked silently, arm in arm across the driveway towards the flats entrance porch, clinging onto each other for the support I knew neither of them really had the strength to give at that point. I hesitated for a moment. I had promised the girls I would wait until the hearing was over and keep my temper in check. I had promised I would not do anything rash or make any impromptu decisions. But I had waited as patiently as I had been physically able for weeks, and unfortunately, my patience had finally run out. The hearing was over, justice had not prevailed, and now my wait was surely over, too. There was nothing else I could do. Calmly, I closed the passenger door of Rebecca's car, walked casually around to the driver's side, climbed into the car and slammed my foot onto the accelerator pedal as hard as those tyres would allow me.

***

I sat in Rebecca's car for over an hour, waiting. I could afford to be as patient as I needed to be now, and that single thought gave me a quiet feeling of satisfaction I found frighteningly exhilarating. My time for vengeance was finally coming, and no longer did I need to hold back the feelings that had been steadily bubbling inside me for the last few weeks. It was the beginning of December now, and I turned up the heater, sitting calmly listening to music on the radio station, a smug deliberation swimming around my head, ready for what I knew would be the most satisfying moment of my life.

They always drank in the same pub together, every single night, seven days a week. It was a wonder they even had livers left inside their pitiful bodies that functioned. In the exact same way that rats gravitate to the same place each day to find scraps of food, those two were creatures of habit as well. I found it quite pathetic, really. I knew they would be inside that place right now, getting drunker with each passing moment and patting each other on the back at how amazing they were. I could hear them readily boasting to anyone within earshot about how fantastic they had been at having triumphed over the justice system.

I couldn't help smiling at the idea of their oblivious ramblings because they would be laughing on the other side of their faces by the time I had finished with them tonight. The odd passer-by occasionally glanced into the car window, obviously curious about my motives, and probably noticing the calculated and scheming look in my eyes. If they had any idea at all what I was contemplating, they certainly would not have been walking away from me so calmly, that much I did know.

As the temperature began to drop, my adrenaline levels

steadily increased. It was as if the cooler the evening air became, the higher my anticipation rose. I didn't at any moment allow myself time to stop and think about how Rebecca or Grace would react if they knew what I was planning because right at that moment in time, I seriously didn't care. I had calmly done what they had asked of me. I had remained silent where I had wanted to scream. I had stayed away from trouble, and I had kept my anger buried deep inside me for long enough. But I would have happily gone to jail for either one of those girls that day. No one should ever have to see their loved ones suffer at the hand of another and feel that helpless, empty feeling inside, knowing you have been rendered powerless to do a damned thing about it.

I was beginning to feel somewhat restless after several hours of waiting, but when they finally emerged from the pub's side door, I physically felt my heart lunge. They were laughing hard, leaning against each other so as not to fall over and staggering around like the deplorable idiots they were. They looked beyond ridiculous, and right then, I realised what it actually felt like to genuinely hate someone. I quietly popped open the car door and reached my hand into the back seat, wrapping my fist around a seven-pound hammer that I had carefully stored safely behind Rebecca's driver's seat. It had been waiting as patiently as I had since the night of her attack. They were both so drunk, they didn't even notice my approach as I charged boldly up to them, ready to swing the heavy hammer straight into the side of Ryan's head.

'Fucking hell,' Justin yelled as he spotted me charging towards them from the darkness. Ryan spun around in shock, and the hammer caught him awkwardly against his shoulder instead of its intended target. He staggered backwards, muttering something I couldn't hear as he stumbled against the pub wall with a thud and slid to the floor. I raised the hammer high. My intentions were to seriously beat every breath they had out of their bodies. As Justin lunged towards me, every ounce of hatred and frustration that had been stored up inside me poured out of my body in that one single moment, and I allowed the hammer to drop to the floor, ready to give my raw anger the freedom it desperately needed.

I punched Justin hard in the stomach, and as he bent forward in response to the pain, I kicked him squarely in the face. He toppled backwards in perfect time for me to bring my knee up between his legs as hard as I could. I wanted that son of a bitch to never be able to use that damned thing ever again, even for pissing out of. I wanted to cause them pain like they could never imagine existed. Pain they didn't even know was possible to experience. I wanted them both to suffer so severely that they would forever remember that it was because of me that they were never quite the same again. Ryan had somehow managed to clamber to his feet and came towards me with fists flying in a somewhat confused drunken state.

Oddly, I have to admit, I actually hate fighting. I am normally the type of person who would rather talk things through wherever possible and avoid physical confrontation. But if I do need to fight, I fight dirty, and I fight hard, and that night Rebecca's honour was at stake. I bought my elbow up to Ryan's jaw and punched him hard in the gut as he lunged backwards, satisfied I had taken the wind clean out of him. I didn't care that it was two on one. All I knew was that whatever it took, both of those men would wish they had never laid a single finger on Rebecca. Justin came up from behind and punched me in the kidneys. A sharp pain shot through my back, and I was thrown off balance for a second, forcing me forward into the pub wall. I spun around and grabbed him by the throat. My intention was to actually strangle him until the last wisp of breath had left his body. I seriously wanted him dead and absolutely did not care about the consequences that followed.

Unfortunately for me, Ryan then hit me across the back of the head with a piece of splintered wood. I have no idea where it came from, but it forced me to release Justin, who fell to his knees coughing and spluttering for breath like the spineless coward he was. We were all breathless by now, and as my knees buckled, Ryan dropped the wood and ran, followed closely by Justin, who was still clutching his throat, clearly struggling to breathe and probably wondering what the hell had just happened. I scrambled to my feet in time to catch sight of Ryan diving into Justin's car face first as they sped out of the pub car park like a couple of maniacs, the passenger door still wide open.

Although I could feel the blood in my hair, my only thought was to go after them and end this thing, once and for all. I had never felt anger like it in my entire life, and at that moment, no one would have been able to talk me down. I was like a raging bull as I ripped Rebecca's car keys from my jacket pocket and sped after them as fast as I could. It was as if a mist had descended over me. I had no consideration for road laws or anyone in my path as the car screamed in response to my reckless driving. My only focus was to keep Justin's car within my line of vision at all times, caring nothing for traffic lights, road junctions or late-night party revellers who I'm ashamed to admit darted out of my way on more than one occasion. We must have looked like lunatics, racing through those darkened streets with no regard whatsoever for anyone else at all.

Rebecca's Toyota MR2 had no trouble at all catching up to the rear bumper of Justin's much slower and older Volkswagen Scorpio. I rammed my foot hard onto the accelerator pedal and heard a satisfying crunch as the two cars made contact. I could hear the sound of tyres screaming as

Justin struggled to keep control of his car ahead of me. I was reckless, unhinged even, but seeing the looks of smug satisfaction on their faces earlier that day had literally tipped me over the edge. I realised I didn't want to cause them pain anymore. I wanted them both dead. As I went in for a second attempt, I successfully forced Justin's car straight into the curb. My timing could not have been more perfect. I slammed on the brakes as I watched almost in slow motion as his car swerved violently back out into the middle of the road and tipped sideways. It rolled over twice, bouncing aggressively onto its roof before rolling again and coming to rest upside down, rocking gently back and forth, an amalgamation of glass, rubber and metal as the carnage that was Ryan and Justin's payback unfolded in front of me.

It was as if at that moment reality hit me because, for a few seconds, I was stunned. The only sound I could hear now was the violent spinning of wheels and an engine that aggressively revved in the darkness as I sat and quietly observed the scene in front of me. My heart felt as if it were about to jump from my chest and lie mockingly in my lap as I surveyed the destruction in the road ahead. Smoke poured from the mangled engine, and as I sat motionless in Rebecca's car, I waited and secretly hoped the whole thing would explode into a ball of flames and be done with them both forever. Seconds felt like hours. I could see no movement. As I visualised two mangled bloodied bodies lying lifelessly up ahead, no longer able to hurt anyone ever again, I felt a quiet sense of justice creep over me. I had done it. I had actually done it.

Almost immediately, a surge of extreme sickness swept over me, and reality came back into blinding focus. It was as if the world had turned from muffled stillness to painful noise. I reversed the car back along the road as fast as possible, making a not so eloquent movie style U-turn in the road. I tore away from the scene, glancing in the rear-view mirror only once to double-check I had not imagined the whole thing.

# Chapter 5

I drove back to Rebecca's flat in a daze, not really fully aware of much around me at all at that point. I could feel her car struggling to respond to anything I tried to make it do and listened in dismay as broken metal rattled against the surface of the road. I parked carelessly on the driveway and climbed out to inspect the damage. My legs felt like jelly and, for a moment, I struggled to stand upright. I had to take a breath. To take a moment to contemplate that any of what I'd been through tonight had actually happened at all. Rebecca's car was her pride and joy, but looking at it now, the mess I had made of the bodywork would surely cause her significant upset. There was a deep dent where the two cars had made contact, and the front bumper was hanging off. The distinct smell of oil was not a good sign either. I was physically shaking and could barely get my legs to walk in a straight line as I headed towards the flat entrance door. My hands trembled, and I honestly felt as if I might be sick at any moment. The only thing that helped keep me calm was the feeling of extreme satisfaction that where the courts and police had not served justice for Rebecca, I had.

In my mind, I was convinced that once their bodies were discovered, the accident would simply be put down to a case of careless drunk driving on their part. I was completely satisfied that no other women would ever be forced to face the same fate that Rebecca had at their hands ever again. I was deluded, I know, but at the time, I couldn't allow my frazzled brain to consider any other outcome. Grace was waiting for me on the landing as I climbed the stairs to the flat.

'Where the hell have you been?' she demanded, as I deliberately avoided making eye contact with her. My clothes were filthy, and the dried blood in my hair from the blow I had taken a short time earlier now looked angry and shocking. I realised I had a headache. It didn't take a genius to work out what I had done.

'Is Rebecca okay?' It was the only thing I could think to say.

'What do you think?' Grace exploded. 'We've been worried sick, for God's sake. Please, Craig, please don't tell me you've done something stupid.'

I looked straight into her eyes. 'Let's just say those bastards won't be bothering anyone else. Ever. Again.' My words were as bitter as I felt at that moment, and yet as I casually stepped passed her into the flat, I didn't really want to see her reaction. It didn't prevent me from hearing the sharp intake of her breath, though, as I walked by.

Rebecca came running out of the bedroom but stopped dead in her tracks when she saw the state of me. 'Oh my God, please tell me you didn't-' she breathed as she collapsed onto the carpet in front of me, fresh tears ready to explode, her legs no more able to hold her up than mine were. My knees crumbled in response to Rebecca's outburst, and I slid down in front of her, reaching my trembling hands to hers as every inch of my body finally released the frustration that had built for weeks.

'What did you expect me to do, Bex?' I croaked, my throat tight with frustration and pain that had nowhere to go. 'You saw the look on their faces today. There was no way I was going to let them get away with what they did to you. No way.'

'But what about you?' Grace stepped into the flat behind us and closed the door, her own voice sounding far too angry for my liking.

'Don't worry, no one saw me-'

'What difference does that make now?' she yelled. 'Rebecca, have you seen the state of your car?'

Rebecca glared at me. 'Craig. What have you done?' She was shaking again as I attempted to pull her close to me. I actually really needed a hug.

'I'm so sorry, Bex. I couldn't help it.' And the truth was, I genuinely couldn't. I had literally seen red and nothing, and no one, would have been able to stop me from going out that night even if they had wanted to. 'I'll get your car sorted-'

'I'm not bothered about the car, Craig.' Rebecca scrambled to her feet and shook her head. The bruises on her face were fading but still a potent reminder of what had happened to her. 'The only thing I care about is you, and the last thing any of us need is you up on an assault charge. Or worse. Please don't tell me you did something worse.' When I didn't immediately respond, she started to cry with that familiar helpless tone I was growing accustomed to. A feeling of restlessness swept over me yet again.

'How could you go behind our backs like that?' she sobbed.

'Are you serious?'

'I begged you not to go after them-'

'What the hell did you expect me to do? Nothing?' My heart was racing with everything that today had thrown at me.

'Yes, because the police were dealing with it, Craig.'

'Oh yeah, and that turned out really well, didn't it?' I clenched my fists, noticing they were as raw and angry as I was.

'I'm not angry at *you*, Craig.' Rebecca softened her tone and put her arms around me. 'If anything, I'm actually proud of you for risking everything, just to protect me. I didn't ever expect anything else from you, to be honest. But what now? What happens now?'

\*\*\*

The following day we had visitors in the shape of two police officers who hovered on the driveway outside the girls' flat, standing dangerously close to Rebecca's wrecked car and talking to each other as if to re-confirm their already confirmed suspicions.

'Craig Marshall?' one of them questioned as I stepped outside to join them.

'Yes?' I answered as calmly as I was able without giving myself away.

'Are you familiar with this car, Sir?' He continued to survey the damaged bumper.

'It belongs to a friend of mine.' I wasn't quite sure how to answer the question without instantly convicting myself, but I knew I had to take responsibility for my own actions, and so would have to tell the truth at some point. Events of the previous night had not happened out of insanity but with precise, calculated revenge in mind, and now I would need to step up and take the punishment that was obviously coming to me.

'We have reason to suspect that this car may have been involved in an incident last night at around twelve o'clock. The other vehicle's driver has confirmed that you had a fight with them outside the Bell Pub in Wellingborne at around eleven-thirty last night. Do you want to tell us what happened?'

Shit. Shit. How the hell could they not be dead? For a

moment, I couldn't think straight. 'Erm-'

'We don't really want to do this here, Sir, so we need to ask you to accompany us to the station to assist us with our enquiries.' He held out a hand, indicating that he wanted me to step into the police car. Was I being arrested?

I closed the front door of the building behind me and looked towards Rebecca's front window. I did not want the girls to see me being taken away by the police, and I genuinely hoped they hadn't noticed what was going on. They had been through enough already. I would call them later if things didn't go well. I tried not to look at Rebecca's car as I walked across the driveway onto the pavement towards the police vehicle. I did not want to be reminded of what I had done, and I did not want to acknowledge what was surely about to happen now. I had started showing clear signs of being in a fight, with a black eye and thick lip as confirmation, and my knuckles were bright red where I had punched Ryan and Justin repeatedly. I knew the police would be putting two and two together, and although I wasn't exactly surprised, I would be lying if I said I wasn't dreading what was indeed about to happen next.

I was interviewed for several hours, and I was as truthful with them as I could possibly have been. I knew there was no point in lying to the police, so I told them everything I could about Rebecca's attack, about the court hearing the previous day, and how I had gone after them with pure revenge the only thing on my mind. They double-checked my story to ensure I was indeed telling the truth and kept me in suspense for what felt like an eternity. Although in hospital with bruising and several broken limbs, Ryan and Justin were still alive. As angry as that made me inside, it meant I could not be placed on any murder charges.

My honesty had persuaded them that my actions had been merely out of anger and bitterness and not the cold, calculated brutality I had actually intended. But it also meant that those two could continue causing trouble, and at that time, there was simply no way I could have fully understood what I had started between us.

'We have a witness that puts you at the Bell pub, fighting with the men in question. However, neither men do not wish, at this stage, to press any charges, so you seem to be having an extremely good day.' The police officer announcing this seemed to assume that I would be pleased.

'They don't want to press charges?' I was shocked to discover this fact. Why the hell would they do that? They hated me. It would have been all too easy for them to see me up on a GBH charge, dangerous driving, causing an accident, leaving the scene of an accident, attempted murder, you name it, I'd probably done it.

'Nope.' He placed his folder onto the table as if he were as surprised by that fact as I was.

'However, Mr Marshall, I have to say that the subsequent road traffic collision that occurred after your alleged fight has been flagged as suspicious, so we do need clarification on your movements once you left the pub if you don't mind.' He looked at me with suspicion in his eyes, a pen in his hand ready to record my next words.

'The collision?' I questioned. I wanted to know exactly what they knew before I accidentally convicted myself.

'Yes, you were seen speeding away from the car park in pursuit of the second vehicle. Care to elaborate on what happened afterwards?'

I nodded my head. I knew the police had already confirmed the damage to Rebecca's car, so I didn't see any genuine point in not admitting that I had chased them after our fight had ended. 'I did chase after them, yes.' I had no idea where this was going, but I went with it anyway. 'And I managed to catch up to them at one point, but although our cars did make contact for a moment, my intention had only been to scare them.' I think they actually bought into my story. 'But I lost them en-route somewhere.' I paused. 'They were driving a bit erratic, to be honest. They'd been drinking.'

I'd already damaged Rebecca's car, so I didn't see the point in making things worse for myself. I knew my story would fit with the damage they had seen on the car, and I knew they also had confirmation that Ryan and Justin were drunk at the time. I conveniently left out the part about having actually caused the accident, though. They were not pressing charges, and so my accidental confession would have done me no favours whatsoever with the Crown Prosecution Service.

I could not think for the life of me why Ryan and Justin had failed to tell the police that it was me who had caused the accident, apparently claiming they had simply been careless on their way home because they had had too much to drink. As no one else had been hurt in the crash other than themselves and their own car, no driving offences were bought against them. I had assumed they would have literally broken their necks to land me in a police cell, and my brain was screaming that none of this made any sense at all.

Although the police had seen for themselves the state of Rebecca's car and didn't honestly believe a word I had said, with no allegations being bought against me by either Ryan or Justin, they could do no more than to let me go under caution. An injunction was soon after enforced, making sure that I stayed away from them both and that they stayed away from us. It would have to do. For now.

***

I should have known it wouldn't be enough for Ryan and Justin to simply let things go. I had taken my revenge, putting them in hospital for several days, and although I could not understand why they would not want to see me rotting in a prison cell, I knew deep down they would now be out for blood. Just a couple of weeks later, the police returned to the flat, and this time, it was serious. I was arrested regarding Rebecca's attack. No one had yet been charged for her assault, and so without warning, my name was firmly in the frame. For the second time in as many weeks, I found myself sitting inside a police interview room listening to a statement that had been provided.

'It has been suggested to us that it was yourself who actually attacked Miss Rebecca Taylor on the evening of October the seventeenth.' I literally could not believe what I was hearing. I know the policewoman conducting the interview would have noticed the shocked look that automatically planted itself onto my face, but she gave nothing away of what she thought about the accusation. 'And, in an attempt to cover it up, a Miss Grace Williams, being a good personal friend of yourself and Miss Taylor, created the story regarding Ryan Miller and Justin Anderson to defer the blame from you. Apparently, you have a shocking temper, Mr Marshall.' I noted she had the file regarding the previous fight and subsequent car accident on the desk in front of her. My recent actions had done me no favours at all, reinforcing the fantasy that I had a terrible temper. Ryan and Justin couldn't have planned it any better. 'According to what we have been told, in a drunken moment of madness, you attacked Miss Taylor when she refused your advances. Do you have anything to say about that?'

'Yes, I do indeed. What a load of complete and utter bullshit.' I didn't care how angry I sounded. How dare they attempt to shift the blame onto me?

'It has been suggested that Miss Taylor went along with the story as an elaborate plan to get back at Mr Miller for dumping her, and apparently Mr Anderson was dragged into the story simply because he had previously cheated on a friend of Miss Taylor.' She looked at her notes. 'A Miss Jade Peterson.' I could not believe what I was hearing, and worse still, I hated how she was formally addressing everyone by their surnames. Wow. It must have taken them all of around five minutes to concoct such a bullshit story.

'Why don't you ask Rebecca, Grace, and Jade yourself.' I spat. I could feel the heat of the room beginning to suffocate me.

'Oh, we intend to, Mr Marshall. We just wanted to give you the chance to tell us your side of the story first. Actually, the girls are being interviewed as I speak.' She folded her arms calmly and attempted to smile at me weakly, something in her eyes telling me she didn't believe a word that had been said to them, yet they still needed to verify everyone's movements and motives all the same.

'I would never hurt Rebecca. She's my friend.' It was the truth.

'I believe you, Craig.' I am sure she wanted to reassure me that I had nothing to worry about, but she simply sat stone-faced next to her colleague who had been recording the interview. A door opened, and the officer suspended the interview whilst she stepped out of the room. It felt like an hour passed before she returned, although it was probably no more than a few minutes.

'Rebecca Taylor has denied the allegations against you.'

'So can I go?' I desperately needed some air. What the hell did they expect Rebecca to say?

'We do have to take every allegation seriously, I'm sure you understand.'

I nodded. 'I know you do.' My words came out almost as a whisper.

'This will be kept on record in case of any further

developments. You are free to go, but just a small warning,' I went to stand up but hesitated. 'Stay away from those two and keep your friends away from them as well.' I hoped she could see straight through their lies, and as a police officer, was able to tell that they were nothing more than soap scum you scrape off the bottom of the shower tray, but her face gave nothing away of what she was thinking. 'You are free to go,' she added as she closed the folder and laid her hand across it.

***

I left the interview room to the sound of Rebecca yelling some feet away along the hallway. It didn't take a genius to work out that she was utterly furious with the police and those two slimy pigs for suggesting I could do anything like that to her.

'It's those two twats you should be locking up, not Craig,' I could hear her yelling. It made me smile, grateful that she was quickly able to set the record straight so I could get out of this place.

'Thank you,' I mouthed towards her as I neared the entrance doorway in which she had been restlessly standing. She threw her arms around me and hugged me.

'I'm so sorry,' she whispered.

I shook my head. 'It's hardly your fault Bex.'

I had unwittingly instigated trouble that was beginning to escalate out of control. Today's accusations became a trigger that would commence a chain reaction and cause some serious problems for us all. Ryan and Justin's friends and family started spreading rumours around the town that I was a violent rapist, even though it was certainly not true.

Although Rebecca came to my defence at every stage, unfortunately, mud tends to stick, and people who did not even know me began whispering behind my back, giving me strange looks wherever I went. Some even crossed the road when they saw me, convinced that some of what they had been hearing must have been true. I am living proof that one tiny lie whispered viciously to another can ultimately ruin a person's reputation, and for several weeks my life became unbearable. My car was repeatedly damaged, with disgusting messages scratched into the bodywork almost daily, among other things. Rebecca tried to stay strong, but she was a shell of the person she had once been, and trusted no one now at all.

We spent much of our time hiding away inside the flat now, neither of us wanting to venture outside for fear of the ridicule we knew we would receive if we did. The lies told about us had become truly unbearable to the point where Rebecca would spend hours peering out through the curtains into the street, waiting for something to happen to her car or for a window to be broken. She was branded all kinds of disgusting names too terrible for any of us to comprehend. And to make matters worse, those tales were being told by people she didn't even know.

In turn, others then heard altered versions of the same story, all of them seemingly finding it easy to believe every word that was said and adding little extras of their own, simply to make the stories all the more exaggerated and shocking. Like Chinese whispers, Rebecca's ordeal was told and retold until eventually, it sounded as if she was the problem. No one had any trouble spreading the idea that Rebecca was nothing more than a common slut, simply because she was a glamour model. She had tried to bring justice to her attackers, and they had hit out at her the only way they knew how.

*\*\*\**

By February 1989, things had calmed down enough for us to

be able to, once again, pick up the pieces of our lives and attempt to gain back some kind of normality. The stories that had taunted us for weeks were told with less enthusiasm each day, yet they left deep scars that none of us would be able to shake easily. In the same way that a newspaper headline becomes tomorrow's discarded trash, we were eventually mostly forgotten about, bitter words meaning no more to the people who muttered them than the changing of the weather. However, it did not go unnoticed how the very two people who had actually committed the attack had not been ridiculed in the way I had. They had somehow managed to completely divert any attention from themselves, their own version of events met with sympathy and compassion.

There were, of course, a few people who remained firmly on our side—the ones who knew me better and knew how crazy the whole situation had become. Rebecca hadn't accepted much modelling work since her attack, her confidence and emotions having become seriously hindered. She was terrified of what people now thought of her and would not leave the flat without me firmly by her side. To make matters worse, she hated being at home alone and did not ever want me to leave her at night at all. Her usual flirtatious personality had been replaced by one of a petrified young girl who would flinch whenever I accidentally touched her without her realising it was me.

One evening she was dozing on the sofa, the television was on low in the background, and as I sat down next to her, I innocently rubbed my hand across her leg. It was something I had done since we were kids, and didn't immediately realise my mistake. Instantly her eyes flew open, and she drew in her breath, pulling herself tightly into a defensive ball.

'Bex?' I yelled. I couldn't help the look of total shock on my face. 'It's okay. It's only me.'

Rebecca took one look at me and burst into tears. 'Oh

God, Craig, I'm so sorry,' she sobbed as she flung her arms around me. 'I'm sorry.' She was physically shaking and didn't stop apologising for the next two hours.

***

Rebecca's attack had changed her, and although I knew she was trying as hard as she could to get back to the person she once was, she was different somehow. For a girl who would typically confidently jet-set across to the other side of the world on photoshoots without a single care in the world, it was seriously upsetting to see her now unwilling to even venture to the local shops without one of the girls by her side or me. Grace and Jade noticed it too and, for a few months, we all struggled to put behind us the incident that had taken place that previous October.

I seemed to be the only male she would speak to now and would literally cross the road when she saw a group of men she didn't know. I was devastated by what she had become, wishing with every inch of my soul that she would, at some point, rediscover the person I loved and respected so much. I had abandoned my motocross training completely, the last few months testimony to the silent suffering we had been forced to endure. I went home only to check that Bella was being looked after well by the other household members and collect some clean clothes, most of which were now actually at Rebecca's flat anyway.

To any outsider, it probably looked as if I had moved in with her, but I was simply taking care of my friend. After everything that had been thrown at us, other people's viewpoint on my relationship with Rebecca was the least of my concern. It was March before Rebecca seemed to turn a corner, emerging one afternoon, fully dressed, her hair and makeup done for the first time in months, and the first genuine smile I had seen on her face in quite some time.

'Come on, you,' she announced as she pounced onto my lap playfully. 'We're going out.' It was a surprise to see her like this, and I didn't for a second want to do or say anything that would send her backwards, so I didn't dare argue.

'Uhh?' my question came out as a groan.

'I'm not going to give those bastards the satisfaction,' she announced firmly. 'I've been letting everything get to me for too long, and I'm not going to do that anymore, Craig.' She squeezed my arm and laughed. 'It happened, yes. But I can't do anything about that now, can I. What I can do is try to get on with things the best I can.' She kissed me on the nose. 'I am so sorry that I have been such a pain in the backside lately.'

'You haven't-'

'Shush,' she whispered as she placed a finger over my lips. I saw something in her eyes then. If it was the beginnings of a sparkle, I dared not hope, but we went bowling that night and had more fun in that single evening than we had in months. Was Rebecca coming back to me? I could only genuinely hope she was.

# Chapter 6

I was seriously relieved when Rebecca found the confidence to begin smiling again, and 1989 slowly became a year of promise and excitement that none of us had expected it to be. Ryan and Justin had caused no further trouble since their attempt to frame me for Rebecca's attack, and things were slowly improving in general for us all. I was grateful to resume my motocross training, feeling confident that the girls would be safe whilst I attended the gym to ready myself for the upcoming season.

I needed to get back some kind of normality and reinstate my motivation to turn the sport I loved into a professional career. I had been feeling quite unfit and neglectful of my body, Rebecca's needs far outweighing my own.

It was during a lazy unassuming evening with Rebecca that things began to shift within our relationship. We had been sitting innocently watching television at the flat, and Rebecca, as usual, had her head resting on my shoulder with her legs across my lap. She was trying not to fall asleep during a programme I was quite enjoying and becoming annoyed because she kept telling me it was boring. Although she had been stroking her hand over my leg for the last hour, I hadn't really taken much notice of its significance. I was used to how Rebecca acted around me and had never really thought much about it at all.

I didn't see what other people saw from the outside because I was utterly oblivious to the way her behaviour towards me must have looked. I was simply grateful at that point for the fact that she no longer flinched when I accidentally touched her and that she was slowly becoming comfortable cuddling me again. I had missed her affection over the last few months, if I'm being honest. I wasn't used to not having that closeness with her, and now that it was returning, everything felt normal again. I glanced down at her and caught sight of the old Rebecca, the Rebecca we all knew and loved. I smiled, and for a moment, nothing else around us seemed to exist. No one had seen that cheeky look on her face in quite some time, and as I casually kissed her forehead, she reached her hand to my face and stroked my cheek.

'I love you, Craig,' she whispered.

'I love you too, shit face,' I teased, trying to bring my focus back to the television. We told each other that we loved each other all the time, so this was nothing different in my mind. However, when she lifted herself onto her knees and wrapped her arms around my neck, I noticed something in her eyes that I tried initially to brush off. 'I'm trying to watch this-' I attempted to say before I felt her lips press firmly over mine, obscuring my line of vision completely.

Our friends had teased us for years about how we could possibly be so close and yet never become more to each other than the best of friends we were. My male friends, in particular, would often ask if I was gay. How could I share a bed with someone like Rebecca and not "do" anything with her? Rebecca's flat had only two bedrooms. Grace slept in one, of course, and Rebecca's hated the idea of me sleeping on the sofa, so I would climb into bed next to her. It was convenient more than anything else. Grace and Rebecca's relationship was far more relaxed than most people understood, and Rebecca hadn't committed herself to Grace as part of a lesbian couple. To them, their affection towards each other equated to a casual liaison when they needed sexual gratification, and as far as I knew, it was nothing more than that.

I had always considered Rebecca attractive, but she was my very best friend, and I would never have dreamt of jeopardising what we had. But when she straddled me that night, wearing nothing but tight leggings and a t-shirt, I laughed nervously and tried not to notice she wasn't actually wearing a bra. She'd always had a flirtatious nature, and she most definitely knew how attractive she was. It gave her an incredible presence that lifted her confidence higher than anyone I had ever known. She was not arrogant in her attractiveness either. In fact, it was her humble attitude to her appearance that I found the most endearing.

I was unsure how to respond to her advances at first. Since the attack, she had not shown a glimpse of her usual open attitude towards sex, and to be quite honest, I was shocked to find it being aimed directly towards me that night. I knew she no longer trusted men at all now, although I also knew she trusted me more than anyone else. I wondered for a split second if this was her way of trying to get back to some kind of normality. There were no other males in her life that she felt safe enough to re-establish her sexual desires with, and I'm only human. Of course, I wanted to help her find her confidence again.

She leaned forward slightly and slid her hips over my legs, brushing her breasts against my face. When she started grinding her thighs across my groin, I couldn't help the arousal I began to feel. Come on. I'm a man. What do you expect? She looked into my eyes and simulated the motion of sex, helping the growth that was taking place inside my trousers. Although I didn't feel exactly right about what was happening, I did not want to be the one to interrupt Rebecca's newly found assurance, so I simply lay back on the sofa and watched her body move seductively above mine. My hand automatically reached under her top to feel the firm swell of her breasts. I couldn't help it. I guess I just got caught up with the moment. Inevitably at that point, I felt a sharp, wet sensation between my legs and instantly knew what had happened. I closed my eyes and groaned, breathing in the orgasm that burst out of me with no remorse whatsoever.

'You bitch-' I breathed as I opened my eyes again to see a wide grin stretched across Rebecca's face.

'You loved every second of it,' she teased as she leaned in and kissed me on the forehead.

I tried to make light of the situation as I pretended to push her away. I loved her so much, and sitting on top of me right then, she looked more beautiful than I had ever seen her. But something felt wrong. It was something I could not place, but it made my stomach churn all the same. She casually climbed off of me and walked into the kitchen, smiling at me with cheeky blue eyes that always seemed to make me melt no matter what she did. I was grateful that I kept spare clothing in the flat, so I went into the bathroom to shower. I seriously hoped she would not suddenly decide to join me and take whatever this new thing was between us to an even greater unexpected level. I was actually quite relieved when she didn't.

I loved Rebecca more than anyone could have possibly understood, but her actions tonight told me that things were moving in a direction I was not at all ready for. It worried me. There was a vast difference between loving someone with all your heart and actually being "in love" with someone, and I knew deep down that I was simply not in love with Rebecca. Our relationship was unique. It was remarkable, extraordinary even. But she wasn't the person I felt I would someday marry and settle down with. It may sound crazy because most couples are happy when they find that particular person with whom they connect personally and enjoy spending time with. But for me, it wasn't enough simply to settle for that. Rebecca's friendship meant too much to me.

Rebecca and I were heading in entirely different directions in life. We were not on the same page at that point, and I was far too young to think about settling down and committing to one person. Somehow it didn't feel right for us to be in that kind of relationship because although we loved being around each other, I could never honestly see myself with her on a permanent, long-term basis. Our personalities were too different. What if we didn't get on well in a fully committed relationship? What if it ruined the friendship that had taken us years to build? We were tied to each other in a way I couldn't have explained to anyone. I loved the fact that we had our own lives yet enjoyed spending time together. It just worked.

It was the first real intimate moment between us, and although we didn't actually have sex, it was as if in that single moment, her personality came flooding back, and she smiled freely as if she had no cares in the world. I was torn between feeling glad to have helped her get back to her old self, yet at the same time worried sick that this change would now seriously affect the dynamics of our relationship. She had been my very best friend for as long as I could remember and had been the sister I desperately needed. We were open and flirtatious, and seeing her naked was completely normal to me, but this was new. This was something I had not intended or anticipated. Were we beginning a love affair? Would this signify an accidental changing point in our relationship?

As I stood in the shower feeling the water running over my body, I could feel our friendship running into the drain along with it. What if a full-on, committed relationship was not for us? We were young. It was inevitable that we would probably break up at some point. I could not shake the thought of losing her friendship. What the hell had I done? Was I so weak that I could allow a moment of sexual desire to destroy everything we had spent so long building? I honestly understood at that moment why so many male-female friendships don't work. Sex always seems to get in the goddamned way. Had Rebecca been my actual sister, sex would never have even been in the equation, but we were not blood-related, and I was terrified of what I may have unwittingly begun.

***

I tried to wash away my thoughts with the hot water that ran down my back. It was true that Rebecca and I had become much closer in recent months, but I had simply attributed this to her attack and everything that had happened to us since that fateful night. I felt that, if anything, it had actually helped strengthen our bond. She was always walking around the flat with next to nothing on. I had seen her naked so many times, and it had never really bothered me before. I certainly would never have considered the idea that she might develop any ulterior motives, yet her actions tonight told a different story.

I knew she had never actually liked any of my past girlfriends, and thinking about it then, I realised she was probably secretly happy that I was currently single because it meant she could have me all to herself. But we had grown up together, and I had always assumed her over-protectiveness had simply been her way of looking out for me. As comfortable as I was around her, though, I had always been careful of her never to see me fully naked. Something inside my brain prevented that much familiarity with her, although until that very moment, I had never stopped to question why. Maybe I already knew that I needed to keep a barrier between us and to keep our friendship just that—a friendship.

Ever since I could remember, Rebecca would never want me to go home at the end of any evening we had spent together. I would often wake up with a cramp in my arm because she was lying fast asleep on my shoulder, only to look over at the clock and discover it was gone four in the morning. Until now, I hadn't given this extra attention much thought. She had always openly shown affection towards me, yet I had no reason to think her intentions were anything other than platonic. Rebecca had been the only thing in my life that made any sense and the one constant that made things better than they would have been without her. Although my stepdad, Michael, had never attempted to hide the fact he couldn't stand the sight of me, my mother wasn't much better at defending me. It had been Rebecca who had filled a void that I didn't actually fully appreciate until tonight.

Receiving little affection from my own family didn't bother me because the girls were the family I craved. To me, the friendships I had forged with them were far more important than any material items, and I valued every moment we spent together. Yet, for as long as I could remember, I had always felt alone. It was strange to think about that as I stood naked and somewhat vulnerable in Rebecca's shower cubicle. It wasn't simply because I had no caring family to support me, but because I had always felt something was missing, deep down. It was something I hadn't quite been able to fully understand. It felt that there was a part of me that simply wasn't there. I had a hole inside me somewhere that I had no idea how to fill, but when I met Rebecca, that hole seemed to disappear.

\*\*\*

When I came out of the bathroom, I found her in the kitchen happily spreading strawberry jam over a sloppily made cheese sandwich. When she gave me one of her usual smiles, I almost sighed audibly, pure relief evident on my face that she was acting totally normal around me and that the events of the evening had not caused any awkwardness between us.

'Want one?' she asked, holding up a sticky jam-coated knife that dripped onto the countertop.

'I don't know how you can eat that crap.' I wondered how anyone could presume sweet and sour flavouring actually worked together, but I laughed anyway, hoping like hell that the last few moments had all been in my head.

'Feeling better now?' she looked sideways at me for a moment with a knowing smile that told me she had enjoyed making me orgasm and, licking her fingers, she slowly walked towards me and slid her arms beneath mine. I don't think she even cared that she had managed to spread strawberry jam over my clean t-shirt.

'What's happening here, Bex?' I tried to sound casual, but the tone of my voice gave me away immediately.

'What do you think's happening?' Her look had changed. I saw something in her eyes that I hadn't seen before. The way she looked at me now was as if she was actually in love with me. It scared me to death.

'We can't do this. I'm sorry.' I shook my head and gently pushed her away, not able to help the sigh that left my lips unchecked.

Rebecca seemed to echo my own concerns then, her face becoming suddenly too serious for my liking. She wiped her jam-coated fingers half-heartedly on a tea towel and discarded it into the sink.

'But you know how I feel about you, don't you?' She leaned in and tried to kiss me. I was actually surprised and taken aback.

Up until that moment, I genuinely had no idea she felt this way. Call it ignorance if you like. Maybe it was my way of shutting out what I didn't actually want to acknowledge. Whatever it was, it took me by surprise.

'I'm sorry, but we can't do this.' I tried to ignore the look of disappointment on her face. 'Please don't get me wrong, I do have feelings for you, Bex, but we just can't.' I tried to explain my feelings the best way I knew, even though I was failing in my quest completely. 'If we cross the line, things could never be the same again between us. What if we split up? I don't want to lose you.' I was deadly serious, and I knew she would eventually understand what I meant, even as she stood looking at me with pouting lips and colossal puppy dog eyes.

'But you will never lose me,' she whispered before turning around and picking up her cheese and jam sandwich from the countertop somewhat half-heartedly as if she had completely gone off the idea of eating it.

I knew I had hurt her feelings and was desperate for things to go back to normal between us. I couldn't bear the tension. 'I hope you know how much you mean to me,' I said as honestly as I could. 'You know I love you more than anything, don't you, shit face.' I had always called her shit face for as long as I could remember, and it seemed fitting that I attempt to reclaim our friendship now. For a moment, it appeared to calm the mood as Rebecca nibbled the filling out of her sandwich whilst I made us both a hot drink.

'Is that really all you're going to have to eat tonight?' I asked as she dropped a clean plate into the sink that she hadn't even bothered to place her sandwich onto. Rebecca usually hated cooking, not wanting the hassle of the washing up pile afterwards, so she would mostly eat junk food, snacks, or takeaways unless someone was around to make sure she ate a decent meal. I often wondered how she managed to keep her figure in check. Models usually don't eat much at all, but Rebecca loved her food, as long as someone else was doing the cooking. She shrugged, and things went back to normal between us as I got out a saucepan and set about making us both a plate of tuna and cheese pasta.

We sat in front of the television together, acting to anyone looking in, exactly how we always had. We chatted about the silly advertising slogans that Rebecca found amusing, disagreed about what channel to watch and tried to enjoy our simple meal in peace, yet the guilt I felt beginning to set in was unbearable. Although we had always been very open with each other, Rebecca and I always seemed to know where to draw the line. Until tonight that was. Tonight had changed everything.

'Are we okay?' I asked eventually when I couldn't stand the pretence any longer.

'What are you still worrying about that for?' Rebecca almost spat her words towards me as she discarded her plate carelessly onto the living room floor and stormed into the bathroom, slamming a dirty towel into the laundry basket with a thud. Her mood had shifted quickly, and I knew we needed to clear the air before things got out of control. 'My God, Craig, it's not as if we haven't been getting closer lately.' She stood in the bathroom doorframe, looking at me as if I had somehow managed to make her feel cheap, and it was then that I realised she was taking things far more seriously than I had first thought. Her darkening mood made me wonder if she actually assumed we would now begin a full-on relationship, with no questions asked or concerns being addressed.

'You're my best friend.' I suddenly felt sick.

'Maybe I want more than friendship.'

I didn't quite know how to respond. 'Let's just see how things go, shall we?' I didn't know what was happening between us, and it genuinely scared me. I certainly couldn't tell her that I didn't want more than friendship. I wanted things to remain exactly how they were right now, the way they had always been. Her friendship was all I had.

'You're acting as if we did something wrong. We didn't even have sex.'

I almost choked on a piece of tuna. 'And why do you think that was?' To be honest, I wasn't entirely confident that if Rebecca had wanted to take things further tonight, I might have actually reciprocated and ruined everything completely. It would have been a terrible mistake, yet I somehow wrongly assumed that by keeping things with Rebecca on an even keel now, I would be still able to keep our friendship intact.

'I have no idea, to be honest, why we didn't have sex.' Rebecca had the same look on her face she often displayed when she sulked. I usually found it adhering, and I had to look away before I made things any worse.

I sighed. Rebecca meant more to me than anything, although being in a full sexual relationship with her scared me to death, and I did not intend to jeopardise what we had. 'Because you're like a sister to me, that's why.'

'Oh, and you squeeze your sister's tits do you?' Rebecca sounded irritated, although it was actually quite funny.

'Obviously not.' Jesus Christ, what the hell had I allowed to begin? 'That was just-'

'Just what?'

I wanted to say, just a mistake, but noted the severe look on her face and anxious tone in her voice. The last thing I needed right then was a full-blown argument. 'That was just my automatic reaction. I find you attractive. Sorry if that offends you.' I was attempting to act jokey and lift this impending argument's mood towards a more relaxed conversation. I did find Rebecca attractive. Everyone did.

'I'm not offended.' Rebecca smiled slightly, and for a moment, I thought I saw her cheeks flush.

'Please, let's not argue tonight,' I pleaded. I genuinely

74

needed to calm things between us. I was dreading the idea of Grace and Jade finding out what had happened, but I would have to deal with that later. Right now, all I wanted was some relaxation. Rebecca nodded and came over to the sofa and sat on my lap.

'Sorry,' she whispered. I was glad she didn't lean in for another kiss.

'So am I.' And I genuinely meant it. I was sorry about the whole damned thing.

# Chapter 7

As Rebecca's general mood improved and things slowly began to get back to normal, I threw myself into my training regime and pushed myself harder than ever to be ready for the start of the motocross season that year. I was almost twenty years old and knew if I didn't soon get the break I needed to move to a professional level, I would be classed as too old to be signed by a high-profile team. I knew if a team like Honda were to sign me up, I would only need to race until I was around thirty-five years old, and then I could retire a potential millionaire. It seemed like the perfect plan, and I didn't even consider that anything could possibly go wrong.

June came around quickly, and so did one of the biggest competition weekends of my career to date. Scouts from Honda, KTM, and Yamaha would be there that weekend, and I was desperate to be spotted as the fresh young talent they needed. I had gone from junior to expert level within just two seasons. It hardly ever happened because motocross requires hard work and dedication, and for this reason, scouts from the big teams were beginning to notice me. It usually takes a young rider several years to progress to senior ranking, and I had managed to do so within a brief timeframe. However, as with most other industries, it can become quite ruthless when you earn money from professional sports. The prospect of making a substantial amount of money within a relatively short amount of time is appealing for most riders but, of course, this concept does not come without consequence.

Over a year, I had managed to break several bones, dislocated most of the fingers on both hands and my left shoulder, painfully ruptured a testicle and spent a couple of days in the hospital with a concussion, having hit my head too hard on the handlebars.

Every rider on that track wanted to win races and earn the money that was on offer, my own dreams of turning professional, not in any way unique to everyone else out there. I was just one of several riders good enough to be signed by the big teams, and it was the reason I had been training so hard. I knew that Rebecca was not happy about how dangerous things were becoming, but the prospect of earning several thousand pounds per week doing a sport I loved kept me going back for more, and I absolutely could not and would not stop, not even for her. I certainly did not want to continue working in a dead-end job for the rest of my life, and I saw motocross as my way of not having to.

***

I was practically shaking with excitement as we unloaded our bikes from the trailer at the track that Saturday morning, the feeling that things were just about to change more firmly embedded in my mind than anything I had experienced before. We were in high spirits, the sun was shining, and I felt stronger and more capable than I had ever felt in my entire life. We had risen early that morning because I couldn't sleep. As I walked the track with the other racers to familiarise ourselves with the angles of the jumps, lines, and corners, I felt sick with anticipation and excitement for a future that, as far as I was concerned, was well within my reach. I could smell fresh bacon cooking some feet away, and my stomach growled, adding to my already churning insides as to what the day could provide.

I glanced around at the growing number of spectators and riders that had gathered for the weekend meeting, including news crews and television broadcasters that would be filming the weekend event and food vans dotted around the place, enticing people of all ages with their wares. I couldn't help expressing an unanticipated grin, and I swear I probably must have looked insane to anyone who didn't know me, a smile planted across my face like a lunatic. For me, this was what life was all about. Feeling alive and free, knowing you are doing something you love and that other people come to watch these races because they love the sport, too. It really felt that, despite everything that had happened over the last few months, today would signal a change in direction for us all, and one we desperately needed. I believed that nothing would be able to bring down my mood at that point. I was literally on a high.

I walked over to where our trailer was situated, keen to share my good mood with the girls and buzzing with excitement I couldn't suppress. I didn't notice the strange look in Rebecca's eyes at first or the way she seemed uneasy, nervous even. She was staring ahead and biting her nails, her mind elsewhere, yet I'd not initially noticed.

'What's wrong with you?' I chided towards her, wanting desperately for the weekend to succeed and needing no distractions whatsoever. When she didn't immediately answer, I followed her line of vision to where a group of motocross riders had gathered. Ryan and Justin were standing a mere twenty feet away from us, laughing and joking as if nothing in the world could possibly touch them. In the very second it took me to lay my eyes onto their smug faces, I felt my heart lunge into my throat. My mood immediately darkened, and I flinched.

Noticing what had just happened, Jade touched my arm. 'Don't you dare,' she warned, giving me a look that if it had the power to kill me, probably would have.

'Shit,' I yelled, not giving a damn who might have overheard me. In my heightened state, I'd totally forgotten that those two would even be there, and yet in the second it had taken me to discover their presence, my good mood had managed to disappear completely. I slammed my helmet into the back of the trailer and swore again. I was convinced that nothing would ruin this weekend for me; my focus only on winning races and getting noticed. The last thing I needed was any distraction from those jumped-up little twats.

It had been because of motocross that I even knew those two existed at all, our circle of acquaintances seemingly smaller than I had realised. Jade had actually met Justin because of motocross. Why the hell I didn't warn her about him before she got mixed up with him, I have no idea, but I couldn't dwell on the past. I was sure their dislike for me had developed out of pure jealousy for my relationship with the girls and the fact that I was damned good at motocross. Better than they were, that was for sure.

'Hey.' It was Grace's turn now to grab my attention. 'Don't you dare let them spoil this for you.' She shook her head knowingly. 'Not today.' I knew she was right, of course, but it didn't change how I felt. Rebecca wasn't looking at all comfortable standing next to the trailer, trying to keep herself upright by leaning against my bike. Although she assured me she was okay, I knew her better than that and knew she was not okay at all by the way her body had started to tremble.

Once Ryan had noticed our presence, he seemed to revel in the concept of making her feel uncomfortable, randomly waving in her direction and blowing kisses whenever she accidentally looked his way. The pain and anger I had felt on the night of Rebecca's attack still bubbled away below the surface, and it threatened now to tip me over the edge completely. I would have loved nothing more than to walk straight up to him and slam my helmet into his face.

'If you even so much as think about it, Craig, you can kiss your motocross chances goodbye.' It was Rebecca. She walked over to me and stood stared into my eyes, trying to assess my thought processes.

'Do you think I don't know that?' I couldn't help snapping at her. I wasn't completely stupid.

'Then take that look off your face. Right now.' She wasn't joking.

\*\*\*

The first two races were endured through gritted teeth as I tried hard to stay out of their way, my entire time spent thinking about how badly I wanted to hurt them. I was concentrating so hard on winning the first race that when Ryan passed me on a corner, I couldn't quite figure out if I'd imagined him mutter the words "you're dead" as he sped by, spraying dirt across my visor in the process. I caught up to the rear of his bike, ready to take him on the last corner and leave him quite literally eating my dirt. He glanced back, grinned at me and misjudged the turning, allowing me to easily pass him by. I won that race, of course, but I was fuming by the time I got back to the trailer.

When I told the girls what I thought I'd heard, they tried to laugh it off. 'They're full of shit,' Jade assured me. 'Don't worry, Craig. Just get on with it. Don't let them bother you.' I couldn't help but let it bother me, and for the rest of that day, I was left with a feeling of discomfort that I simply could not shake. I couldn't tell if it was their presence that was creating my anguish or the fact that my gut was telling me something was off, but whatever it was, it wasn't leaving me alone.

***

When I woke up on that Sunday morning, something just didn't feel right. As I pulled my bike out of the trailer, it didn't respond in the way it usually did. I had cleaned off all the mud from the day before and had checked the brakes, tyres, and engine, twice. My mechanic Jerry had checked all components and had been satisfied that everything was in good working order when he had wheeled it back onto the trailer for the evening. Everything had been working fine, but as I wheeled my bike across the grass that morning, I had a niggling feeling I simply couldn't shake.

'Are you okay?' Rebecca asked, seeing the look of concern on my face.

'I don't know,' I answered as honestly as I could. 'I've got a weird feeling.'

'What kind of feeling?'

'I don't know. My bike doesn't feel right.' I glanced around at the tents and trailers surrounding us as if I expected to see a menacing face staring at me from somewhere, anywhere.

'What do you mean? What's wrong with it?' Rebecca sounded anxious then, too.

I looked away from her quickly, realising I had probably worried her unnecessarily. 'Don't worry. It's nothing. I'm probably just being silly.' I tried to shake off the growing feeling in my gut, but it didn't work. Something was wrong, and Rebecca knew I knew it.

'Craig.' She said sternly. 'Talk to me-'

'It's nothing,' I answered again. 'Forget about it.'

'Do you need Jerry to take another look?'

'No, it's fine.'

'You don't think-'

'No, I don't,' I stepped in, not giving her time to finish her words. I knew exactly what she was about to say and I didn't want to hear it.

'How do you know?' She was actually starting to sound angry. 'You said they threatened you yesterday.'

'To be honest, Bex, I don't know what I heard. It was noisy out there. I probably didn't hear anything.' I didn't need this stress right now. Rebecca folded her arms and raised a worried eyebrow. I sighed then, not quite realising the significance of my own intuition. 'I'm sure the bike is fine. But if it will make you happy, I'll get it checked over in a bit.'

'Promise?'

'I promise.'

Rebecca motioned to walk away but changed her mind and sighed. 'Don't race today.' It was not a passing request, and it seemed to come from nowhere.

'What? Don't be so bloody stupid. I've got to race.' I could not believe what I was hearing. 'Today is the most important day of the season. If I don't race, I don't get spotted. If I don't get spotted, that's it. Forget it. I've got to wait another year before I get another chance.' There was absolutely no way I was about to let several months of training be all for nothing.

'It doesn't matter-'

'Of course, it matters.' I dragged my bike back over to the trailer, still concerned that it seemed to be limping somehow, its wheels not turning as freely as they should. I leaned it against the back of the truck. 'I'll be too old next year. They won't even look twice at me.'

'Who cares?' Rebecca tried to grab my arm. 'What does it matter about scouts and money if you get hurt in the process? Who's going to sign you then anyway?'

'Who cares!?' I yelled, ignoring the part about getting hurt completely. At that point, I didn't care who could hear me. 'I care, Bex, that's who. I've been working hard for this all year. I'm not about to let some jumped up twats ruin my chances of a better future.'

'I don't give a damn about motocross, Craig. I care about you. Of course, they'll sign you next year. You are only twenty years old, for God's sake.'

'I should be already signed up with a team by now, though.'

'Jesus Christ,' she spat. 'Don't be so stupid.'

'Stupid? How stupid is it to want to make something of my life? Is it stupid to want you to be proud of me?'

'I'm already proud of you,' she yelled. By now, we were actually drawing a crowd.

'This is my big chance. Don't you understand that?'

'Please *don't* race.'

'I'm racing.' It wasn't negotiable.

'Craig, please-'

'Fuck off.' It was my final word on the subject. I caught sight of Rebecca as she stormed off and climbed into her car, driving off so fast that mud and grass sprayed out from under her wheels as she mouthed something under her breath that didn't sound very ladylike. It left me physically shaking. We had not argued like that for quite some time. How dare she do this to me, today of all days?

\*\*\*

My anger at the way things had been left between us increased, and as time drew nearer to the start of the race, I actually began to feel quite nauseous. Rebecca had a volatile temper and would often storm out of the flat during an argument. It was a standard way of diffusing an otherwise tense situation and allow things to cool between us. We got on so well most of the time but, like anyone else, we too, had our moments. Under no circumstances could I let her affect this race. Not today.

It was too important to me. As I wheeled my bike to the starting gate, I retained a feeling that something didn't seem right with it, but I was not about to let anything, especially Rebecca's words, stop me from getting through this weekend and emerging as a new recruit for Honda.

Jade carried my helmet for me down to the starting gate, as she always did, her own concerns clear to see across her face that I tried to ignore. 'I haven't heard you two fight like that for ages,' she told me as we stood on the line.

'What does she expect me to do?' I grabbed my helmet from her grasp and spent too long fiddling with the fastening. 'She knows how important this race is today.'

'She just wants to make sure you're okay,' Jade replied as she squeezed my arm. I knew she was trying to calm me down, but it wasn't working.

'Well, I'm not now, am I?' I pulled my helmet over my head and fastened my goggles into place, my hands unapologetically trembling.

As I mounted my bike, I could feel my heart pounding against my ribcage, and I could barely swallow my own saliva. I couldn't figure out if it was due to my overwrought nerves or the sheer amount of dust on the track, but whatever it was, it made my head ache with anticipation. Bikes to the left and right of me were screaming, jumping forward in desperation to be set free, their riders as anxious as I was. I glanced along the line of bikes next to me and caught a glimpse of Ryan's smug grin as he pulled his helmet over his head. It was as if he had been waiting for me to notice him. I felt sick. He must have heard the fight between myself and Rebecca and had no doubt been gloating ever since. Smug bastard.

I had never hated someone as much as I hated him at that

moment, and I knew it was adrenaline alone that was keeping me upright as I pulled back the throttle as hard as I could. My head was screaming contradicting thoughts that I did not know how to handle. Should I race? Was Rebecca right? Why didn't any of this feel right to me? My bike's engine screeched angrily in response to my thoughts as I held a tight grip firmly on the brake. I realised I had forgotten to ask Jerry to check my bike, but it was too late for me to worry about that now.

They say we all have an inner voice that makes us feel strongly about a situation and tells us when something is wrong or right. The type of gut feeling that tells you deep down when you need to take immediate action or avoid a situation altogether. Some call it intuition. Whatever it was, right then, my gut was screaming at me, telling me I was about to make the biggest mistake of my life. Yet I was only twenty years old. I was arrogant, cocky, and way too damned sure of myself for my own good. What the hell did I know about intuition and such things? I wasn't about to let some weird sickly feeling in my belly stop me racing that day. I had come too far, and I had worked too hard. I simply assumed that I would win that race and then happily kick the shit out of that son of a bitch once and for all.

As the race began, everything else faded from my mind, and the task ahead became my only focus. I had trained so hard and for so long. As we came into the first bend, I was already in the lead. Thoughts of Rebecca and my uncertain fears disappeared as the roaring sound of engines around me took control of my senses. As far as I was concerned, this was my chance, my time to make something incredible happen on my own terms. My bike responded to my demands, and together we raced around that track, both determined to show everyone just how good we actually were.

I could hear the crowd cheering encouragement as we threw ourselves into the race. Every single rider that day wanted to impress, knowing that this single event could change our lives forever. It's a shame that I could not have realised at the time that this race was actually about to change my life, just not in the way I had assumed. As I powered my bike towards one of the most significant tabletop jumps on the track, I opened the throttle, determined to produce as much distance between myself and the ground as possible. I wanted Honda to see me and think, "Wow, this guy is impressive. We've just got to sign him." I allowed nothing else to cloud my mind, and as I came towards the jump, my bike lunged from the ground in anticipation of an impressive finale that I knew would surely wow them all. It was at that exact moment I knew something was seriously wrong.

I had performed many jumps previous to that day, executing perfect flips and kicks as I projected my bike over twenty feet into the air, showing off my stunt skills to excited onlookers and roaring applause. I loved the feeling it gave me, and I loved the approval of the crowds below. I was convinced that today would be no different, but as my tyres left the ground, I felt my bike's back wheel suddenly lock up behind me. The engine roared frantically as my bike began tilting dangerously forward. I tried to regain the correct position for a safe landing, but I had no control at twenty feet in the air, and gravity was fighting back rapidly.

I have no memory of what happened next, but I was later told it was the most horrific crash the motocross organisers had ever witnessed. I didn't open my eyes again until three weeks later, and when I did, things were very different.

# Chapter 8

At first, I could neither make out where I was or what had happened to me. I was lying flat on my back, and I could feel something uncomfortable digging into my skin, but I did not have any idea at all where I was or what was going on. I could vaguely make out the shape of someone in a white coat who said something about me having been drifting in and out of consciousness for over a week, but few words spoken to me seemed to make any sense, and I struggled to keep my eyes focused long enough to take in any of my surroundings.

I could barely make out the shape of a girl standing next to a bed I seemed to be lying in, but I didn't recognise her, even when she held my hand and told me everything would be okay. Who was she? Where was I? And more importantly, what the hell had happened? I tried to pull my hand away from her grip and felt a sharp pain shoot through my head.

'Oh, please don't do that,' the girl whispered quietly, trying to smooth my hand back down onto the sheets in some strange assumption she was actually calming me. Although I could vaguely understand the words being spoken to me, they sounded blurred, slow, and weirdly unreal. I felt somewhat detached from my senses. It was a challenging situation to comprehend. 'It's okay, babe,' the unknown girl kissed my forehead and smiled at me, her eyes a telling validity that none of this was okay at all.

Why was she calling me babe? I didn't know her, so why was she acting so familiar with me? I tried again to pull myself free from her grasp, not knowing who she was or what she wanted from me at all. She had a puzzled look that matched my own, but at that moment, I seriously didn't care. I glanced down at my right arm, wondering why it hurt so much. I caught a glimpse of a needle protruding from the back of my hand attached to some kind of drip.

My ears were making an alarming screeching sound that only aided in emphasising all other noises around me. It was as if someone had turned on a radio at full volume without considering anyone else whatsoever. In a panic, I tried to force myself into an upright position. I needed to gain some perspective and shake this growing sensation that my brain wasn't functioning correctly, but I was instantly met with excruciating pain in the back of my head I wasn't expecting to feel. Jesus Christ. I tried again, and the same pain almost made me vomit. I felt something wet on my face and realised, with an alarming jolt, that it was saliva dribbling from my mouth. What the hell was going on?

By this time, the girl had retreated into the corridor to call for help. I had to get up, to get some air. I could make out vague shapes around me, but everything felt surreal, the screeching in my head growing more intense the longer I remained conscious. Someone came into the room and spoke to me, but I could not precisely fathom any words being said. It was as if they were speaking a language I could not understand. Curiously, it was as if I was watching a movie where words had been purposely placed into extreme slow motion for dramatic effect. Even if I could have understood anyone, the shrill ringing I felt in my ears dulled any senses I usually had, making the humdrum goings-on around me impossible to deal with. My head felt as though a bomb had exploded somewhere deep inside it, and I automatically leaned over the edge of the bed in an attempt to calm myself. I genuinely thought I was going to throw up.

I could sense people coming in and out of the room and watched in slow motion as some white-coated shape spoke to me. Why I could not understand a word he was saying to me, I simply did not know. The girl standing next to my bed only moments earlier leaned forward in an attempt to retake my hand. I must have looked blankly at her because she burst into tears.

'It's quite normal, Rebecca,' I thought I heard someone mumble. 'It should pass in a few days'.

My heart was pounding and literally felt as if it could burst out of my chest at any moment. A disgusting taste of iron in the back of my throat made me gag, and I desperately needed a drink of water and a major explanation. I tried to open my mouth to speak, but I was shocked to discover I could not form any words and the sound that emerged from my throat sounded strangled and ridiculous. No one could understand what I was trying to say, and I was met with what I could barely translate as snippets of "It's okay, Mr Marshall, just relax and try to keep calm." But I didn't want to relax, and I certainly didn't want to keep calm. The only thing I needed right then was for someone to tell me what the hell was going on. I felt something press into my arm, and everything slipped into oblivion.

***

When I opened my eyes again, I instinctively tried to sit up but was shocked to discover that I could not move a muscle. I panicked. What in God's name was happening to me? Something had drastically changed, yet at that point, I simply had no idea what it was, and I couldn't figure out how to deal with anything that was happening around me. Someone entered the room and drew back the blinds from the window allowing daylight to flood the space. My eyes immediately felt as if they had been poked out of my head with an iron rod, and I involuntarily cried out in pain. Each time I closed my eyes, I caught tiny glimpses of memories new and old, and I could clearly see random items from my lifetime. An old toy stuffed dog that for some reason only had one ear, motocross bike parts, carrot cake.

I tried to shake off these crazy visions, convinced I must have been floating in and out of consciousness and hoping like hell I wasn't going completely insane. The blinds were pulled closed again, followed by a muffled apology before I was left alone, none the wiser as to what was happening.

At that exact moment in my life, I fully understood what it must be like to feel as if you are literally going mad. For the majority of time, we are usually entirely oblivious to the thousands of tiny connections our brains need to make for us to function on a normal level. It is incredible to consider that the human brain processes more than fifty thousand thoughts in any given day. This equates to approximately one random thought every two to three seconds or thereabouts, and ninety per cent of these thoughts go completely unnoticed by our conscious minds. Those little actions that our brains perform on a subconscious level, including moving our hands, scratching an itch, or simply being able to breathe, are things we hardly stop to think about at all. And yet, for me, I was now fully aware of everything that my body needed to do. I could feel my own blood pulsating through my veins. I could hear every single beat of my heart inside my chest and could even sense the flushing of oxygen through my lungs.

If I wanted to move my hand, I had to physically think about the idea of doing it before I could make it happen. It felt as if I had somehow, without warning, turned into a machine, a robot, processing everything manually to be able to function, and it genuinely terrified me. I fully understood what it feels like for that unassuming person sitting in the corner of a room somewhere rocking backwards and forwards, their brains not correctly able to connect to their bodies at all because of the sheer volume of thoughts racing through their brain. Right at that moment, my body was doing anything but connecting with my brain. It was the most horrific thing I have ever experienced, yet one I was unable to tell anyone about.

I could hear a hollow, slurred voice somewhere in the distance, although the voice actually seemed to be coming from a person standing next to my bed that I struggled to understand at all. She had probably merely asked if I was okay, but I couldn't quite place her words into any correct order in my brain. My heart lunged. Why the hell could I not understand words being formed by the people around me? The nurse standing next to my bed had a sympathetic look on her face that made me want to scream at her. She continued to speak in that annoyingly slow, slurred way as she wrapped a piece of canvas around my arm. She squeezed a plastic ball, and my arm tightened. It felt as if something was draining the blood from my entire body.

I wanted to ask her what day it was and why my head was hurting so much, but I couldn't figure out how to translate the words going around inside my head and get them to come out of my mouth in the correct order. I had questions I did not have the faculties to answer, and every time I tried, I simply could not correctly form any words into speech. I was terrified. It was as if I had become trapped in a dream-like state. Nothing around me made any sense, and I could not get anyone to understand what I desperately needed to say.

I had visits from two people that day, neither of whom held any recollection in my mind. One of them I remembered as the girl who had been holding my hand previously, but I did not recognise the man who sat by the side of the bed for over an hour, smiling at me and seemingly asking every few minutes if I needed anything. I later learned that it had been my boss, Andrew. He had sat next to my bed with a very concerned look on his face, although at the time, I had no idea why. They apparently chatted to me for a short while before leaving me to sleep, although I do not recall a single word that either of them had said.

Days must have passed quickly because when I awoke with the feeling that I could finally understand words again, it was told to me that I had been in hospital for almost three weeks. When Rebecca and Jade came into the ward, arms wide for a hug, I was surprised to see their relieved faces smiling back at me. I had no genuine recollection of the last few weeks at all, and I didn't even realise that I had failed to recognise Rebecca during her previous visits. They looked relieved to see me awake and fully alert after what must have felt like a highly frightening time for everyone.

'I thought I'd lost you,' Rebecca was attempting to sound casual in her tone, although she failed to hide a tear that made a break for it down her cheek. We both knew she was hiding the seriousness of what had happened to me.

I smiled at them both, grateful that the fog I had been experiencing was now slowly beginning to clear. I opened my mouth to speak, but my words came out as a jumbled mess. My tongue did not form the words I wanted to say. I tried again, yet the only thing I could achieve was a strained groaning noise that made me sound like a simpleton. Rebecca held my hand and smiled, a silent fear behind her eyes that I did not like and could not understand. I began to panic. *Help me, someone, please,* I desperately tried to say several times. I had no idea what was happening to me.

I leaned forward, desperate to get out of bed. I felt that if I could get up and walk around, I could shake off this dream-like feeling and snap myself out of whatever it was that was happening to me. All I could think about was stretching my legs for a moment, and I would be just fine.

I tried to move my legs, but to my horror, they wouldn't move. Panicking, I dragged them to the edge of the bed in an attempt to stand up, but in my haste, I slid from the edge of the mattress and collapsed onto the floor, my feet only making contact briefly with the tiles before my knees crumbled beneath me. Lying on the cold hospital floor that day, I genuinely thought I had been paralysed, and terrible thoughts raced through my mind. Jesus Christ, what the hell was happening to me?

A nurse ran into the room, followed quickly by a doctor, who both mirrored a similar look of concern. I was still trying to force my mouth to form words as they helped me from the floor and back into bed.

'Don't worry, Mr Marshall,' one nurse said. 'It's perfectly normal.' It was the second time I had heard those words, and I had had enough. I could see the girls standing to one side, neither of them able to offer any help, and both looking almost as panicked as me.

'Why can't I walk?' I desperately tried to ask them, although my tongue caught the back of my throat, and it came out more like 'Hye are ey lowg?' I hoped like hell they could understand me, and by now, I was actually starting to have a genuine full-on panic attack.

I was settled back into bed and given some drugs to calm me down, but at that point, I just wanted to be left alone. My breathing felt shallow, as if someone was crushing my chest, and because I didn't understand anything that was going on, I just wanted the girls to go away. I didn't want them to see me like that.

'It's okay, Craig,' I heard Jade say, but nothing about any

of this was okay at all.

\*\*\*

Once everyone had gone, and I was finally left alone with my own thoughts, I allowed myself to lie back so that I could finally try and create some well-needed clarity on this strange situation I had found myself in. I closed my eyes, wondering why all I could see were images and memories from my own life. They bore no relevance at all to my current location or situation, and I couldn't figure out why I couldn't turn them off. It was as if a slide show had been turned on in my head, and I had no idea how to pull the plug. I glanced around the hospital ward at the other unfortunate patients surrounding me.

I hated hospitals; that distinct stench of disinfectant and the sensation of impending death around practically every corner. As I lay in that bed feeling sorry for myself, a feeling of dread began to creep over me. What if this was it? What if I was destined to lie on my back for the rest of my life whilst someone else fed and bathed me like a child who has no faculties to speak of? Yet even as I thought it, the idea sounded completely stupid to me. I felt ridiculous for even considering such a thing. I knew that eventually, I would be just fine. I had to be. Nothing else seemed possible at all.

I felt that to shake off this fog, all I needed was to get up out of bed and get some well-deserved fresh air. I tried to pull myself up against pillows that weirdly rustled and made me think of those plastic sheets often used when children wet the bed, shocked to discover that my legs would not move. It was as if someone else had control of them, and I was simply along for the ride. I reached down to touch them, terrified I would not be able to even feel my flesh and relieved when I felt my fingers pressing into my thigh. I tried to wiggle my toes, but nothing happened. I tried again only to be met with the same outcome. What was going on? I was too spaced out at that stage for any doctor to adequately explain what had happened to me, but it didn't stop me from fretting, nevertheless.

I could not understand why I saw random images and pictures that constantly flicked through my conscious moments. The sensation was as if someone had stuffed a projector inside my head, randomly loading photographs into my eyeballs. How could this be possible? It almost felt as if I was dreaming somehow, even though my eyes were open, and I knew I was clearly awake.

It's strange when I think about it now, but many of my early memories have been dislodged and fragmented, and I struggle to recall certain things from those early times in my life. To be suddenly bombarded with vivid memories from my early life now was unnerving. It may be that some aspects are just too confusing for my brain to process because there are large pieces of that time missing, and little things that should be obvious to me simply do not exist in my memory. It made the entire process even more terrifying now because I had no idea which of those images were true, and which ones had been created by my brain, purely for effect.

For instance, I don't seem to be able to recall a single time in my entire childhood when my mother ever cuddled me, held me in her arms or told me she loved me. It may sound ridiculous, but the more I desperately try to remember these simple acts of parental affection, the less I can actually recall her ever showing me any fondness at all. The truth is that I honestly don't understand what people mean when they talk about what it's like to have a family. I guess that is why I held onto what I had with the girls so closely because, as far as I was concerned, they were my family.

I don't know how actual families are supposed to act

because growing up, my family never really bothered with me at all. I didn't learn to love the people I knew as my parents because they simply didn't give me the chance to feel anything other than insecurity, anger, and repulsion for my own existence. I genuinely thought they hated me, and I had literally no idea what I had done to deserve such condemnation.

It's funny what you recall when you are small, and I don't actually remember much about my dad at all. The only thing my brain remembered was that he was a sullen faced, skinny, ginger-haired man who never liked to wash. He wouldn't change his socks or underwear from one week to the next, and for all her downfalls, it must have driven my mother crazy. It obviously became too much for her because she disappeared from my life when I was just five years old. I learned later that she had left us, for another man apparently. She had simply packed a suitcase one morning after my father had gone to work and walked out. I had a horrible vision for a long time of her storming along the footpath, suitcase in tow, almost breaking out into a run as she left our lives in a hurry. I felt that it must have been because of me.

The worst part of all was that I was immediately put into foster care after mum had gone, although, for some reason, my older brother and sister remained in the care of my father. I had no idea why this had happened, and I had no way of asking questions I understood nothing about. It was two more years before my mother came to take me home.

I didn't want those old memories in my mind. They were long gone, and there was literally nothing I could do about any of it now anyway. I cursed my brain for showing me those old wounds that I realised had never truly healed. It was reasonably amusing on the occasion when random images would pop into my thoughts. I was reminded of an old, knitted sock with a hole in the toe that made me cry so hard and a stuffed toy monkey called Mickey, who, as a child, I remembered vividly. He was much older than I was when I came to own him and already showed distinct signs that he had seen a lot of love before he came to belong to me.

I have no idea where he had come from or how old I was when I acquired him, but I took him everywhere with me, and he shared every pain that I had been forced to endure. He had been my best friend and my earliest memory. I wondered for a moment what had happened to him—good old Mickey the Monkey.

# Chapter 9

I had been in hospital for over a month by the time someone was finally able to actually explain what had happened to me. When a doctor came into the ward and offered a brief smile that seemed entirely staged, I tried to ignore it, pretending for a moment that this was happening to someone else.

'How are you feeling today, Craig?' he asked, his strong foreign accent doing nothing whatsoever for my sense of understanding. I couldn't answer him directly, so I simply shrugged my shoulders. It would have to do, and it ironically fitted exactly how I felt anyway. 'You have suffered a severe traumatic brain injury, young man,' he continued. 'You've damaged the blood vessels that connects your brain to your central nervous system, and your brain is extremely bruised at the moment. We will, of course, need to do further tests to determine an exact diagnosis.'

He was going through my notes as he spoke, and yet I am sure he was completely unaware that I could not understand much of what he was saying to me. His words filtered off into the distance, my mind still unable to determine what was actually happening around me.

Rebecca had been allowed to remain in the room while the consultant talked to me, and for that, I was extremely grateful. They assumed correctly that having a second person in the room would allow me to better understand what was happening because of my injuries' severity. They were not wrong. Although I could hear words that were being spoken, my comprehension was muddled, and when Rebecca squeezed my hand, I wondered if she had heard something I simply wasn't able to absorb.

'You are currently unable to walk because your brain is severely swollen, and your speech problem is due to your brain literally being scrambled inside your skull.' The doctor made a little jiggling action with his fist. 'You have a severe bleed in your brain, and we had to keep you sedated for a while in an induced coma to help the healing process.' Bloody hell, this was actually serious. 'I do have to tell you, Craig, that unfortunately, you might never walk again.' Had I heard that right? I could feel my insides turn to jelly as Rebecca took a sharp intake of breath that I tried and failed to ignore. I would have given anything at that moment to have wholly misunderstood those words entirely.

I could not take in what he was trying to tell me. As he spoke, all I could focus on were random images and memories from my life that flitted across my mind like a silent movie playing over and over again without remorse. Some beach I'd visited years earlier, a rusty barbeque that had been left out in the rain, Bella's chew toy that she hated because it squeaked. The consultant looked at me as if he did not know what else to say, and no other words from him would have, in any way, helped me understand the devastation of his evaluation. 'We will need to keep you in for further tests, of course, and to see if your brain heals by itself,' he added before leaving us alone to process the information we had been told.

I stared at Rebecca, desperately hoping she would understand what I wanted to say. What did he mean, *if* my brain heals? Was he actually serious? She looked so tired, as if she hadn't slept for weeks. I tried several times to speak to her before I gave up and closed my eyes in frustration, nothing making any sense to me at all.

'I can't tell you how thankful I am that you're awake, Craig,' Rebecca sighed, squeezing my hand tightly in hers. I knew she was trying to ignore the doctor's last words in some apparent ditch effort to protect me, but I didn't want her to ignore them. I wanted her to confirm that I had heard him wrong and that every one of the doctors had got this completely wrong. 'They said it was touch and go for a while and that if you even woke up at all, you'd probably be a-' Her voice trailed off, and I couldn't help glaring at her lost looking face sitting blankly by my bedside. I wanted to ask her what exactly it was they thought would I be, and she must have seen the look of desperation on my face because she closed her eyes and finished her sentence too quickly. 'They said you would probably be a vegetable for the rest of your life because your brain injury is so severe.'

Jesus Christ. I couldn't believe what Rebecca was actually saying to me. If I could have found my voice at that moment, I probably would have screamed at her, laughed even at the total lunacy of her words. I knew I was not exactly helping my self at that point because, with every attempt to speak, I was simply confirming to the doctors that their predictions were correct. They probably assumed I was already in some kind of vegetable state and that my brain was too damaged for me to ever communicate appropriately again. Yet, I certainly had no intention of being anything other than completely normal. No doctor would tell me what I was or wasn't going to do— vegetable my backside.

I really wanted to talk to Rebecca about my accident and ask her views on what we had just been told. I had no fundamental concept of what had actually happened to me; the last thing I remembered of that day was being twenty feet in the air and thinking that this was really going to hurt as gravity started to fight back. No one seemed to be saying much to me at all other than to go through the motions of politeness. I was already getting quite sick of it.

'Awk u ee?' I hoped that Rebecca would understand what I was trying to say to her.

'Talk to you?'

'Eeess.' Why would my goddamned words not come out right? I gripped the bedsheets tightly, hating everything I had become.

'I don't want you to worry about anything at the moment, Craig. You're going to be okay, I promise.' Rebecca sounded sincere, yet something in her eyes told a completely different story.

***

The first time I saw myself in a mirror, I could not believe what I was witnessing. My hair had been shaved off so probes and wires could be attached to my scalp to monitor my condition, and my face was swollen and bloated out of proportion. I hardly recognised the person looking back at me. I actually felt like a circus freak that had been locked inside a cage. Although none of the girls seemed to take much notice, I did not want to be seen by anyone else who knew me under any circumstances. It was bad enough that my body no longer functioned properly, but knowing that my looks had completely altered as well was too much for me to take. I could not believe how my life had changed so dramatically, now unable to hold a conversation or use my legs at all.

I had understandably been feeling quite sorry for myself during those first few weeks in hospital, but when two paramedics walked onto the ward to see me, they singlehandedly elevated my mood enormously. As they approached my bed, they seemed genuinely overwhelmed to see me sitting up and watching television, unaware of the carnage that had been my accident. They smiled broadly when I gave them a blank look. I had no idea who they were.

'You won't know us,' one of them began as he pulled a chair next to the bed and sat down. 'But we were the ones who brought you in here.'

'Yeah,' the other added. 'And I have to say you look a hell of a lot better than you did the last time we saw you.' They both laughed then as if they genuinely couldn't believe I had actually survived.

I smiled back, hoping they wouldn't ask questions they actually expected me to answer, yet desperate to ask them so much about my accident that I did not yet know.

'You're bloody lucky, that's for sure.' The guy sitting next to my bed was nodding his head as if he seriously didn't believe I would actually make it out alive. 'If your friend hadn't been in the back of our ambulance with you, I don't know what might have happened.' I looked puzzled. Friend? What friend? He looked at me and winked. 'Jade, I think she said her name was,' talking as if he actually understood my non-verbal communication gestures. 'We advised her against travelling to the hospital in the ambulance due to the severity of your condition. But she was like a madwoman possessed. She had an incredible determination to keep you alive, that's for sure.'

The other paramedic pitched in again. 'At one point, she actually slapped me because she said I wasn't working on you hard enough.' He was laughing when he mentioned the slap, but I could see in his eyes the severe upset that day had caused. They described the scene that had faced them that day; the reality of my accident was bought to shocking life as I realised my fate had rested entirely on those men's shoulders. 'We couldn't even remove your helmet because your head was so swollen. I've never seen so much blood, and believe me, we've seen some terrible sights in our time. It was

pouring out of your eyes, your nose, ears, and mouth. Christ.'
He took a moment of contemplation. 'In fact, your head
looked like a running tap that had no way of being turned off.
To be honest, I think your helmet was actually stopping your
head from exploding. I thought you were going to drown in
your own blood at one point.' I was genuinely shocked to hear
this and grateful they had taken the time to visit me.

'You hit the ground pretty hard, that's for sure, and your
bike came down right on top of you.'

'Yeah, you're actually quite lucky that we were on
standby because several other riders rode straight over your
body, not even realising you were there.' Both men seemed
upset by that comment, yet it at least explained why every
inch of me ached. Saint John's Ambulance crews usually
attended standard race meetings, but because that weekend
was a professional competition event, full ambulance crews
had been in attendance. I suddenly realised I was actually
extremely lucky. As good as Saint John's were at their job,
their training was pretty basic beyond patching up cuts,
bruises, and assessing broken limbs. I struggled to
contemplate the idea that if my accident had happened during
a routine practice weekend, they would not have had the
training to save my life.

I sat and listened as they told me that I had died three
times in the back of their ambulance before they finally got me
to the hospital and the realisation of just how lucky I had been
hit home right then. They also admitted that after a second
attempt to re-start my heart failed, they had been ready to
actually call time on my life and give me up for dead. They
believed my injuries had simply been too severe and therefore
didn't see any point in continuing. They genuinely looked
quite ashamed and guilty about that concept.

It had only been due to Jade's constant screaming and
frantic demands for them not to give up on me that had forced

them to try for a third time. My heart did stop again in the operating theatre at the hospital, but luckily for me, a fourth kick start managed to bring its rhythm back on track.

'You have one excellent friend there, mate,' one of the medics said as he joked casually about Jade's perseverance, and although he was trying to sound blasé, I knew he meant it sincerely.

I wished I had the faculties to thank them for everything they had done for me, but I knew it was Jade that I really owed my life to. I would not be here now had it not been for her. I nodded, smiled, and shook both of those guy's hands, even going as far as attempting a thank you that I knew didn't sound anything close. I had no idea if they, like the doctors, assumed my brain injuries had left me permanently disabled, but I was grateful at that point simply to be alive.

When Jade and Rebecca came into the ward later that day, I gave Jade a hug that I wanted her to never forget. I cried with gratitude that she had saved my life. Jade cried for the fact that I had survived, and it was an honest and genuine moment that we both knew would stay with us for the rest of our lives.

*** 

I endured many painful tests in silence and continued to feel like my insides had been ripped out as I was constantly pumped with drugs I could not pronounce the names of. No one could explain why my mind was racing with images and memories from my life, and no one seemed to care that I was suffering in silence because they literally could not understand what I was dealing with. Something had happened to my brain, and although the doctors never actually said it to me in person, I could see what they were thinking every time they looked at me. Thoughts including;

*He's never going to come out of this to live a normal life again,* and *If he lives through this, there's a good chance he'll be a cabbage for the rest of his life.*

If I could have spoken, I would have asked them outright why they felt I would be anything but normal. There was no way anyone would tell me what my body was or wasn't going to do. I was furious with them for looking at me with such pity, and I was determined that no matter how long it took, I was going to get myself completely back to normality. Besides, there was simply no way I would give Ryan and Justin the satisfaction of knowing I might never be the same again.

Nobody expected me to ever regain the full use of my legs, least of all my doctors. After all, I was having a hard time stringing a sentence together, so what chance did I have of being able to do much else? And yet, every day, I tried hard to wiggle my toes. The nurses would look at me and roll their eyes as if I was crazy, but I didn't give up. I couldn't give up. How could I possibly envision a future in a wheelchair? That was not for me. No way.

Eventually, one morning whilst lying propped up on pillows and willing my toes to bend, my big toe actually moved. It was a single muscle twitch, and if I blinked, I might have actually missed it, yet I knew at that moment I was going to be just fine. 'Hey, nurse,' I tried to yell, although it obviously didn't sound anything of the sort. The sound of my grunts bought her casually over to my bed, but the casual smile on her face slipped completely when she witnessed me actually bending my big toe. Twice.

\*\*\*

Rebecca was initially thrilled for me, although she urged me not to get my hopes up too much in case I found myself unable to do the things I wanted. I could clearly see the fear in her eyes when I showed her that I could bend my toe, but I wasn't concerned at all by her apparent disbelief. If my toe could move, then so could the rest of me, and slowly over the next week, I actually managed to bend my knee a little. It was only a slight movement, but it was precisely the result I was aiming for. I was elated, yet with each new thing I could get my body to do, the doctors became even more baffled. They had convinced themselves and everyone else around me that I would never walk again, and yet there I was, proving them wrong, daily.

Realising I was not going to be beaten and against everything they had presumed would happen to me moving forward, they started me on an intensive physiotherapy programme to help me learn to walk again. It was a much more complex challenge than I realised it would be. Never in my life had I had to think about putting one foot in front of the other to coordinate my attempt to walk in a straight line, and although the physiotherapist was very patient with me, I was far from patient with my own progress. I lashed out at myself for not getting my legs to automatically do what I was telling them to do. I felt like a child learning to do the simplest of tasks all over again. I could not coordinate my feet and hips at the same time and spent several frustrating hours dragging my legs across the room in a ridiculous attempt to remain upright. Because I could not form words properly either, I felt like the very freak they all assumed I would eventually become, and quickly slumped into a state of depression.

'It's okay, Craig.' Rachel, my physiotherapist, was standing at one end of a double rail, and I was at the other. 'Take your time.' It was as if she was telling me that I wasn't good enough to walk and that I should try and take things at a slower pace. It was all the encouragement I needed. I dragged my left foot forward, grasping hold of the rail with both hands and probably looking as if I had had way too much to drink. My left foot twisted beneath my weight, but I didn't give up, forcing my right foot into position next to it. I didn't care if it took me all day to walk those blasted three metres to the other side.

I was exhausted after only three steps, and Rachel seemed extremely happy with what I'd achieved, but I did not want to give up until I actually got my legs working again.

'Please don't overstretch your muscles,' she said to me as I dragged my legs carelessly towards her. But I wasn't listening. I had pushed my body in motocross, and I was damned sure the thing wasn't going to let me down now. I did make it across those parallel walking bars, but I spent two days in bed recovering afterwards. It was a starting point, at least. The only way I could go from here was up.

I had spent several weeks in hospital at this point and was getting used to seeing patients with severe injuries coming in and out of the trauma ward, their stories unfolding in front of my eyes as doctors worked to save their lives in the same way they had saved mine. It didn't prepare me for James, though. I never actually saw his face during the four days he lay in a bed opposite me, but I will never forget the sounds of pain that erupted from his mouth on the odd occasion whenever the drugs wore off. He was covered in bandages on almost ninety-five per cent of his body; the only area unscathed was weirdly his left foot. He didn't make it through that fifth night, and it never fails to unnerve me just how unyielding fire can be. Lying in my bed as they wheeled James's body away made me feel lucky to be alive, no matter how much my voice and legs eluded me.

# Chapter 10

When the girls came to see me the day James died, I couldn't talk to them about it, and I couldn't tell them how grateful I was to be alive. Although it had been my love of motocross that had bought me to this place, I would not have changed a single thing that had happened to me. I would have probably ignored my instincts, anyway, even had I known the outcome.

The possibility of death is all part of the equation in motocross and the reason you get such a rush when racing. The feeling of being so alive whilst knowing that death can take you at any moment gives you a feeling that you can't describe to anyone. Adrenaline junkies feed off this energy. It's addictive.

The girls were sitting on plastic chairs next to my bed, reading a bike magazine they had supposedly bought for me. Occasionally Rebecca commented on the "ridiculously underdressed girls in some of the photographs". Her words, not mine. It made me smile, considering what she did for a living. Grace leaned across my bed and winked.

'Need plumping?' she asked, leaning over me and placing two hands on my pillow, ready to give it a good shake. I shook my head. I wished I could say something to her. Anything would have made me happy at that point. But I was locked inside my head, unable to explain anything I was thinking or feeling to anyone, even had I wanted to. I could do nothing more than express simple gratitude that my three best friends were there for me right then. We had been a part of each other's lives for so long, I couldn't imagine life without them.

I closed my eyes, listening to Rebecca's continued rant about some girl with a staple through her head whose bikini, in her opinion, was way too tight and that she would never be seen dead wearing such an outfit.

I smiled to myself as I lay back, listening to a conversation that wouldn't have meant much to most people but meant the absolute world to me. As we had grown up, our friendship had not only remained intact but was actually developing in a way that neither of us could have expected. We were closer than we had ever been, and I believe that our utter determination to be a part of each other's lives was the main reason we had remained such good friends. I thought about that night in the flat and felt a pang of guilt shoot into my gut for the mistake I had convinced myself I'd made. I would never do anything to deliberately ruin our friendship. As far as I was concerned, Rebecca was the sister I never had. She was better than any family I had ever known and one of the few people who had actually cared a dammed thing about me in my entire life.      Maybe it was because our lives were so similar, but we leaned on each other, supported each other and somehow, because of that, things seemed easier to bear for both of us, knowing we had each other to depend on no matter whatever happened in our lives. Looking at her now, sitting next to my bed, I honestly hoped she had put our moment to the back of her mind. She hadn't mentioned it to me since that night, and I don't think she had told Grace or Jade because if she had, I certainly wouldn't have heard the end of it.

At the age of seventeen, someone had suggested to Rebecca that she try glamour modelling. She had a great body and with a natural girl-next-door look that agencies were always keen to find, we all knew she would have no trouble getting work. At first, she was unsure, knowing the stigma that surrounded glamour models in the 1980s, but when she attended a professional photoshoot for the first time, her sister Emma tagging along for support, she quickly changed her mind.

She lied about her age and secured her first topless modelling job posing for a men's motor magazine, earning more money in that single shoot than I made in an entire year. Her natural good looks and confident persona placed her in high demand with photographers, and reasonably soon, she began receiving job offers from New York, Miami, St Tropez, and London. The modelling world was a totally different place in the 1980s. The money was fantastic, and the girls were highly paid and well looked after because of the enormous demand for attractive models willing to bear all for the camera. I could still recall Rebecca's excitement the day she announced ecstatically that she had earned enough money to buy her first property. She moved into the top floor flat of a large, converted white-fronted house with Grace in October 1986 with nothing more than an old bed, a sofa and a suitcase full of clothes between them.

\*\*\*

As much as I was aware of my general surroundings, my accident had changed something deep inside me, and I struggled to communicate properly with anyone. Although I could vaguely understand what people were trying to say to me, I could still not give anything back to them or place conversations in the correct order. I would often miss words altogether, and sentences didn't sound quite right, even though they sounded absolutely fine inside my head. It was frustrating, and I spent many sleepless nights lying in that hospital bed waiting for answers I felt would never actually come. I was given a sleep test whereby hundreds of tiny probes were attached to my skull to ascertain what was going on inside my brain. I was connected to a machine for twenty-four hours so that doctors could monitor my brain waves and the results came as quite a surprise to my consultant.

'Craig, your tests have indicated that you have somehow managed to wake up the area of your brain usually only reserved for the period when the human body is asleep.' He was standing next to my bed with his attention set firmly on the notes in his hand. I stared at him, grasping what he was saying yet unable to ask any questions about it, the discarded magazines on the table in front of me remaining unread through lack of ability. He seemed genuinely baffled by the whole thing and entirely animated by his findings. I wished for a moment he could actually experience what I was going through because he might not sound so happy about it. 'You have damaged the part of the brain that allows us to dream and keeps our internal organs functioning normally throughout the night whilst we are asleep.'

I wasn't too bothered that he had continued talking without waiting for my reaction because I couldn't speak to him anyway. 'It's why some babies die of cot death,' he continued. 'Their subconscious brains simply forget to tell their hearts to beat.' He shrugged, sounding almost amazed at how complex the workings of the human mind is. 'You see, Craig, there are two parts to the human brain. The front part and the back part. Your accident has somehow caused the area of the brain reserved for sleep to become activated when you are awake, and unfortunately, we can't understand why it is not switching off.'

My consultant spoke to me as if I was a child as he turned over a piece of paper and sketched a ridiculous looking brain shape for me to see what he was talking about.

'If you think of the human brain as being connected by several billion tiny electrodes, just here, where the damage is.' He drew a squiggle around the base of his drawing, indicated the brain stem. 'Electrodes are firing across one another in a way that shouldn't be happening, and it's now managing to keep the subconscious area of your brain awake even when you are not asleep.' I didn't really understand much of what he was telling me at the time. Apparently, my condition had a long name called Brain Dural Arteriovenous Fistula. It is where new pathways grow around damaged areas to allow blood flow to continue its course unhindered. The word fistula actually means "abnormal connections between two structures that are normally not connected".

'You will no doubt be feeling quite low at the moment,' he continued after prescribing me with too many antidepressants amongst other drugs I couldn't fathom the reasons behind. 'Your brain can't go through something like this without it affecting your mental state of mind.'

But it wasn't just my mental state that I was having a problem with. It was because the rest of my body was refusing to cooperate that was really getting me down. After being in hospital for a couple of months, my frustration was increasing. It was made worse when the doctors determined that no operation could be safely performed because my brain's damage was too deep and close to my spinal cord for them to even consider attempting surgery.

They explained that my brain was extremely bruised, and until the swelling had fully subsided, they would be unable to determine the next course of action. I was devastated. I pleaded with the hospital staff in my slurred voice to discharge me. I was desperate to get out of there and gain back some self-respect and normality in my life.

I was tired of being poked and prodded, and I was tired

of lying on my back in a hospital bed with no answers as to why they assumed I wouldn't get any better. They reluctantly agreed to let me go home, although I could not be by myself because I needed round the clock care. I could hardly walk. I could not eat solid food, and I could not use the bathroom facilities without help.

They had a look of pity in their eyes when they discussed my daily care needs. They seriously believed that my head injuries had been so severe that, if I was lucky, they determined I had an approximate estimation of around five years left to live. Again, I was left completely baffled. How on earth could they come to a conclusion so quickly about what I was or wasn't going to do?

They had told me I would probably never walk again, and I had proved them wrong about that, so their negative connotations about my life expectancy was not something I was about to absorb either. I am in charge of my own body, and I determine when I will or will not die; thank you very much. Rebecca stepped in and offered to temporarily have me go and live with her and Grace at the flat. I moved in with the girls in August 1989 with no hair on my head and very little use of my faculties, but glad at least to be out of the hospital I could no longer stand to be in.

***

As expected, my first few hours living at the girls' flat consisted of a barrage of overprotective pampering and fluffing of cushions as both girls flitted around me like headless chickens on steroids. It had taken the hospital transport staff several attempts to get me up to the flat, the wheelchair I was forced to use, nothing more than a metal straight jacket that, in my opinion, made me look weak. I hated what I had become, and I hated having to rely on these people for the support I felt I simply didn't need.

I was glad that I couldn't speak because I didn't wish to make small talk with those poor men struggling to lift me onto each step. I knew it was their job and that my safety was their priority, but it didn't make me feel any better. I was utterly mortified. At that moment, I wished I could close my eyes and disappear completely for a while, at least until my body was functioning again.

I could not swallow properly because my brain could not communicate with my digestive system, and my throat muscles were simply not working. Every couple of hours, Rebecca would emerge from the kitchen carrying some strange orange liquid that the hospital had taught her how to place inside the feeding tube in my belly. It did not smell at all nice, and I was slightly grateful I didn't have to actually eat the stuff, despite the fact I would have given anything to have been able to chew food again. It genuinely felt as if I had regressed backwards to infancy.

As you can imagine, going to the toilet was an even worse endurance and an extremely embarrassing one at that. That orange liquid apparently helped calm things inside my gut lining. But it had the side effect of making my bowels react badly. I quickly became frustrated because my best friends regularly had to clean up after my unavoidable toilet movements. They did not complain once. It was actually quite a miracle.

I tried to respond the best I knew how, but nothing at that moment felt real. My head was in constant and excruciating pain, and I was locked inside a distant fog I could not shake. I had been given strong medication to take, but the drugs only made me feel worse, and I spent most of my time asleep. I was grateful that I was safely tucked up in Rebecca's flat instead of a hospital ward, but this was not the life I had visualised and hoped to God I could find the strength to get back on my feet quickly. Whenever I did wake up, I would be met with a terrible screaming noise inside my head that I could not stand. Even the sound of one of the girls placing a cup onto the coffee table in the living room would make my ears ring as if they had thrown the whole thing across the room. No matter how hard I tried, I just did not feel like myself anymore, and I knew I desperately needed help I was unsure how to even ask for.

My first night out of the hospital should have been a wonderful experience. No nurses chatter in the middle of the night or groaning patients to disturb my well-needed peace — no clanging of bedpans or machinery noises or loud snoring. No being shaken awake after I had actually finally managed to fall asleep, only to be given more medication to help me sleep. As it was, I felt more vulnerable at the flat than I had ever felt before. Although the doctors could offer no more support than the girls could, I had a ridiculous notion that because they were trained medical professionals, the nurses would somehow know what to do if I needed them. I was literally in a no-win situation.

Rebecca was, of course, as attentive as she could be, bombarded me with endless queries as to my wellbeing and genuinely doing her best to show me that no matter what happened, she would always be there for me. If I could have strung a sentence together, it would have been to tell her to stop fussing. She meant well, of course. She just wanted to ensure that I was okay, but none of this was okay at all, and I had absolutely no way of telling anyone how I really felt. As I settled my head onto Rebecca's freshly washed pillowcase, desperate for the pain to ease, even for one moment, she climbed onto the bed next to me and lay her head against my shoulder.

We lay together in silence for a while, neither of us needing to offer any comfort to the other. Ever since we were children, she had liked me to hold her until she fell asleep. It made her feel safe and knowing that I didn't have to get up and go home after she was settled always helped me feel better. Tonight it was Rebecca doing the comforting, and it felt good.

'I'm glad you're home,' she whispered to me after she realised I was still awake. I squeezed her hand in response. 'We will get you back on track again, I promise.' She turned her head so she could look into my eyes. 'I won't let this break you.' I thought I saw a tear, but she smiled anyway and closed her eyes. I wanted to tell her that I wasn't about to let this thing break me either. I would get better. I was determined to become me again. 'I love you,' she whispered as she turned out the light. I wanted to tease her, to tell her that I loved her too and call her shit face. I wanted to hear that familiar giggle as she rubbed her hand playfully across my chest in the way she always did. But instead, I lay with Rebecca's head on my shoulder for over an hour, listening to her gentle breath and unable to thank her for everything she was doing for me. She was the strongest person I had ever known and yet lying next to me right then, she seemed so fragile, so small. I would always be there for her no matter what happened in either of our lives, and I was glad she had been there for me tonight.

I smiled to myself about how our bedtime arrangement would come to an end if either of us ever got married, but at the time, thoughts like that felt such a long way away. Although there had never been anything sexual in our relationship until recently, it wasn't something that other people could ever have understood. We had been this way with each other since we were kids, and nothing would ever change that, although even I had to admit we did indeed have a very unique type of friendship. Eventually, I drifted off to sleep. I was glad to be there with the girls that night.

# Chapter 11

A few days after coming out of the hospital, some friends from the motocross club visited me. They looked at me as if they were expecting me to suddenly spontaneously combust, offering shallow, sympathetic words that, to me, sounded unrealistic and forced. I had not realised until then just how other people would look at me, my own turmoil being somewhat diffused by the girls' lack of judgment. It was not lost on me that this was the first time they had seen me since the day of the accident, but I could have had no idea how bad their reaction to my appearance would actually be.

'How're doing, mate?' Andy stood at the bottom of Rebecca's bed, leaning a leg against her ottoman and looking as if he didn't quite know what to do with his hands. He had a nervous look on his face that told me he wasn't expecting to see me with tubes coming out of my body and stubble on my head where my hair used to be.

I nodded and smiled, yet every time I blinked, it felt as if someone was poking my eyes out of my head. Upon my request, Rebecca had kept the curtains closed, but I could sense that both Andy and John were uncomfortable standing in front of me now in her darkened bedroom.

'He's okay, aren't you, Craig?' Rebecca's cheery voice filtered into the room, momentarily shifting the boys' attention from me. I was not good company. That much I did know, yet I had no idea how to change how I felt. My unwillingness to be seen by them, or anyone else for that matter, was very much apparent, and they stood in front of me on tenterhooks, totally unsure what they should actually be saying to me. Usually, we would be sharing a joke by now, bantering back and forth between us and generally putting the world to rights. Now I could not even imagine sharing a cup of tea with these guys.

Unfortunately for me, they noticed my unease and left after around twenty minutes of forced conversation with the girls. I could hear them in the living room asking how long I would be like "that" as if my condition was a disease they were unsure how to deal with. I quickly realised I no longer enjoyed other peoples' company because of how I felt they would all react to me now. I knew that no one would be able to understand that whenever they spoke to me, words became jumbled in my mind, and I couldn't really understand much of what anyone was saying to me anyway.

I did not feel comfortable holding a conversation because the words I had lined up in my head simply refused to come out of my mouth in any coherent order. How could anyone understand how that feels? I certainly could not expect any of my mates to get it. It made me feel isolated, and I found myself just wanting to be left alone. I wasn't coping very well with the constant slide show that now plagued my waking moments, twenty-four hours a day, seven days a week. Rebecca did her best, of course, to help however and whenever she could, but I felt more alone during that period than I could have ever explained to anyone. How do you explain to people that even when you are looking out of the window or quietly watching television, you are technically dreaming, with memories new and old and images of random items flicking into the forefront of your consciousness? I could no longer read, not even a passage in a newspaper. My mind would not allow me to concentrate on a single thing long enough to absorb any information. Words became mixed up with images of cartoon characters and random flowery curtains, and quickly I began to feel extremely frustrated.

***

It took several months before I slowly began regaining my speech, but my brain would forget to tell me when I needed to swallow, and I would often find myself dribbling into my lap. It was terribly embarrassing. Because of this, I did not want people to see me, and I spent months locked inside Rebecca's flat with only her, Grace, the occasional visit from Jade, and the television for company. Even though my hair was growing back, I didn't feel good about how I looked and rarely looked in the mirror at all. I was grateful that the girls could see past my looks, yet it didn't help my low mood one bit. I received daily visits from district nurses who changed tubes, replaced urine bags and ensured the girls had enough medical products to keep my progress moving forward.

My physiotherapist came in every two days to strengthen my now weak and skinny legs, and the girls were shown exercises to do with me every few hours.

Although my walking was improving slowly, I continued to feel like a small child, learning to do things all over again as if I had never known any of it in the first place. I found myself bursting into tears at the slightest thing and developed a severe dislike for the tinned soup that Rebecca insisted I eat. I had been so relieved when my feeding tube was finally removed, allowing me to eat foods again, albeit soft ones initially, but I would have happily plugged it back into my belly myself to avoid the taste of that soup.

Going to the toilet was still extremely embarrassing, and I had to have one of the girls with me at all times for them to wipe my backside and keep me upright because I had no strength in my legs to support my own weight. I had no grip either, so they would have to pull down my trousers and physically sit me onto the toilet. It was humiliating, yet not once did they complain or act in any way as if they minded taking on such responsibility. When I did actually begin to string words together into sentences, I still sounded as if I had lost my marbles, often stumbling over words I usually would have no trouble finding. And yet, throughout all this, Rebecca and Grace remained confident it was all part of my recovery process, steadfast in the support they gave me. I honestly do not know where I would have been had it not been for those amazing girls.

Despite my slow journey to recovery, I had moments where I thought about Ryan and Justin and the words that Ryan had said to me on the day of my accident. 'Try not to overthink that,' Grace said as she handed me a glass of juice that I almost didn't grip properly.

'I can't help it,' I slurred. And I genuinely couldn't. I knew I couldn't speak to Rebecca about my concerns either because the last thing she needed was reminding of those two pigs' existence. Still, inside I knew they would be out there somewhere, laughing at what had happened to me and enjoying the thought of my injuries and subsequent poor health.

'Just focus on getting better. That's all we want for you right now.' Grace had a good heart, and I loved her for her patience and support, yet I needed to show them all that I was not the type of person who stayed down for long. It made me all the more determined to do everything I could to get back on my feet. I spent hours with my legs elevated on Rebecca's floor cushion whilst attempting the sit-ups my physiotherapist had taught me. I needed my spine to strengthen enough to walk normally without constantly feeling as if my legs belonged to someone else.

\*\*\*

It took several months before I felt confident enough to leave the flat, but I realised swiftly that going outside would be more difficult than I assumed after only one attempt to walk to the shops alone. I could literally feel every single element around me as if the world had changed into something grotesque in my absence. A leaf, scrapping its weightless form across the pavement, annoyed me. A dog, barking so loudly that I thought my ears would burst made me want to scream. Cars sounded like express trains. Even the breeze sounded like a hurricane that threatened to overthrow my sanity. I panicked and almost broke into a demented run as I stumbled back to the flat in a hurry. Rebecca was furious that I had gone out without her.

'What if something had happened?' she yelled at me that evening. Something had indeed happened. I had all but destroyed the person I had once been.

It was as if the invisible shield I felt had always protected me had finally broken. I'd always acted as if I was invincible because I always thought I was. Now, with a frightening jolt, I realised I was anything but. I had always made fear work for me. I loved the feeling I got during a motocross race, literally holding my life in the palm of my hands, but now that same fear was getting the better of me. I felt as if the damage inside my head was evident for everyone around me to see. I was convinced that they all could see the pain I was in and the slide show I was forced to endure, and because of this, I felt like a circus freak that had been left on display by mistake. To add insult to my very serious injury, because the swelling in my brain was taking quite some time to heal, my head felt huge, as if someone had stuck the end of a bicycle pump inside my ear and inflated it. I desperately wanted the pain to stop. To say that I felt exposed would be an understatement.

The medication helped, but only enough to send me in and out of continued oblivion that made me question my surroundings on a daily basis. Days and nights blended into an endurance that threatened my sanity, and yet throughout that entire time, Rebecca never left my side. She had taken a break from her modelling, although, at the time, I hadn't even noticed. To make matters worse, the swelling in my brain had caused me to begin having seizures. I was told that this was normal and they would subside as the pressure on my skull reduced, but it didn't help my declining state of mind one single bit.

I did not see my bike again after the accident, but it was bought to my attention just a few weeks after the crash that it was now only worth ninety pounds scrap. It had cost six and a half thousand. Because the race was a championship meeting, professional television camera crews had been present and had videoed the entire thing. When Andy walked into the flat with a copy of the video in his hand, I could see the uncertain look on his face and knew exactly what he was thinking before he had even closed the front door. I hadn't seen him or John since that awkward moment after I came out of the hospital, and although I now had some hair growth and was no longer bed bound, I still walked with crutches and couldn't exactly hold a proper conversation.

'I warn you, it's not a pretty sight,' he said as Grace pushed the video into the recorder. I sat down on the edge of the sofa, and Rebecca placed her hands on my shoulders. No one spoke. To be honest, I am not sure what any of us expected to see. I had no memory of the accident at all. Although the girls had been present that day, Rebecca had already driven off in a complete huff before anything had happened, so she didn't actually see me again until I was in the hospital fighting for my life. The race on the screen now seemed a far distant memory, and I couldn't wait to get well enough so I could resume my training and get back on a bike.

I recognised the colour of my bike and the design of my helmet, and when Rebecca yelled, 'There you are,' I was already feeling quite nervous. I tore around the corner and hit the largest jump on the track flawlessly. It looked for a moment as if I actually knew what I was doing. I watched almost as if I was having some kind of out of body experience as my bike began to flip forward. I began to lose the battle with gravity as my bike headed towards the ground, now almost completely upside down with me still attached to it.

I hit the ground hard, the unexpected sounds of shock emanating from the crowd. It was something I did not anticipate would upset me. I could not believe that it was my body being tossed around like a rag doll on the screen in front of me. As I fell to the ground, smashing my head into the dirt from twenty feet in the air, my bike hit me full force across the back of my head, just above my neck.

Several other bikes rode straight over me without even realising what had happened. It had all happened so fast. I sat and watched helplessly as this lifeless body lay limp in the dirt. Jesus Christ that surely wasn't me. How could it be?

We all sat in Rebecca's living room for a moment, silent, as if we couldn't quite fathom what we had witnessed. 'Fuck me,' I let out the words without warning. Everyone laughed. It was the most normal sounding thing I had managed to say for months, and I couldn't help but smile too at the irony of my own sentence.

'That was so similar to how poor Liam's accident happened,' Andy suddenly chipped in.

Rebecca looked at him and then at me. 'How is he doing?' she asked, a weird look suddenly creeping across her face as if she had totally forgotten about him.

'Not good, apparently. He's paralyzed from the neck down and will never walk again.' Andy looked straight at me as if my own circumstances could have been far worse. 'Poor sod. John went to see him last week actually, but his mum wouldn't let him in. I think he's been suffering from depression.'

I knew exactly how he felt. The most frightening part about the whole thing was that Liam's accident had happened just a month before mine. I looked at Rebecca. She knew exactly what I was thinking and turned away. I knew she didn't want to acknowledge what I was thinking any more than I did.

'Didn't he have the same type of bike as Craig?' Andy asked, sounding entirely innocent in his tone and not realising the magnitude of his words.

'Yes,' I managed to say. 'He did.' I wondered for a moment. Was it at all possible that Ryan and Justin had already tried to set up my accident on a previous occasion? I felt sick at the idea of some innocent person being paralyzed because of me.

'Yeah, and his bikes back wheel locked up in precisely the same way that yours did, Craig. Weird that, hey? Must be a problem with the brand or something.' Andy genuinely had no idea what he was saying. How could he? How could he know the hatred that lingered between Ryan and Justin and myself? 'He'll never be the same again, that's for sure. Poor bugger.'

Although I knew I had been lucky to have not ended up in the exact same position as Liam, in the back of my mind, something felt very wrong. He had owned the exact same bike model as me, and it had very similar colour markings. To me, it seemed a little too convenient that we should both suffer a similar fate, merely one month apart. There had been an inquest after my accident, of course, although the outcome was ruled that the tabletop jump on that track was simply too dangerous. As a result, it was lowered. They said it was nothing more than a freaky coincidence that both accidents had occurred similarly, with the same thing happening to both bikes. The fact that we had the same make of bike was ruled as immaterial. I suggested to Rebecca that it was no coincidence, and, although she understood exactly what I meant, neither of us had any proof. If the first bike had been rigged, mistakenly believing it to be mine, we had no way of proving it, and that thought worried me.

***

I spent the next few months going back and forth to different hospitals for endless tests and sessions that ended the same way, with no one knowing any more than they did before my appointments and no further answers being offered. Once the swelling had subsided enough, a routine CAT scan at a hospital in Birmingham finally revealed the truth after they took detailed sliced images of my brain. I had crushed my pituitary gland, compromising the connection between my brain and central nervous system, and it meant that my adrenal gland was now on permanent overdrive. This may have happened due to the high level of adrenaline racing through my veins on the day of my accident, but it meant that my adrenal gland would continue to create too much cortisol and permanently put me at high risk for heart and other health problems.

They also discovered a deep brain aneurysm that had formed at the base of my skull just above my spinal column on the brain stem. I was given two choices. They could operate; the chances of me surviving, fifty per cent, the chances of me becoming a vegetable and living the rest of my life neither knowing anyone or able to feed myself, fifty per cent. Or, I could live with the condition and try to get on with life the best I could. I chose the latter.

I was in the care of a neurologist at the Royal Birmingham Hospital who was very good at his job and quickly realised the extent of my dealing with it.

'Craig,' he told me during one of my routine appointments and looking almost stunned. 'I have to be totally honest with you. Everyone I ever had the misfortune to deal with who has had to live with this sort of condition are either now in mental institutions, or they took their own life at some point.' It bought home to me the extent of my injuries, like a fist to the face. A mental institution, or suicide. Great choices I had there. I could not believe what I was hearing. 'How are you managing to separate your waking moments from your fake dreams?' He could not understand how I had managed to compartmentalise my brain into sections to determine what was real and what was not.

'I don't know,' I shrugged because, for me, it was the only thing I could do. Most of what was going on inside my head did not feel real, and I knew that if I were to get any kind of normality back in my life, I quickly needed to sort out the fictitious areas from what was actually going on around me. Before I left his office that day, he told me that if I could figure out how to shut off the images and the white noise to get on with my day, I would become a millionaire by saving hundreds of lives. The irony of that statement wasn't lost on me at all.

The truth was, though, I didn't have a clue how I was able to separate reality from the images that swam in my head. I can only describe the feeling as if I am sitting in a room surrounded by a dozen television sets that are all turned on at full volume and on different channels. I have to focus on the one I want to watch and hope to filter out the rest to not lose focus on what I am doing. It is something I had to get used to doing every single day.

I get out of bed every morning and start all over again, concentrating on what is real and not. Some days get the better of me because my head hurts so much, and it can become overwhelming. Those are the days I understand fully how the idea of taking your own life can have its appeal.

# Chapter 12

For the next few months, I was continually poked, prodded, and made to feel like an experimental rat in a glass box. Although I was told they only had my best interests at heart, I was left to endure endless tests with no explanation as to why my brain was behaving the way it did, the likes of which often made me physically sick. Every new appointment brought different faces for me to get used to and new people I had to try and listen to. When I met two consultants from a hospital that had been deemed specialist, I knew exactly what they meant.

'You want me to go to a mental hospital?' I asked, still unable to comprehend the words I had just heard.

'We would really like the chance to study your condition, Mr Marshall,' they said. 'We have the very best facilities at Millhouse, so you will be in good hands. We promise you will not be under any obligation to stay for long.'

I wasn't sure I actually trusted anyone's' so-called promises at that stage, but I needed some answers, and so I agreed to go along for a visit to that place with little resistance. Rebecca insisted that she come with me, not wanting to leave me alone with those people even for a moment, just in case there was an outside chance I didn't come back out again. I stepped out of her car in the car park, feeling nervous but thankful that at least I wasn't alone. The building itself looked far too much like one of those old-fashioned asylums you see in movies, but I tried to push that thought to the back of my mind as we walked along the driveway towards the main entrance. However, as soon as we ventured inside, we realised we had made the most horrendous mistake.

Two male nurses were on the floor, their knees and fists pressed into the torso of a young man who was screaming for what I could only make out as his "bowl of leaves". A woman smiled at me as we walked past. She was dressed in a bathrobe that she had on backwards and was wearing a pair of slippers that did not match in colour or size. I glanced at Rebecca, and she squeezed my arm.

'Over my dead body,' she whispered as she steered me straight back out to the car.

***

I stopped taking my medication not long after my brief visit to the psychiatric hospital. They made me constantly tired, and I did not feel like myself at all when I took them. I would not let this thing in my head beat me under any circumstances and was certainly not about to end up like the people I had seen in that terrible place. Yet, this only enforced my consultant's fascination with my inept inability to succumb to my injuries.

'When did you stop taking your medication, Mr Marshall?' I was asked on one of my endless visits to the hospital. I was sitting in a tiny room, perched on the edge of a very uncomfortable chair that made me feel somewhat hot and irritated.

'I need to try and get back to normal,' I answered, attempting to be as honest as I could. 'They make me tired all the time, and I don't like how I feel when I take them.'

My consultant leaned back in his chair. 'Well, I have to

say, as much as I do not agree with your decision to stop taking your medication, I find your approach to your condition very intriguing.' I thought he was going to lecture me for a moment, but he surprised me with his following words. 'There are, of course, others like you, living with a similar type of brain injury. But I'll be honest, most of them are living in specialist hospitals with round the clock care.'

I looked straight at him. 'I know all about the specialist hospitals you're talking about, and I have already witnessed your idea of "care."' I didn't mean to sound so sarcastic. It just came out.

Oblivious to my words and maintaining his fascination with me, he continued. "The ones not already institutionalised take powerful medication to help them cope, and they are not able to function nearly half as normally as you seem to be.' He tapped his pen against my file that lay open on his desk. 'You are not only coping with your condition, Mr Marshall, but you are doing so without the help of drugs. I swear that if I didn't have your medical notes in front of me right now, I wouldn't have a single clue that there was anything actually wrong with you.' I'm sure he didn't mean it, but his words came out quite cold, matter-of-fact like. The way he sat, blankly looking at me as if I was wasting his time purely because I had managed to heal myself well enough to function again.

I was already receiving awkward and confused looks from people who didn't understand the full extent of what I'd been through and, therefore, didn't appear to believe I was injured because, from the outside, I looked reasonably normal. Now my own doctor was telling me that he, too, was having a hard time believing what I was dealing with. He flicked through my notes for a few moments before looking me straight in the eye.

'Would you consider donating your brain to medical science?' He asked this with a finality in his tone that I was not expecting.

'I beg your pardon?' Had I even heard him correctly?

'We are currently unable to understand how you are coping with your condition,' he said. 'And we would very much like to be able to slice your brain into sections to study how your neurons are firing. It would be good to see what exactly is allowing you to distinguish between normality and everything else that must be going on in your head.' I must have given him a puzzled look because he pulled out a notepad and started drawing a picture. 'The human brain is very complex, and there is a fragile line between sanity and insanity. Because your subconscious brain does not settle down when you are not asleep, technically, you are dreaming whilst you are awake. There is a conflict going on inside your brain that should be driving you literally mad.' He genuinely looked surprised. He wasn't wrong.

'It does,' I stated firmly, wondering how the hell he could possibly understand how I felt or how they actually thought they would be able to slice open my brain. Wouldn't that kill me? He was right about one thing, though. It did indeed feel like a conflict. I could no longer read because my subconsciousness was constantly throwing images and memories into my mind. And I couldn't hold conversations with people for long because I could be thinking one thing one moment, and something totally different the next.

He nodded and scribbled something onto his notepad. 'If you would sign an agreement allowing us to study your brain, Mr Marshall, you would be helping hundreds of people who haven't been quite as lucky as you.'

Panic started to rise in my stomach. 'But I need my brain,' I told him. I was very serious. I suddenly had a vision of someone slicing open my brain whilst I lay cold on an operating table.

He smiled and lay his pen down next to his pad. 'No, I'm

talking about when you die.'

A horrible thought flew into my mind then that if ever I needed to be resuscitated again for any reason, would they try as hard as they had previously or allow me to die so that the hospital could get a hold of my brain? 'I'm not planning on dying for some time yet,' I stated. 'The answer's no.'

*\*\**

Because of my continued seizures, I was now undergoing tests for Epilepsy. My driving license was temporarily revoked. I was forced to undergo another twenty-four-hour sleep test whilst doctors watched for fluctuating brain patterns, among other things that I didn't understand. Because I had stopped taking my medication, the conscious part of my brain was no longer being allowed to turn off, and I barely slept at all. Although my eyes would regularly become heavy, needing to close just like anyone else, my brain simply would not allow me to actually sleep.

My subconscious mind was already awake and giving me random dreams whilst walking around and going about my everyday life, so it did not realise that anything was amiss. When I needed to rest, I would be almost forced to keep active, as if someone was standing behind me constantly shaking me and saying, "wake up Craig, come on, keep going, we're not done here." The doctors and consultants simply did not know what to do with me because this was not something they saw often. It was unusual, and I knew something would have to give eventually. I was prescribed yet more tablets to help me sleep.

The old pattern began to emerge fairly soon, and I began to fall asleep at the most inconvenient moments. I would fall asleep mid-conversation with the girls before I even managed to finish a sentence and I once drifted off whilst holding a hot cup of tea in my hand. That was not a pleasant experience for anyone. Because of this, I was not able to return to work immediately. Luckily for me, Andrew was very supportive. He paid my total wages during the entire time I was off sick, even though, in the end, I was actually off work for almost a year. I fully expected my job to be given to someone else, but he told me that my job would be waiting for me when I felt well enough to return, no matter how long it took. I was genuinely grateful for that, but I only wanted to get back to normal as quickly as possible.

I stopped taking my second lot of tablets after only being on them for around three weeks. One piece of advice was given to me by one of my neurologists, and it is something that helped keep me going even on the worst days. He told me that if I could cope, I should try and do so without medication. He said that prescribed drugs would eventually weaken my body, and in time I would become dependent on them. I was determined that nothing would make me weak, and so I only took painkillers on the days when the pain was too much for me to cope with.

After every possible test the hospital could provide had been completed, I was referred to my local hospital for ongoing outpatient support. It genuinely felt as if I was being passed along a conveyor belt with no one willing or able to offer much help. To make matters worse, none of these people seemed to care about how any of this made me feel. To them, I was nothing more than an NHS number. By the time I was due a routine check-up at The George Miles Hospital in Milborough, I had already seen too many head injury specialists, none of whom had helped me much at all.

Jade came with me to my appointment that day as none of the girls were comfortable with the idea of me doing very much by myself at that point. Rebecca had been offered a modelling job that was simply too much money for her to turn down, and because I was slowly getting my faculties back, I told her to go. As far as I was concerned, the sooner we got back to normality, the better. Jade and I walked into the consulting room expecting to see my usual consultant welcome us in, but I was surprised to see a young understudy sitting behind the desk. As we sat down, he did not even look up from the pile of notes he was randomly flicking through, turning over page after page of medical nonsense in some kind of attempt to understand my condition. The clock on the wall behind me ticked relentlessly, mocking me with its intense clatter. The sound of rustling papers on the desk in front of me became louder and louder in my head. It felt as if I was surrounded by noise, and yet nobody had spoken a word.

Jade noticed the anxious look on my face and took hold of my hand. She winked at me and smiled, knowing how I was probably feeling and obviously guilty that she couldn't really help me other than to simply be there for me. After what felt like a decade of annoying page rustling, I could stand it no longer.

'Well?' I asked sharply, not even caring that my tone sounded off. 'Do you have the results or not?' It was another test result in a long list of scans I had endured over the last few months, and I was getting tired of being poked and prodded.

He glanced up from my notes briefly, his face young enough for me to assume he was fresh out of college and not much older than me. 'It appears that the results of your last test have been mislaid,' he offered calmly.

'What is that supposed to mean?' I could feel the heat of the room close in around me with the distant mannerism of his voice.

'We don't seem to have them here,' he continued. 'But judging from previous tests, everything looks okay-'

'I beg your pardon?' I couldn't help glaring at him. 'What

sort of pathetic thing is that to say?' I looked at Jade for confirmation that I had heard him right and shook my head. 'You don't even know what's wrong with me, do you?'

The understudy calmly glanced at my notes as if my irritation was of no consequence to him and began flicking through the papers again. 'Yes,' he answered finally. 'You have been undergoing tests for Epilepsy.'

In that instant, something inside me snapped, and I scrambled to my feet too quickly. 'Oh my God,' I yelled, not caring who in the building overheard me. 'What an absolute joke.' Jade tried to intervene, but I was having none of it. 'I'm not going to sit in front of some jumped up little twat who doesn't even know my medical history and all you have you tell me that everything is okay.' I could feel the anger rising in my stomach that I didn't know what to do with. 'No one knows what the hell to do, and you're just passing the buck.'

'Mr Marshall, please, there's no need-'

'I need to see someone who knows what they're talking about,' I interrupted. 'I'm fed up with all this bullshit. I need some straight answers. Now.'

As the understudy got to his feet and left the room, Jade frantically stroked my arm in an attempt to keep me calm. She didn't say a word. She didn't need to. My head was pounding by this time, and I knew if I wasn't careful, I'd probably keel over at any second. A few moments later, the understudy returned, his face giving nothing away of what he was thinking. 'The consultant will be with you shortly,' he said casually as he sat down behind the desk and continued flicking through those bloody notes. No one spoke another word, yet that damned clock mocked me with each stroke for almost ten minutes.

When my actual consultant finally arrived, he had a look on his face that told me immediately that he was not in the slightest bit impressed at having been interrupted from whatever it was that he had been doing. He was followed closely by a security guard who stood behind him in the doorway, obviously wondering if I was about to cause much trouble and readying himself for some kind of confrontation. I noticed that several people were beginning to stare.

'What seems to be the problem, Mr Marshall?' the consultant asked, standing with his arms folded across his chest in defence.

'I just want to know what's going on with my injuries and what's going to be done about it,' I spat. Everyone could sense the bitterness in my voice, but I was beyond caring.

'Mr Marshall, you already know what the situation is.' He spoke with a patronising tone that did not become him.

'And what exactly is that?'

'You know that your aneurysm is inoperable.'

'I know that,' I yelled. 'I'm not an idiot. But if that is the case, why do I keep having all these tests?'

'Well,' he closed the door to prevent anyone else from overhearing. 'For one, it helps advancements in medical research, and of course, we need to monitor your brain to make sure it's not getting any worse.'

'If it does get worse, what can you do about it?' I asked, trying to calm myself but failing miserably.

He looked at me blankly. 'I'm afraid there is nothing we can do.' His answer was cold, flat.

I looked at Jade to make sure I had not imagined his last words. She looked just as surprised as I did. Oh. My. God. 'Then what's the point of me even being here?' I yelled, wondering why I hadn't punched him yet. He stood in silence for a few moments, obviously not knowing what to say to me that would make any difference at all. 'What papers do I need to sign to get me the hell out of all this bullshit?' I added firmly.

'You do realise the seriousness of what you are asking to

do, Mr Marshall?' The consultant actually looked surprised.

'Well, you're not going to do anything to help me, so it doesn't really matter, does it?' I spat. 'I may have a brain injury, but I'm not an idiot, and I know my own mind.'

'You do realise that the hospital will take no responsibility for you if anything happens?'

'You haven't helped me much anyway, have you, so it doesn't really matter.' I just wanted to get out of that place and get some air before I passed out.

'You will, of course, need to sign the discharge papers-'

'Fine. Get them, and I'll sign anything I need to.' I could feel that my head was about to go into a full-blown seizure, and I needed to get outside before I collapsed. The last thing I needed to do was wake up in another goddamned hospital bed.

'You will have to make an appointment to come back next week to sign the papers. We can't just get them like that.'

I got to my feet hastily and pushed open the door. At this point, I had heard enough. 'Nothing new there then,' I yelled as I stormed along the corridor with Jade close behind me. She had remained silent during the entire conversation, but I knew she agreed with everything I had said. Rebecca phoned for the appointment when she returned from America a few days later, and the following week I was free. Free from constant prodding and poking and free from the bullshit I'd been fed by the hospital for almost six months. The only reason I had quietly endured the endless tests was that I had been waiting for the doctors to give me the all-clear, so I could get my motocross license back. It was looking unlikely this would ever happen now, so I saw no further reason to keep up the pretence.

# Chapter 13

I tried to return to work around eight months after my accident, desperate to get back to normal, but just four hours of forced endurance was enough for Andrew to send me home again. He could see that I was no more ready to go back to work than he was to sell his business and move to the moon. As I worked with heavy machinery, the noise was unbearable, and as no one there really understood what I was suffering, I didn't last too long. He was good about everything, though, allowing me to come in on the days when I felt up to it and to stay at home on the days I didn't.

He continued to pay my total wages and allowed me to take things as slowly as I needed.

It was just as well, really, because I found it extremely difficult to go outside, even simply to step outside the front door for some well-needed fresh air. Without warning, the entire world now felt strange and frightening, and I couldn't understand why everything had changed in my mind to such a colossal extent. My mates had initially wanted me to get back out socialising with them as soon as I was out of the hospital. They were all relieved to see that I was okay and wanted things to get back to normal as quickly I did. 'Come out for a drink, Craig,' they'd said on several occasions. 'Thank Christ you're an okay, mate. Let's get hammered to celebrate.' But the truth was, I was far from okay. Andy and

John had discovered that much on their visit to see me at the flat, and everyone else now seemed to be catching up.

By the time I found the courage to go to a nightclub again, it had taken only a few minutes for me to have a major panic attack and spiral out of control. Everything felt wrong. I couldn't stand the noise of the music, the volume of people swarming around me like flies or the claustrophobic atmosphere that threatened to choke the very life out of me. I put up with it for around an hour or so and then made my excuses and left. I had to get out of there. My head felt as if it was going to explode along with the rest of me, leaving nothing but carnage in my wake. I was given a few strange looks as I left, but I didn't care. The only thing I needed right then was fresh air and silence. 'What's wrong with him?' I could hear the guys sneering as I hurried out of the building in a daze.

Because my injuries were on the inside, it meant that I looked absolutely fine from an outside point of view. My hair had grown back, and I walked around, stringing sentences together as if nothing had happened at all. I couldn't have expected them to understand. So, sure enough, one by one and over a relatively short time frame, they drifted out of my life, asking me less often to join them whenever they got together until eventually, no one asked me to join them at all. As my motocross days were now well and truly behind me, they no longer saw any reason to socialise with me. I found it relatively shallow because only the girls stood by me and watched me try to rebuild what was left of my life.

People began telling me that I had changed, although inside, I still felt like the exact same person I had always been. I was well aware that I lived every day with pain unlike anything I had ever experienced. Of course, my waking moments were now swamped with stupid images and memories that flicked across my mind like a slideshow. But I was still the same person inside.

I did not feel as if my personality had changed at all, and neither did I feel different than I ever had. My head injury had not removed my dry sense of humour or my openly flirty nature. I still enjoyed the same foods and laughed at the same jokes.

Rebecca would tell me not to worry, but it didn't help. I simply could not understand how I could seemingly have a wide circle of friends one moment, yet in the time it took me to hit the ground from twenty feet in the air, they all disappeared. It didn't even happen suddenly. It happened in slow motion so that I could see it in glorious technicolour detail.

Of course, I recognised that certain things had changed, but I initially tried not to take much notice because they seemed unimportant, insignificant. Before the accident, I wore only trousers and sports jackets, always ensuring I looked as smart as possible to stand out from the crowd and be noticed. And yet, the idea of wearing trousers now made me uncomfortable, and I only felt satisfied slobbing around in jeans and t-shirts.

It might have been because I was convinced my injuries were visible, which made me vulnerable to the outside world. Dressing low key seemed to help me disappear into a void that I hoped no one would notice. It didn't help either that only the girls seemed to understand why I was no longer the life and soul of the party. People literally could not grasp the idea that I was dealing with something they simply could not see.

I felt that the rose-tinted glasses I had once looked at my life through had been sharply removed from my eyes. Up until that point in my life, the friends I knew had formed a large part of my existence, and I never dreamed for one moment that I might ever find myself without that all-important support network. But after watching them disappear out of my life one by one, it quickly dawned on me that most people are never actually your friends at all unless they are getting something of value from you. Only then do they hang around, gaining from your existence. For me, it may have been the fun and carefree attitude that I wore proudly for all to see. I guess it made them feel good about themselves too for a while, and yet when I could no longer offer this, they slipped away quietly without giving me a second thought.

It may sound terrible, but I started to see their ulterior motives, and I looked at people differently. I wondered how many people can genuinely say they have friends who care about them for who they are and not just because of what they might be getting out of them at any one time? I questioned how many of those friends would be there in challenging times because I realised with a jolt that most of my friends were anything but. The only people that stayed around long enough to see me recover as much as I was ever going to were Rebecca, Jade, and Grace. I didn't have to hope that they were my real friends. Their actions had proven beyond doubt that they were the best friends I would ever have.

***

Things quickly began to escalate, and eventually, it got to the point where I could not even step outside the front door without having a panic attack. Although I desperately tried to push myself, I couldn't shake the feeling of anxiety that was steadily growing inside me. I had changed from being an outwardly confident guy who didn't care what anyone thought of me, to someone who couldn't even open the front door without a massive fear of being seen in public. I was convinced that my head injury was visible, and I was a complete freak. I thought that people could see my condition and was confident they would all point and laugh when they saw me.

By now, Rebecca and I were much closer than we had ever been. I initially assumed it was because we were now living together, but as time went on, I realised that she was the one person I needed the most in my life. She had felt terribly guilty about having left me on the day of the accident and spent far too much of her time attempting to make up for things she had no control over whatsoever. She felt if I died that day, she would never have been able to forgive herself, and although initially, I was thankful for the support she gave me, as time went on, her good intentions became somewhat overbearing. Of course, this wasn't something I could ever actually tell her. She had been my rock at a time when no one else could possibly have understood what I was going through. Ironically, in an attempt to ensure her happiness, by the time Christmas came around, our relationship was inadvertently ready to move to the next level.

We were due to attend an awards ceremony for the conclusion of the annual motocross season. Although it was the last place on earth I wanted to go, Rebecca somehow persuaded me that it might actually be a pleasant experience.

'You'll be okay,' she said casually as we were getting ready. I was standing in her bedroom, fiddling with buttons on a shirt that made me feel as if I was going to suffocate. 'I'll be with you the whole time, and if it gets too much, we can always come straight home.' She helped me with a dickie bow that I felt made me look ridiculous and smoothed the edge of my collar before smiling at me in a way that only she was able to do that helped calm me down. I wanted to tell her I wasn't up to it, to explain I couldn't possibly go out looking like a penguin because it made me feel stupid.

But, of course, she was right, and as it turned out, we

enjoyed a delightful evening. I picked up an award for *The Most Spectacular Crash of the Season*. It was ironic how they managed to make something so horrific sound amazing as they announced quite proudly how, against all odds, I had overcome such a harrowing ordeal in order to be with them all that evening. There was much gratitude towards me because I had lived through a terrible experience and everyone wanted to speak to me and offer words of support. We even managed to completely ignore Ryan and Justin's presence as if their existence held no consequence whatsoever. What more could I have possibly asked for?

I knew, of course, that it was my way of showing them that despite everything that had happened between us, they had not beaten me and would never beat me. I was alive, I was healing, and I was getting back on my feet quicker than anyone could have thought possible. They did not need to know the horror that lived inside my head, and they certainly would never see me on those bad days when I couldn't even get out of bed. We caught each other's attention only once before Rebecca diverted me swiftly towards a group of people from her modelling agency that had been sponsoring me for the last year. I graciously accepted my award that night and kept that plaque on Rebecca's shelf next to a photograph of me before the accident as a reminder of who I once was, and who I desperately needed to become again.

I was surprised that I actually rather enjoyed the evening, despite returning home exhausted and needing a lie-down. It was the first proper night out since the accident that I had managed not to run away from, and when we returned to the flat, Rebecca had a look in her eye that I couldn't quite fathom. She stood in front of me wearing a black sparkling backless halter neck dress that she had purchased especially for the occasion, looking beautiful with her blond hair scooped up softly below her neckline. She stared at me for the longest of moments as if she wanted to say something but didn't know where to start.

'What?' I asked eventually, wondering why she gave me such a strange look and genuinely only wanting someone to point me towards my bed.

'You,' she answered coyly as she tilted her head sideways, still looking at me with a weird glint in her eyes.

'What about me?' I took off the dinner jacket that Rebecca had insisted I wore and placed it over the back of the dining chair so I wouldn't crease it.

'Are we ever actually going to get together?' It was a serious question and took me by surprise.

'Oh, Bex,' I sighed loudly, trying to sound as sincere as I knew how and hoping she wouldn't take it the wrong way. I was too tired for such a serious conversation; my head was pounding from the evening's noise and interaction. 'We've been through this before. What if we broke up? You know how I feel about all that.' I was in no mood for this conversation again tonight.

Without saying a word, Rebecca untied her dress strap and allowed it to drop to the floor in one single motion. She stood in front of me wearing nothing but the skimpiest pair of knickers I had ever seen.

'We won't split up,' she whispered, truly believing her own words as she walked towards me expectantly. 'Not ever.' The attraction between us was so strong at that point and the intensity of our emotions so high, we both knew eventually something would have to give. When Rebecca and I finally got together that night, it was like a dam had finally broken and the subsequent flood allowed to rush in swept over us like nothing before. With all the messing around and teasing we had shared over the years, we had never gone beyond a certain point, but that night changed everything as we allowed our passions to take over and had sex right there and then on Rebecca's dining room table.

\*\*\*

The weeks that followed saw Rebecca's personality take on a lease of life that no one could have anticipated, especially me. As stupid as it sounded when I actually took the time to think about it, it never had entirely crossed my mind that it had been her intention all along for us to, at some point, begin a full-blown sexual relationship. I truly believed that because we were so close to each other, our fooling around was simply part of the way our relationship worked.

I shouldn't have been surprised that things would now change drastically, but I was caught totally off guard by the whole thing. I was genuinely happy to see her in such high spirits, but inside I was petrified that our friendship would be lost forever if we split up. I knew I would not be able to bear that at all, yet equally could not shake the happy feeling that surrounded Rebecca's flat now. The atmosphere was electric. Her friends were pleased for us, and Grace and Jade practically jumped all over me when Rebecca broke the news to them.

'Oh my God.' Jade yelled into my ear excitedly. 'About bloody time, too,' she joked. 'We thought you guys would never actually get together.' I quite literally had no idea that it was apparent to everyone else how Rebecca felt about me. Who was I to burst her bubble?

\*\*\*

Although things were slowly beginning to calm down and my head was getting accustomed to its new way of life, the panic attacks I was suffering seemed to worsen. I was absolutely fine if Rebecca or one of the other girls was with me, but if I had to go out alone for any reason, just getting to my car seemed a near-impossible task. I would actually mentally work myself up into a frenzied state before I could open the flat door, car key in hand, as if it was a lifeline that connected me to the outside world. I honestly felt that if I could get to my car quickly enough, I would be safe. It was a terrible feeling. I could barely remember the carefree guy who could happily go to nightclubs, chat to everyone around him, then drive from the club straight to work the following morning without a seconds thought about it. It felt as if I was no longer myself anymore, yet the more I tried to shake the feeling, the stronger it became.

I pushed myself hard to relieve my own anxiety, and eventually, my brain settled down enough for me to return to work on a full-time basis. Even though Andrew was still paying my wages, I was growing tired of depending on Rebecca's kindness, and I genuinely didn't feel at all right in doing so.

I wanted to move back home to Somerton Village, but she would not hear of it, saying she needed me close so she could look after me. I suspected the truth may have been because she was keen for us to begin a committed relationship and live together as a proper couple. A few weeks after our first night together, she started receiving offers of work in America and reluctantly started flying over to Miami. She needed the money, and I needed an excuse for things to return to normal as quickly as possible. She would call me whenever she could, of course, usually two to three times a day, and would never really settle until she was home again.

*** 

The day Rebecca came home after being away on a two-week photoshoot, something felt different. She sat in the flat in silence for too long, seemingly on edge about something I had not been a part of, not her usual happy self at all.

'What's wrong, babe?' I asked as we were cuddled up watching television. I kissed the top of her head, and she sighed as if there was something on her mind that she didn't know how to tell me. 'Are you okay?'

I couldn't reasonably interpret the blank expression on her face as she turned and looked straight into my eyes. 'I'm fed up with living in England,' she announced out of nowhere. 'Why don't we move to America? Permanently.'

'Are you serious?' I had no idea where this statement had come from, and I was not expecting it at all. I sat upright, moving away from her in response to her sudden declaration.

'Yes, Craig, I'm deadly serious,' she answered. 'I want us to move to Miami. I've been thinking about it for a while.'

I glanced towards the ceiling and sighed without meaning to sound so irritated. 'Bex, I'm having trouble getting outside the front door at the moment, let alone being capable of moving to the other side of the Atlantic Ocean.' I had no idea how she could spring something like this on me now. I may have been getting my faculties back, but it was a prolonged process, and I was a long way from being as normal as I knew I needed to be.

'You'll be okay. I'll be with you. It'll be a fresh start for us. Anything's got to be better than this place, surely.' She waved her arms in the air as if she genuinely hated her life in England.

'No, babe.' I couldn't take in anything of what she was saying. 'We can't.'

'Why not?' Her tone came out aggressively, too aggressively in fact. She folded her arms across her chest tightly.

'Well, for a start, I've never actually been overseas for a holiday, let alone anything more permanent. I don't even have a passport. How can I go and live in another country? My job is here. My life is here. England is all I know.' I was shocked by her sudden revelations and had no idea where her random idea had come from.

Rebecca looked as if she was going to cry. 'But-' she started to say.

'No buts, babe. I can't go and live in America. And that's the end of it.'

# Chapter 14

By the time April came around, Rebecca's behaviour had become increasingly erratic and incomprehensible to the point where I knew something would have to give eventually. Knowing her as well as I did, I was sure there was more going on with her than a simple desire to move to the states. She snapped at me twice before breakfast one morning for something I had or hadn't done, becoming irritated by the tiniest of things that generally wouldn't bother her. Even the ring my teacup had made on the kitchen counter seemed to send her into a fury I simply couldn't understand. She was spending much of her time teetering on the edge of some kind of explosion, and I was walking around on eggshells just wondering what might upset her next. She complained about things far more than I had ever known her to do. It was totally out of character, and yet whenever I asked her about it, I was met with even more irritation that created arguments I was in no mood for.

We had arranged a night out to celebrate our upcoming birthdays that I knew we both desperately needed. It was my way of trying to work through the agoraphobia I could no longer tolerate. I also wanted Rebecca to regain the usual brightness that had always surrounded her existence. *Life is for living*, she would say. She was the life and soul of any party and made friends quickly yet, looking at her lately, I couldn't help wondering if she felt the pressures of being with someone who struggled to cope with a painful head injury. I considered the idea that it was my fault her mood had altered, yet my brain was still oblivious to what was going on outside the confines of my own head. I had enough to cope with already and genuinely didn't spot Rebecca's changing mood until it was all but too late.

Our birthdays came around quickly, and we enjoyed the evening out we had planned. I tried my best to hide the anxiety that lingered below the surface of my typical façade, for the first time since my accident, actually feeling genuinely comfortable with being out of the flat, even if it would only be for a couple of hours. By the time we returned home, Rebecca was actually smiling again, and I allowed myself to relax slightly, assuming my plan to cheer her up had worked. I made us a hot drink, and we settled down on the sofa together.

'What can I do to make you change your mind?' Rebecca was staring at her cup of coffee, swilling the liquid around in the mug absently.

'About what?' I asked casually as I flicked on the television, the commotion of the restaurant still ringing in my ears and not immediately noticing Rebecca's darkening mood.

'Moving to America?'

I shot a look towards her, and my heart plunged. She hadn't given up at all on her crazy idea. 'Oh, for God's sake Bex,' I groaned. 'Please, can't you just stop talking about that?'

'No, I can't.' Her tone was clipped, and I knew instantly we were heading for an argument.

'I don't want to move to America, Rebecca,' I answered firmly. 'Why can't you get that into your head? Don't you understand how difficult everything is for me at the moment?' I sat upright and moved away from her towards the edge of the sofa, my own irritation growing and our otherwise pleasant evening now well and truly ruined. 'Why is it so important to you anyway?'

'I've got some big jobs coming up, and I need you to be there-'

'So? Nothing is stopping *you* from going. You've had big jobs before, so what's the difference now?' I didn't feel like drinking my tea anymore.

She paused for a moment, and I wondered what was going through her mind right then. 'I don't want to leave you here, Craig. That's the difference.' Her tone was sharp, yet her voice seemed to hide a sadness I couldn't have understood at that moment even if I wanted to.

'So you're actually blaming my head now?'

'Jesus Christ, no, of course, I'm not.' Rebecca ran her cold hand over the back of my neck as if she didn't want to fight with me any more than I did. 'But I can see how much better you're feeling. I thought it would be the fresh start we both need. I just want to be with you. What's wrong with that?'

'Rebecca. I don't want to go to America. Why is this all such a big deal for you? You're not making any sense at all.'

'Why don't you want to come with me?'

'It's not as simple as that. I can't just drop everything. My job is here. How would I get a job in America? I've never even been to the place. I don't know anything about being in a different country. I would feel totally out of my depths over there. And I've also already told you, I don't have a passport.' I felt as if I was repeating myself, and this conversation was getting old. Surely she understood what I was currently dealing with in my head.

'Firstly, you won't have to worry about getting work over there because I'm earning more than enough for the both of us, and we can get you a goddamned passport easily enough.' She was starting to lose it. I hated it when she got like that because there really was no reasoning with her.

'No, Bex.' England and my life here was literally all I knew. I had enough to cope with as it was without having a whole new country to contend with. I thought she knew this. I thought she understood.

'For fucks sake, Craig.' Rebecca got to her feet and slammed her cup onto the table, spilling coffee and chipping a piece out of the rim in her haste. 'I want us to move to the states and get the hell away from this place. I know we can get better treatment for you in America. And I don't want to leave you. Please, Craig. Please say you'll at least think about it?'

'So this *is* about my head after all?' I yelled at her. I couldn't help it. I had developed a terrible headache now due to the pressure I felt I was being placed under.

'Not just that-' She paused as if she wanted to add something but didn't quite finish her sentence. 'I just hate Britain and everyone in it,' she added firmly. 'Unless you're-' her voice trailed off.

'Unless I'm what?'

'Unless you're having second thoughts about us, and that's the real reason you don't want to come with me?' She folded her arms across her chest as if she had made a startling discovery that even took me by surprise for a moment. Yet the more I thought about it, the more I realised her words weren't strictly untrue. I had been having second, third, and even fourth thoughts about us being together ever since the night of the awards ceremony. I knew she was happy to be with me, but I personally didn't feel exactly right about the direction our relationship had turned. Up until that moment, I simply hadn't felt able to speak to her about it. Now was as good a time as any, and I knew I wouldn't be able to hold it in forever.

'I sometimes wonder if we crossed the line too quickly.' I'd said the words before I could stop myself and now needed to verify my thoughts. 'Maybe we might be better off as best friend's again, babe.' The words had left my mouth in such a hurry. I wondered if I had said them how I had meant them to sound.

'Oh my God, I knew it.' Rebecca grabbed her car keys from the coffee table and stood up sharply, turning them around in her hand as if pondering her next move.

'Oh, shit, sorry that came out wrong-' I got to my feet in response to Rebecca's sudden realisation, but it made no difference to her response.

'No, it didn't. You just said it all. You don't want to be with me, and you don't want to move to the states with me. What more do I need to know?' She ran a shaky hand through her hair as if she was about to burst into tears. 'I get it now completely.'

'No, Bex, you really don't-'

'I said. I get it.' She stared at me for a few seconds with her teeth clenched together before she muttered something under her breath that I didn't quite catch. She shook her head as if my words had confirmed something she needed to hear before storming out of the flat in a blatant attempt to get as far away from me as she could. She slammed the front door so hard that it bounced back out of the latch and vibrated against the wall, leaving a dirty mark on the paintwork.

Feeling wobbly and somewhat shaken, I sat down on the edge of the sofa and visualised her body language as her footsteps echoed down the stairs to the front doorway. Women. Why did they always have to make things so complicated? Thoughts of what I feared would happen if we ever split up came flooding into my already crammed mind, and I sighed loudly.

I had known all along that this was going to happen. Why the hell did I not listen to my own instincts and stop this before we got to this point? And why the hell was America so goddamned important to her? I had never seen her act so irrationally before and had no idea what was going on in her head. I leaned back against a cushion in an attempt to prevent the room from spinning wildly. My head was pounding, and I knew it would be unable to cope with any further upset tonight. I vowed that I would get to the bottom of things when she returned, but right at that moment, the only thing I needed was for my head to calm down. I closed my eyes. We could talk when she got home.

\*\*\*

I have no idea how long I lay on the sofa or that I had at some point actually managed to fall asleep, but I was woken sharply by the sound of someone banging on the flat door. I sat bolt upright, taking in nothing of my surroundings and momentarily forgetting my earlier argument with Rebecca. I drowsily glanced at the clock. It was already gone seven in the morning. For a moment, I couldn't quite grasp where I was or that I had finally managed to drop to sleep after several hours of pacing around the flat, churning over words unsaid. I staggered to my feet as the incessant knocking continued, growing louder with each passing moment the door remained closed. I assumed that Rebecca must have forgotten her keys. Either that or her mood had not abated. By the sound of the banging, I presumed it was the latter. Why the hell she had to make such a commotion, I did not know. She knew how sensitive my head was and was usually more considerate. I pulled open the door, about to tell her not to be so loud, when I came face to face with Emma, Rebecca's sister, standing ashen-faced next to two police officers. She looked as if she had been crying.

'Good morning, sir.' One of the police officers spoke to me quietly. He did not smile. None of them did.

I glanced quickly between them, still not quite awake and

wondering for a moment if I might have been dreaming. 'Can I help you?' I offered, my voice sounding slightly shaky and a worrying feeling bubbling in my gut that I couldn't shake.

'Can we step inside for a moment, please?' the police officer asked. By this time, he had removed his hat and was standing somewhat awkwardly in the doorway. I stepped aside to allow them entry, glancing briefly at Emma for some kind of explanation that didn't come as they strode past me into the flat. I automatically looked towards Rebecca's bedroom door, expecting to see her emerge at any moment asking who the hell had woken her at this hour. I was unsure if she had actually come home at all last night or if she had spent the night with Jade. My heart began to race.

'Is everything okay?' I asked, not really expecting the answer I was about to receive. They motioned me to sit down, but I refused. I simply stood expectantly in the middle of the living room floor, wondering what they were doing here and wishing they would hurry up and get to the point.

The policemen hovered for a few moments in front of me, obviously looking for the right words to say yet not knowing where to even begin. 'I am very sorry,' one of them offered after what felt like an eternity. 'But I'm afraid I have to tell you that the body of a young woman was found in the early hours of this morning.' For a moment, the words I heard didn't quite seem to reach my ears. I took a deep breath as I felt my entire body tense. As he continued speaking, I felt my body grow numb, as if it had been frozen to where I was standing. 'Her car registration matches one belonging to a Miss Rebecca Taylor.' Was that a question or a statement? 'We understand that she lives here. I am terribly sorry, sir, but her sister-' he gestured towards Emma, 'has asked that you come with her to the hospital to formally identify the body.' He paused for my response, but no words he said made any sense to me at all.

'I beg your pardon?' I was seriously trying to take in the information that had been given to me but failed desperately. 'Where's Rebecca?' I had no idea what was going on, and as I darted looks between both the police and Emma, who still had not even looked at me during the entire time she had been there, I had absolutely no contemplation of what I was hearing. When Emma finally found the strength to look my way, tears were already perched for a significant explosion.

'I am so sorry to be the one to have to break this news to you, sir,' the police officer offered. 'But I am afraid it looks as if she took her own life.'

My head snapped towards him sharply. Had I actually heard him right? They must have got this completely wrong. Surely they had the wrong information or the wrong flat entirely. I waited for Emma to offer a contradiction to his words, but her tears started flowing with the sound of his voice.

Suicide? No way. What the hell were they talking about? I wanted to laugh straight in their faces because this had to be a huge mistake. Nothing else made sense to me at all. I opened my mouth to speak, but no words would find their way out. I must have been dreaming, surely. Any second now, I felt that I would be waking up to the sensation of Rebecca jumping all over me with a hot bacon sandwich and her infectious laugh filling the room. I wanted to pinch myself. I wanted someone to actually pinch me. I wanted to scream loudly at them, please, for Christ's sake, someone pinch me.

After noticing the look of horror on my face and realising I needed further collaboration, the police officers turned to look at each other. They then proceeded to describe the circumstances that surrounded this poor victim's demise.

'She was found in her car early this morning by a gentleman walking his dog. Her car was parked some way along Bay Lane.' He paused and swallowed. 'A hosepipe was leading from the exhaust into the driver's window. I am so very sorry.'

Although I could hear his words and could see the look of sympathy on his face, he couldn't possibly be getting any of his facts correct.

*Rebecca?*

*Dead?*

*Suicide?*

I stood dumbstruck as if someone had ripped out my entire insides for a laugh. The usual throbbing in my head now felt as if it was going to explode, and at any moment, I could easily have passed out had it not been for the pure adrenaline pumping through my veins. It must have been sheer shock that kept me upright because nothing else made a single shred of sense at all.

When Emma eventually found her voice, it emerged like a small, frightened child who simply did not know what to do next. 'Craig, please, will you come with me? I don't want to do this by myself.' I stared at Emma as if she wasn't even there. What in God's name was going on?

\*\*\*

We arrived at the hospital in total silence, the police giving us both the time they thought we needed to absorb what was happening. As I stepped onto the tarmac outside the hospitals mortuary, my legs did not feel as if they belonged to me at all. My head, usually numb anyway with everything going on inside it, was now completely blank. I could not get my brain to function correctly, and I could not think straight. We were ushered into an uninviting corridor that smelled of something I didn't want to think about. As soon as we stepped through the door, Emma broke down and refused to go any further.

'Are you okay to do this, sir?' The question was directed at me from some voice I didn't recognise, and I wondered if I had even heard the words at all. All I knew was that I had no choice but to go in alone and prove that Rebecca was not inside that room. I held my breath, allowing my head to nod somehow as if it were attached to a string that someone else controlled. I swallowed hard as a door was pressed open in front of me. It must have only taken a few seconds to walk the three steps into that tiny room, but it felt as if I was walking down the longest tunnel that had ever been created. I did not know what to expect. Nothing was making any sense whatsoever, and I felt that I might actually vomit at any moment.

The only thing that I absolutely, one hundred per cent, knew with all my heart was that Rebecca would not be in here. They had made a terrible mistake, and I would soon be able to tell them all and get on with my day in peace. As I stood in front of a covered sheet, someone carefully peeled it back so that I could view the unfortunate body that lay cold on the slab in front of me.

For a moment, I didn't quite understand what I was looking at. I took in a sharp breath as my brain began to register what I was witnessing, my eyes contradicting the poor retched image in front of me. Rebecca's eyes were closed, shielding the brilliance of her usually bright blue eyes. She was asleep. She had to be. Nothing else made sense. Nothing else could be possible. Someone was talking, I think, but I could hear nothing beyond the buzz of my own brain as I desperately tried to make sense of what was happening. My head felt numb, hollow as if I had been underwater for too long, and no one had bothered to tell me that I had drowned.

It genuinely felt as if my heart had stopped beating. I wanted to shake her awake, to tell her not to lie there like that playing such a cruel joke on me.

'Is it her?' I was asked by a voice that sounded far too calm and patient for the magnitude of this moment. I didn't want to say yes. I didn't want to believe for a moment that any of this could be real. I wanted to ask him if this was some kind of sick joke that had been set up to push me over the edge completely. Yet all I could do was nod my head as if it really didn't belong to me at all. Rebecca's face was covered once again, and I realised with a painful stab that I would never see her again. Oh. My. God. As I was led back out of the room, I dreaded the moment when one look at my face would tell Emma everything I knew she was not ready to learn.

'I am so very sorry for your loss,' a suited man offered after Emma had let out a blood-curdling scream that didn't even appear to come from her body at all. 'I know how much of a shock this must be for you.' He looked me straight in the eyes as he added, 'I'm terribly sorry about the baby.' As those words reached my ears, something profound inside of me snapped.

'*Baby*? What baby?' I couldn't speak properly. I couldn't think properly. I could hear someone crying. It wasn't me. When the suited man gave me his condolences, my knees buckled, and I sank to the floor. As soon as the words left his mouth, I was sobbing, crying like I'd never cried before. I felt as if I'd been punched in the stomach by a sledgehammer. I didn't know how long I was on the floor, but it felt as if I might seriously never be able to get up again. I tried to look up at him, desperate for some kind of explanation that never came.

'I'm terribly sorry for your loss,' I heard again. I felt the room spin, then everything went black.

# Chapter 15

I opened my eyes to the sound of dull sobbing that was mixed with the occasional sharp intake of breath, and I wondered for a moment if it might have been coming from me. My heart was still beating, but inside I was already dead. My body numb, my arms and legs no longer responding to anything my brain instructed. I was lying on a stretcher in a tiny room, and as I glanced around, I noticed Rebecca's sister, Emma, sitting next to me on a plastic chair. Her eyes were red, swollen beyond recognition through tears she was unable to hold back. She got to her feet when she saw that I was awake and took hold of my hand.

'I'm so sorry, Craig,' she sobbed. 'I should have told you-'

I attempted to sit up, pulling my hand away, but I no longer had the coordination to control my own body. I felt sick and was having severe trouble breathing without feeling an incredible pain in my chest cavity with every intake of breath.

'What the hell's going on, Emma?' I somehow managed to stutter through my own laboured breath.

Emma closed her eyes, fresh tears breaking free that left streak marks in her makeup. 'She didn't want to tell you yet,' she began. 'She wanted it to be a surprise.'

'A surprise?' I wanted to laugh at the irony. 'Jesus Christ, are you actually kidding me?' I edged myself onto the floor and stood shakily on legs that threatened to send me sprawling to the ground at any second. 'How long had she known?' I knew my words sounded bitter and angry, but that was nothing compared to how I felt inside right then.

'Only a couple of weeks,' Emma sobbed, her own words sounding strangled and tight. 'To be honest, I was the only one who knew. Even Grace didn't know yet. Oh my God, she was so happy, Craig.' A fresh burst of pain erupted from her then, and she collapsed onto the floor, allowing fresh tears to stream down her face. Instinctively I knelt down by her side and pulled her close. Holding each other, our tears came freely, and it was quite some time before either of us was able to speak again. I had discovered two devastating things that were beyond my comprehension, and neither made any sense to me at all.

'How the hell can she be dead?' I couldn't believe I was even saying the words aloud. Emma shook her head. 'Was that the real reason she wanted to move to America?' I asked. 'Because of the baby?' Even as I allowed myself to say the words, they felt alien to me, wrong somehow. It was a notion that my already messed up brain could not contend with.

Emma nodded then and sniffed loudly. 'She called me as soon as she found out she was pregnant. She kept dancing around, and I could hardly get any sense out of her. She was so happy.' She attempted a laugh that didn't quite reach either of us. 'You were the only one she ever loved, Craig. She always knew it, even when you guys were kids. She always knew that one day you would be together. This last year has been the happiest of her life, and the only thing she ever wanted was to be with you.'

I was still unable to comprehend the words I was hearing. 'But why didn't she tell me?' I snapped through clenched teeth that I wondered might actually break.

'She really wanted to. She was desperate to tell you, but

she needed to know that you wanted her as much as she wanted you. She thought that if you agreed to go to America with her, it would mean that you really did want to be with her and then she would have told you about the baby.'

Those words stabbed me like a sharp knife to the chest, and I clambered to my feet, sending my already unsteady body sprawling backwards against the wall. It suddenly made sense as to why she had been acting so snappy recently. I had been busy trying to figure out where our relationship was heading, and how I could bring it back on track in the way I genuinely needed to. Of course, I loved her. I loved her more than anything in the world, but there is a vast difference between loving someone and actually being *in love* with them, and the truth was that I simply was not in love with Rebecca. I thought she knew this. I thought she understood. Rebecca was my best friend and the only family I had ever truly known. How could I have been so stupid? How could I allow one moment of pathetic weakness on my part to ruin everything we had together? Now to find out that she was pregnant? What in God's name had I done?

'I would have gone to America if she had told me about the baby,' I whispered. And I genuinely meant every word.

'She knew that, Craig, that's exactly why she didn't tell you. But she wanted you to go to America because you wanted to go, not simply because she was pregnant. She knew you would always look after her and step up to your responsibilities no matter what. She knew you would always do the right thing by her. That's why she loved you so much.' She took a deep breath before continuing. 'But deep down, she felt that you were not quite as committed to the relationship as she was; that something was holding you back.' Emma was right. I was being held back. I didn't want to lose the friendship that had taken us years to build. I leaned over and vomited on the floor.

\*\*\*

We left the hospital in total silence, neither of us ready for a future without Rebecca. As I stepped into the morning air, it felt like poison in my lungs, and I staggered sideways, my heart ready to stop beating in that single moment. I don't remember getting back to the flat that day, but when we stepped through the front door, Rebecca's perfume hit me straight in the face, and in the time it took me to step inside the room, my legs had given way, and I collapsed onto the carpet before I was able to stop myself. I was completely hollow inside, totally and utterly empty. I was still alive, but the blood flowing through my veins had already turned to ice. I was dead. Truly dead. How the hell was I going to break this awful news to Grace and Jade? How was I going to live without Rebecca in my life? Nothing made any sense, and we were both feeling the same thing as I helped Emma to the sofa.

'I don't understand why they kept telling us she had killed herself.' Emma was wiping the back of her hand over her tear-streaked face.

I shot her a look, feeling an all too familiar pain stab me in the back of my head. 'You don't seriously believe that she would do something like that, do you?' I couldn't contemplate that notion at all. 'If she had been as happy about the baby as you say she was, there's no way on this earth she would do that to herself. You know it. I know it.' My own words sounded strangled and hollow, and my guilt about our earlier argument erupted suddenly. 'If I hadn't been so stubborn about going to America, she would still be here, alive and well, with me. It's all my fault.' Even as I spoke the words, I could feel every ounce of strength leave my body. My hands were shaking, and I didn't try to stop them.

'How the hell can it be your fault?' Emma sobbed, her own grief mixed with anger for what I had just said. 'Don't talk like that. Of course, it's not your fault. No, Craig, you're absolutely right. She wouldn't have hurt herself. She loved you too much, for God's sake. She needed you more than I think she ever needed anyone. She was having your baby, for crying out loud. There's no way suicide would even enter her head. Why the hell would it?' We looked at each other for a moment, the realisation of what had happened taking a painful amount of time to sink in. I don't know if it was the sheer shock of events that I had no control over, or my own adrenaline that kicked in at that moment, but I suddenly found my feet and my voice.

'None of this adds up!' I yelled so loudly that I made Emma physically jump. I began pacing the room, not knowing what to do with myself or how I should react to any of my surroundings at all. Every single item in the flat reminded me of Rebecca, and I wanted to smash the whole place up without remorse. 'It just doesn't add up.' My anger began creeping into my veins like poison, and Emma looked on helplessly as I slammed my fists into Rebecca's kitchen door, splintering the framework unapologetically. With everything that had happened over the last couple of hours, my brain had not had time to process any information, but in that split second, the realisation of what had happened to Rebecca hit me like an express train, and I knew exactly what they had done to her. 'Oh. My. God. They wouldn't-' I stared at Emma then, my body shaking violently and my brain contradicting every thought I was having. 'Surely they wouldn't-'

I grabbed my car keys, not stopping to listen to Emma's helpless pleas as I fled the flat, not even bothering to close the door behind me. As I climbed into my car, a familiar feeling welled up inside me as events of a previous evening flooded my mind. My hands were shaking, but I could feel nothing beyond a single thought that threatened to erupt my entire brain, right there and then.

\*\*\*

As I pulled up outside Ryan's dad's house, I was unsure what I was actually going to do. The only thought racing through my mind at that moment was what Rebecca's last moments on this earth must have been like before her life was brutally taken from her, and it drove me almost to the point of insanity. I knew in an instant what they had done, and it all suddenly made perfect sense. It had all been planned in every minute detail. My accident hadn't killed me or left me completely paralysed, so of course, it would not have been enough for them to let simply let things go. They had obviously assumed my initial injuries were severe enough to cause life long problems. Yet, they had seen me at the motocross events evening, happy and smiling with Rebecca, my outer appearance seemingly unaffected. I had wanted them to see that their actions had failed to hurt me, and yet it now appeared they still wanted revenge. They must have been devastated to see us together like that. Happy. Unaffected by their poisonous plotting. Killing Rebecca was, of course, the ultimate way of achieving that goal, and even as I considered this notion, the idea that any human could be so callous simply did not sit right with me at all. I raced up the path and pounded on the front door, ready if needed, to break the thing down. A few seconds passed, and when Ryan's dad finally opened the door, he did not look happy to see me.

'Where is he?' I demanded, a look on my face I couldn't have predicted a few hours earlier.

'How the hell should I know?' he spat back at me. 'I don't know where he is, and I don't really care.' I felt by his tone that he was not hiding anything from me. It was no secret that

Ryan and his dad did not get along. He knew precisely the type of person his son was and wanted no more to do with him than I did. Their relationship had become somewhat strained over the last year or so, and he believed nothing of his sons lies, knowing full well about his involvement with drugs and Rebecca's attack. He must have noticed my desperation because he sighed slightly when he added, 'Believe me, Craig, I would tell you if I knew 'where he was.'

'Well, when you do see him, you had better tell that bastard to watch his back because I'm coming for him.' I didn't care how menacing my threat sounded. It was meant to. As I stormed back to my car, Ryan's dad stood watching me, and for a brief moment, our eyes met. His face displayed the pain of a father who had lost his son a long time ago. With a broken marriage behind him and his family in tatters, he looked like a man that had nothing left to lose. I knew he had no reason to lie to me. Although he had no idea at that point why I was so angry, we both knew what would happen if I caught up with Ryan before him.

My next stop was to Ryan's mum's house. Ryan was a mummy's boy, and I knew he would probably be here if nowhere else. When I was given an abrupt dismissal, I was in no mood for games.

'Get that twat out here right now,' I spat as we stood in front of each other, eyes locked, my leg jammed inside her front porch, preventing her from closing the door on me.

'He's not here, but even if he was, I certainly wouldn't allow him anywhere near you.' She had her arms folded in defence, and I hated her at that moment almost as much as I hated him. 'Now get off my property.' She slammed the door into my leg a few times until I relented and stepped outside, allowing her to slam the door and lock it. Despite my continued banging for a further three or four minutes, my efforts went unrewarded. I climbed back into my car, fists red raw as I gripped the steering wheel, wishing like hell that it was Ryan's throat my hands were holding onto.

I drove around the immediate area for quite some time, scrutinising every inch of every street in case he was held up somewhere, trying to hide like the rat he was. I was like a sniffer dog on the scent of a dangerous drug substance, and in my case, the substance was a complete scumbag who, in my opinion, did not deserve to breathe good air.

I visualised what his last moment on this planet would be as he lay on his back in the dirt, my face staring down at him as his last breath left his body. I wanted to be the last thing that he ever saw, and it gave me a quiet feeling of impending satisfaction. It was all-consuming. I could not anticipate what I had become. Overnight my calm, friendly nature had been replaced by a reckless need to commit murder. Eventually, though, I ran out of places to search and had to admit an unwanted defeat. His car was nowhere to be seen, but I knew him well, and I was convinced he wouldn't be able to hide for long.

When I returned to the flat, I had nothing in my mind apart from finding Ryan and Justin, and serving them the cold justice they deserved. I knew what they had done without a shadow of a doubt, and yet I was having serious trouble believing that even they could sink that low. How would I be able to prove any of it anyway? What could I say to the police that would make them sit up and take notice? My mind was racing as I climbed the stairs to the flat, and when I opened the front door, my heart sank as I was confronted by Grace and Jade standing pale-faced and staring straight at me. We looked at each other for a lingering moment before Jade's cries erupted, and she ran across the room and flung her arms around me.

'Is it true?' Grace whispered, not quite ready for the answer I was about to give her. I nodded, and she let out the most devastating scream I have ever heard. I closed my eyes. I could barely cope with my own pain at that moment, let alone have strength enough for the girls. I couldn't do it. I couldn't be the person they had always been able to depend on. Not this time. Prizing Jade's arms from around my neck, I slowly pushed her away and headed towards the front door. I couldn't be there right then. I couldn't stand there and listen to the sound of devastated cries I did not know how to appease. I heard Grace call my name, but I did not respond. As I closed the door of Rebecca's flat behind me, I wondered if I would ever be able to go back inside again.

*** 

I climbed into my car, feeling that nothing in the world seemed real. I still did not quite understand what had happened, and the words of the police and coroner created a buzz inside my head that I could not shake. I certainly could not process any of the information that had been thrown at me. Rebecca was dead. Rebecca was pregnant. Neither of those two statements made any sense in my mind. She had told me she was on the pill, so I momentarily convinced myself that I couldn't understand what had happened. Yet, who the hell was I even kidding? I wasn't stupid. I should have been more careful. I could still see the look of disapproval on the police officers' faces as they silently contemplated how suicide affects those left behind. But I knew Rebecca, and I knew she had not killed herself. No matter what it took, somehow, I had to prove it. I could think of nowhere else to go but to the police station, my mind still racing with everything that had happened. How could I get them to listen to me? Would they even care? Images and thoughts of what Ryan and Justin had done to her whirled around my head, along with scenarios I didn't want to think about.

I drove to the place where they said her body had been found and sat in my car, the afternoon haze creating shapes in my mind that I didn't know what to do with, as I wondered what it was I expected to find there. I didn't know what I was doing. The only thing I could think about at that moment was how desperate Rebecca's last moments on this earth must have been. I climbed out of my car and slowly walked towards the muddy grass verge where her car had been discovered. It was in the middle of nowhere, a good quarter of a mile along an old disused farm track.

They had planned this perfectly. No one would have disturbed them here. No one would have been able to see what they were up to or hear Rebecca's potential screams. The mere idea of it made me shudder. I walked around aimlessly, looking at the ground for any sign that would provide me with the evidence I felt I needed. It was as if I expected some kind of revelation to suddenly jump out at me, to tell me what I needed to know. The ground was wet, and my boots quickly became covered in mud. I could see several footprints around the grassy verge. Prominent boot prints were dotted around where officers and ambulance crew had attended the scene. I visualised their desperation. Had she been alive when they found her? Did they think they could save her life?

With grotesque ideas creating scenes in my mind, I walked into the police station and explained to the officer behind the desk who I was and re-counted the events that had happened that morning, detailing in full how I knew it had been no suicide. I was desperate for him to hear me, to help me. The officer on the desk gave me a look of sympathy but could offer no tangible assistance or advice. He went to 'check' his records and came back with a dismissive tone.

'We appreciate how you must be feeling at this time, sir,' he said. 'But without evidence to prove her death was anything other than suicide, I am afraid there is nothing more we can do.' He genuinely looked saddened for my pain, but it didn't soften the blow.

'But I don't understand any of this.' I tried not to yell but failed miserably.

'Please, sir.' The officer came out from behind the reception desk and took me into a small room so I wouldn't disturb anyone else. He was carrying a file of some kind. 'When the young lady in question was found, a length of hosepipe had been taped to the driver's window from the exhaust pipe.'

I shot him a cold stare. 'But that can't be possible!' I screamed, not really able to take in a word he had said. 'There wasn't any hose pipe or tape in Rebecca's car yesterday.'

He sighed as if he thought I was crazy. 'You can't say that-'

'I *can* say that,' I spat back. 'I can say it because it happens to be true. Don't you understand?' I cut him off before he had the chance to dismiss me. 'There was no hose pipe in Rebecca's car. Please. You're not listening to me. I cleaned her car yesterday, and I vacuumed out the boot. I'm telling you, it was empty.'

I was literally shaking as I stood in front of the police, trying desperately for them to hear me and understand that what I was saying was the truth. I could see the blank expression on the officer's face. It did not fill me with confidence that they were in any way taking my words seriously. 'Did you actually find any tape in the car?' I didn't stop to hear the response. 'No. Because there was no tape in the car.'

'I believe there was a roll of tape in the back of the car, yes,' the officer continued speaking as if my words hadn't registered with him at all.

I didn't care who heard me at this point or who I upset in

the process. The officer went to open his mouth, but I cut him off sharply. 'I'm telling you now for a fact. There was no hose and no tape in Rebecca's car after I cleaned it for her yesterday. There's no way she could have got hold of that sort of equipment when she left her flat at eleven o'clock at night. We were together all day yesterday, so there was no time for her to have purchased those items even if suicide had even been on her mind, which it most certainly was not.'

'Sir, we have spoken to the coroner who dealt with this incident.' The policeman was totally ignoring the obvious. 'There was no evidence to suggest any foul play. She had no bruises on her body, and there did not appear to be any kind of a struggle.'

'But if they drugged her, there wouldn't have been a struggle would there because she would have been unconscious.' Were these people really so stupid? 'They wouldn't have had any trouble getting what they needed. They were drug pushers, for God's sake.' By this time, I was actually shouting. I desperately wanted to make them understand the type of people Ryan and Justin were. 'Did you even check her shoes?'

The police officer stared at me then with a slightly confused look on his face. 'Her shoes?'

'Yes. Apparently, she was found along Bay Lane, wasn't she? It's as muddy as hell there. I know this for a fact because I went there today, and I saw it for myself.' I pointed to the mud that had gathered on my boots, now drying slowly, mocking my every movement. 'Please,' I pleaded, cupping my hands together in desperation. 'Did you even check her feet? I know she didn't kill herself, and I know that her shoes were clean.' My distress was slowly threatening to tip me over the edge. 'And did you check inside the car for any mud?' My questions were coming thick and fast. The more I thought about it all, the less any of it made any sense at all. 'When the hospital returned Rebecca's belongings to us earlier today, her shoes were clean. How can this be possible when the ground surrounding the location where she apparently killed herself is wet and muddy from several days of rain? Her shoes would be covered in mud too because she would have needed to get out of her car to get this imaginary hose and tape from her boot.'

'Sir, I am going to have to ask you to calm down.' The officer had been joined by a colleague, neither men seemingly pleased I was taking up their valuable time.

'Please, I have her shoes in the back of my car. I can get them for you-'

'Wait just a moment,' he held up a hand in an attempt to try and calm me. He placed the folder that he had in his hand on a table and opened it up for me to see the contents. He slid some photographs that he obviously didn't want me to see underneath a plastic wallet and placed the police report in front of me.

There was so much that just did not any make sense. Even reading the words in front of me gave no conclusions at all. 'Okay, so one of her shoes was found in the passenger seat foot-well.' I glared at the police officer. 'That proves that someone dragged her unconscious body over into the driver's seat.'

'No, I'm afraid it does not.'

'Hang on. It says here that there was no mud found in the car at all.' I knew it. 'What did I tell you? Did she somehow fly out of the window and back again just to protect her stilettos?' I could sense that the police officer was beginning to listen to me. How the hell had they discarded all the evidence in front of them so quickly? 'According to this here, she was also found wearing her seat belt.' I stabbed my hand onto the paper as if I wanted to puncture a hole straight through the table. 'Okay so, answer me this question if you can. Why the hell would she, during a suicide attempt, worry about getting her shoes or her car dirty? And why would she fling one of her shoes into the passenger foot-well? I suppose she then hopped around to the back of the car, attached the hose to the exhaust pipe with tape that she didn't even have, climb back into the car, somehow manage to wipe clean her one dirty shoe, discarded whatever it was she had used to clean it and then put her seatbelt back on before starting the engine? Who the hell would do that?'

The scene had clearly been staged, and the evidence was clear for all to see, yet the police simply did not appear interested. It was plainly evident that they had made it look like a suicide, and, not wanting or caring to burden themselves with more paperwork, the police had closed the case as if Rebecca's life didn't matter. I was in utter turmoil.

The officers looked at each other for a moment, unsure why that had not been flagged up. 'I know this all seems very-'

'Don't you understand that they killed her?' I screamed, finally losing it and wondering why the hell none of them were even listening to me. 'I know they did.' I slammed my fist into the police station wall and, after being warned that if I did not calm down, I would be arrested, I stood back against the doorway and broke down.

'I'll see if I can speak to the investigating officer for you, but I can't promise anything.' I was then asked to leave. I was unsure if they would take my words seriously, and I felt even more desperate than I had been, to begin with.

# Chapter 16

The following morning a local newspaper printed a story about a young woman in Milborough who had tragically taken her own life. They mentioned her baby and the dog walker who had found her at around six o'clock in the morning. As Grace read the words on those pages, I cried tears as if I had never cried before. I was sobbing, shaking so uncontrollably that for a moment, Grace considered the idea of calling a doctor. She tried to comfort me, but I was in no mood for company and pushed her away. I yelled at her when she tried to speak to me, and eventually, she disappeared into her room to be alone. We continued like this for three days, neither of us knowing what to say to the other or trying very hard at all.

Rebecca's parents had never held a very high opinion of me, and now that their daughter was dead, they wasted no time in pointing the finger directly at me. In a visit to the flat just days after her death, they did not hesitate to tell me that my presence there was no longer welcome. As I was the last person to have seen Rebecca alive, it was obviously my fault she was now dead. It was another nail that would drive me deeper into the coffin that I could already feel building around me. They were angry, bitter, and although they had never found much time for Rebecca when she was alive, now she was dead, they were suddenly taking a very keen interest in her assets.

'Don't worry,' I spat as I stood in the middle of Rebecca's living room. 'I don't want a thing. It's all yours.' Rebecca was worth a lot of money and owned several properties, including her flat in Milborough, one in New York, a riverside apartment in London, and a beach house in Miami. I had helped her choose that Miami property via a brochure she had been overly excited about. I now realised she hoped we would eventually one day live together in it. Selling these properties would net her parents a tidy sum, and it made me sick to think of their sneaky revelations. I had always hated the way people clung to Rebecca because of the money she earned, and although she had helped support my motocross in the early days, I had worked hard to pay back every penny she leant me.

Standing in front of Rebecca's parents now made me want to run away and never be seen by anyone ever again. We had been closer than anyone could ever have possibly understood, but at that moment, it didn't matter to them at all that she had been carrying my child. In fact, they wrongly assumed it was my fault that she was dead.

They wanted me gone, and I was happy to oblige. 'What did you do to her?' they spat in my face, their bitterness aimed directly at me. 'You were the last person to see her alive. You must have done or said something to her for her to kill herself.' I could not believe what I was hearing. How dare they assume they knew the facts? I knew damned well she had not taken her own life, but how could I begin to explain to them things they knew absolutely nothing about. They knew nothing about Rebecca's life, and they knew nothing about me.

'She didn't kill herself, you idiots. She was murdered,' I screamed words into the void of Rebecca's flat towards ears that were unable to listen and voices that could speak no truth.

'Did you kill her, Craig?' Rebecca's mother shot back at me, her dad on the verge of punching me merely for existing. How could they believe I could do such a thing to the one person who meant the most to me? They honestly did not know me at all.

'Oh, I know exactly who killed her, and I intend to prove it,' I replied, my own voice no longer sounding like mine at all. I could see Grace standing in the kitchen doorway. She did not speak a word. I had no idea if she was unsure how to respond or if, being gay, she too was afraid of the repercussions from Rebecca's family. I knew that if I couldn't get the police to open an investigation, they would be forced to live the rest of their lives believing that their daughter had killed herself with no logical explanation as to why. At that moment in time, they would not have listened to a single word I said anyway, no matter how much I yelled and screamed.

*\*\**

My desperation grew at an incredible rate, and without actually noticing, I began lashing out at everyone around me. Unfortunately, it was poor Grace and Jade who bore the main brunt of my anguish. Next to me, they were the ones who had been closest to Rebecca, and that was a fact I could no longer stand. We had been the best of friends for so long. They were the only family I had ever known. But every time I looked at either of them now, all I could see were the memories we had built with Rebecca, and I hated it beyond rational thinking. Hours passed slowly for me, and every time either of the girls spoke, it was as if every inch of their souls reminded me of her. I could not escape the ache that was threatening to destroy me, and I could not explain to anyone how I felt. We were all suffering.

Grace was sitting quietly crying into a large glass of red wine, flicking through some photographs of Rebecca one evening, oblivious to everyone around her, including me. When I glanced down and saw Rebecca's smiling face looking up at me from an old greying photograph where we were all at a party some years previously, I felt physically sick. How in God's name could she be gone?

'Do you have to do that now?' I snapped at Grace without remorse, causing her to flinch and spill wine onto the carpet. 'Put those things away, will you.' It might have been evident to anyone watching that I could not cope with my grief, but it was not apparent to me, and Grace bore the full brunt of my turmoil that night. I rarely argued with any of the girls, and this new me was hard for either of them to witness. We had spent so long laughing, caring nothing beyond the carefree lives we were living, that now it was all gone, neither of them could see how they could possibly reach me. We were all devastated, but I was living with the fact that Rebecca had needed me more than I could have perhaps realised on the night she died, and I truly felt that I had somehow failed her.

I had spent so long wrapped inside my own problems and trying to deal with my head injury that I had forgotten to put her needs first. The last thing I would ever remember of her would be a stupid argument that should never have happened. If we hadn't argued, if she hadn't stormed out of the flat like that, if I hadn't have been so wrapped up inside my own thoughts, I would have spotted that she was desperate to get away, and I might have been able to ask her the real reason why. I might have even agreed to move to the states had she told me about the baby. It actually did feel as if I had killed her myself.

Thoughts of Ryan and Justin took over my thinking without warning, and I began to scream and shout at the top of my lungs. I screamed for Rebecca, I screamed for everything that had happened to us both and I screamed for the pain in my head and my heart that would not stop. I was closer to the edge that night than I had ever been, and as Grace sat curled up on the carpet in front of me, terrified by what I was becoming, I knew our friendship was over. This was it. This was the end of everything I knew. The end of the life I had loved for so long.

*** 

After that night, I began sleeping in my car, Rebecca's flat holding nothing for me other than pain and memories I no longer wanted. I could see the desperation that grew inside the girls each day, but I now saw them as part of my problem. I felt that if I could break free from everything that connected me to the memory of my best friend, then I could erase her from my mind forever. It would be as if she had never existed, and then the pain would disappear. I could be free. It was totally illogical, I know, but at the time, my grief was so raw, I had nowhere to focus any of my attention. As I sat in my car one afternoon, Jade drummed on the window in an attempt to arouse me from the vacant state of mind that now engulfed my every waking moment.

'Craig?' she called to me, but I wasn't really listening. It had started to rain, and she stood outside shivering in the late April haze. I did not look at her but remained statuesque, staring ahead as if I could no longer see anything of the world around me. 'Craig?' she called louder, this time forcing my attention towards her.

'Fuck off.' I genuinely didn't mean to sound so callous, but they were the only words I could offer as I caught a look of disappointment in her saddened eyes.

'You can't stay out here forever, you know,' she said to

me calmly as she folded her arms around her body. I knew she was only trying to help, but it genuinely didn't reach me.

'Do you wanna bet?' I snarled as I automatically started the engine. For five days, I had barely eaten, food tasting like acid that burned the back of my throat with no remorse whatsoever. Neither had I slept, my brain creating painful images that swam like poisonous darts across my thoughts. As I drove away from Rebecca's flat that afternoon, I knew I would not be back. I had nothing left inside me and nothing that held me here anymore. Rebecca was gone, and as far as I was concerned, so was everything else.

***

It was as if trouble wanted to find me and would stop at nothing to get its way. I no longer cared about how I looked or that I had not eaten a decent meal in days. When I spotted Ryan's mum walking along the street just feet from where my car was parked, I was in no mood for confrontation and tried to slide down into my seat so she would not see me. I need not have bothered. She had already spotted my car before I had even registered her presence. As she crossed the road, I caught the smug look on her face and considered driving away. The last thing I needed at that moment was to hear the venomous tongue of that woman.

However, before I could react, she was already tapping on my window, obviously ready for a full-blown confrontation. I wound down my window, and we looked at each other for a moment before she opened her mouth to speak.

'Look who it is,' she spat, her words nothing more to me than the bark of a stray dog. 'Just look at the state of you,' she sniggered, seeing my unshaven and unkempt appearance.

'What do you want, Yvette?' I asked, really not giving a

damn what she thought of me at that precise moment and not really needing any kind of response to my question.

'Nothing much. I was just passing and thought I would say hello.' She looked far too smug. I didn't like the tone she was adopting one bit. If she was spoiling for a fight, she had come to the right place. She had been one of the main ringleaders in spreading the rumours about Rebecca's rape, and I knew she would not hold back now.

'Good for you,' I sighed. I did not want to continue this conversation, and I started winding up my window.

She sniggered again. 'I told Ryan that you were looking for him.' I shot her a look. If she knew of his whereabouts right then, she was about to tell the wrong person. 'It serves you right, actually, what happened to that girl,' she continued as if my sarcasm had not even registered on her radar. She was oblivious to the pain I was in and blatant in her following statement. 'Because now you haven't even got that bitch anymore.'

Without thinking, I swung open the car door, climbed out and bought my hand up, slapping her hard across the face. 'How dare you?' I screamed. I wanted to hit her again but stopped short of grabbing her arm. 'You complete and utter bitch.' I didn't care who overheard us or the fact that I had just lashed out at a woman. Did she really hate me that much? Did any of them?

Yvette pulled herself free from my grip and staggered backwards, a stunned look plain to see on her face. She stood and stared at me for a few seconds clutching the side of her cheek with her mouth wide open in shock. I had never hit a woman before, and as angry as I was at that moment and as much as I hated Yvette, I felt terrible that I had done so now. Reeling backwards, she turned and ran along the pavement, her cheap high heels scraping the concrete in her haste. My actions had silenced her, wiping the smug look from her face.

Although she turned around once to scream in my direction that I would be sorry for that, I was momentarily glad to have shut her up.

As she walked away, I already knew it would not end there, and that very same evening, two of her brothers came looking for me and proceeded to beat me black and blue. Usually, a dirty fighter, if provoked, I allowed them to do their worst, lying motionless on the ground whilst they kicked and punched me. I did not try to defend myself at all against their vicious attack, allowing them to vent their frustration until they had nothing left inside of them to project towards me. I genuinely felt I deserved it all. As far as I was concerned, it was my fault that Rebecca was gone, and I had absolutely nothing left inside me to fight for.

***

Grief can make us do and say the strangest of things, and my sorrow was beginning to consume me in more ways than at that time I could have possibly understood. I had spent those first few days after Rebecca's death walking around in a daze as if someone had hit me over the back of the head with a sledgehammer that had failed to knock me out. I had attempted to speak to the police several times, but after my third visit to the station in as many days, I could see that they were getting rather annoyed with me. I couldn't just sit back and do nothing. It was driving me to the point where I actually wanted to kill someone. I was so desperate to make the pain I was feeling go away.

I knew where Justin's local was, and I sat in my car the following evening with an intention that I don't mind admitting was laden with pain and suffering, the likes of which even I could not have adequately explained to another soul even if my life depended on it. Although my heart was pounding and my throat was dry, I felt calm, too calm. They had crossed the line this time, and somehow they were going to seriously pay for what they had done. When I saw Justin emerge in his usual drunken state from the pub, I crept around the side of his car and grabbed him by the throat, forcing him against the side panel of his door.

'Don't move,' I spat into his ear as I slammed his head hard onto the roof, kneeing him in the stomach at the same time to make sure I knocked enough wind out of him so he wouldn't fight back.

'Oh yeah? What are you going to do about it?' Justin was almost laughing at me, even with his head firmly planted into his own paintwork and blood staining his jacket.

'I want to know where Ryan is, and you're going to take me to him. Now.' I was beyond anger. I do not think that even Justin could have comprehended my mood at that point. Just being in his presence made me want to strangle the very life out of him.

'Fuck off twat,' Justin sneered at me, and so I punched him hard in the face purely for the hell of it.

'Car key. Now.' I snatched the key from his hand, not caring about the moaning he was doing in protest of his own pain. I opened the car door and jammed Justin's scrawny body in through the passenger door, pushing him over the central console and into the driver's seat, crushing his legs between the seat and the steering wheel in my haste. I didn't know at that point what my exact intentions were. All I could think about was getting them both together, in front of me. I knew that I would figure out my next moves as I went along, yet I knew it would not end well for either of them tonight.

'Let's go,' I snarled as I practically threw Justin his car key.

Justin shook his head and sighed as if I was acting out a crazy fantasy, and at some point, he would get rid of me and get on with the rest of his night in peace. 'You really think that I'm going anywhere with you. Get the fuck out of my car, dickhead.' At that point, I pulled a knife out of my pocket and jammed the tip into the side of Justin's stomach below his ribcage, just far enough for him to understand that I was not joking around, yet not enough for it to actually penetrate the skin.

'Shit-' Justin realised what was happening and glared at me. To be honest, I did not remember having even picked up the knife and had no real idea where it had come from. I assumed I must have taken it from Rebecca's kitchen drawer at some point.

'I said, let's go.' Justin must have seen a look in my eyes that unnerved him because he reached forward and started the engine, not daring to look at me at all. As we drove out of the car park and into the night, neither of us spoke, yet the tension inside that vehicle was deafening. He could have had no idea about my intentions at that moment. If he had, he would have dived out of his car and ran for his life.

# Chapter 17

It took Justin a mere few minutes to relocate his ego and his mouth. 'You're such a twat, you know that?' he chided, obviously assuming I was bluffing. I knew he was trying to press my buttons so he could provoke me, and it was working perfectly. 'What do you think you are going to do, hey? It's not going to get you anywhere.' His words were cocky. Arrogant. I hated him so much at that moment. We had turned onto a country lane. I guess he assumed I wouldn't have the guts to use the knife at all.

'I told you to take me to Ryan.' I genuinely wished he could have known what I was thinking right then because he probably would have wet himself.

'Yeah? Well, I thought we would go for a little drive first.' He glanced over at me briefly, a grotesque grin displayed on his pathetic face, before hitting the accelerator pedal and causing his car to lunge forward. 'You think you are such a big man, don't you?' He laughed again, confidence suddenly finding its undeserved place. 'I hate to break it to you, mate, but I think you'll find I'm the one in charge here, not you.'

'Oh, I get it,' I nodded my head and subdued the urge to laugh. 'Feeling cocky suddenly, are we?' I leaned over and elbowed him in the lip forcing his car to jerk violently towards the oncoming lane. I was still holding the knife to his stomach and wondered for a moment what would happen if I simply jammed it into the soft flesh of his belly. Would it make me feel better? Something told me it would actually make me feel ecstatic.

Justin pressed his foot hard onto the accelerator pedal. I knew he was trying to scare me, but I was so numb inside at that point, I literally couldn't feel a thing. The road in front of us was pitch black. It was late enough for there to be no other traffic using that country lane which was probably a good thing considering the way Justin was driving. As we raced along winding roads, and around hazardous corners, it would have been evident to any onlooker that oncoming traffic wouldn't stand a chance if they encountered us lunging towards them on the wrong side of the road.

We exchanged more bitter words, his tone becoming increasingly erratic with my own rising anger. 'She deserved everything she got,' Justin laughed directly into my face, and I knew there and then that whatever happened tonight, this night would be his last. I could have easily reached over and throttled the life out of him, plunging my knife into his belly without apology, but it was Ryan I really wanted, and I needed Justin in order to find him. I knew I could quickly deal with this little prick afterwards. I owed Rebecca that much, at least.

'Why did you kill her?' I screamed into his ear, my emotions raw and my fists resonating with my every word.

Justin shrugged. 'She was a slut and deserved it.' I couldn't believe he was actually saying those words directly to me. What the hell did he think I would do with that knowledge? He glanced towards me as if he had remembered something else. 'I'm surprised you're still alive, actually. After your little *accident*.'

He aimed the word 'accident' towards me as if he knew it had been anything but. 'I knew it,' I spat, my face too close to his for comfort.

'It worked out better than we had planned to be honest. Because you were not meant to survive.' He was still laughing as if his words had no consequence. 'But now you get to live with that time bomb in your head. Tick tock, tick tock.'

'You paralysed Liam?' I seriously hadn't expected him to admit to any of this.

'Oh shit, don't beat yourself up about him. We thought it was your bike, not his. It was a simple error to make. It could have happened to anyone.' Justin had no concept of what he was saying, his own emotions nothing more than passing words that meant nothing to him at all.

'You absolute bastard.'

'Yeah, so I've heard.'

I couldn't help it when I punched him hard across the cheekbone. He'd not only openly confessed to killing Rebecca, but had also confirmed that mine was indeed no accident. To add insult to the entire thing, that poor lad who had been paralysed a month earlier would never walk again because they had rigged his bike by mistake. I knew those two had been behind it all. The car lunged sideways, veering across the road and back into the middle violently. 'Hey,' Justin yelled as if the punch was putting him off his driving ability.

It was lucky that I knew those roads well because I could anticipate every bend and twist that Justin approached before he knew they were even coming. I also knew that he was driving too fast in his sudden psychotic manner to be able to safely make a sharp bend that was now only a few hundred feet ahead. I glanced at him hastily, but his eyes were set dead ahead. I wondered what his intentions were right then. I could see his speedometer. It was tipping almost ninety-five miles an hour.

'What the hell are you doing?' I screamed into his ear as the realisation hit me that either he hadn't noticed the sharp turn approaching, or more probable, he intended on crashing

186

his car with the actual likelihood of killing me in the process. A moment of shock flashed across my mind, not for the idea that I was about to die. At that point in my life, I would have gladly welcomed death. No. The thought hit me right then that if Justin killed me tonight, I would never be able to get to Ryan and serve the justice I knew he deserved. I didn't care what happened to me, but there was no way I was going to let that piece of shit get away with murder. He had gone too far.

I glanced up and noticed the shape of a large oak tree looming in the distance. This was it. This was the sharp bend in the road I knew was coming. I stared at Justin. He had a look of pure aggression on his face that I couldn't fathom. Surely he would slow at any moment and skid around the corner. I didn't for one second believe he would have the bottle to crash his own car. And yet, he did not slow down. He kept his foot flat on the accelerator pedal, his eyes set dead ahead. It was as if something had taken over his rational thinking completely.

'What the hell are you doing?' I yelled again, but he didn't respond. I knew we had mere seconds left before we hit that tree, so without hesitation, I flung open the passenger car door.

Justin glanced my way, unprepared for my upcoming actions, as his car veered off its intended course for a second or two. I didn't wait for him to utter any further revelations as I closed my eyes and jumped. For a few seconds, I did not even register my own body as it flew into the night air, an icy wind hitting my senses the moment I left the assumed safety of the car. I hit the ground hard and felt a crack as my left arm took the full force of my weight.

Everything went quiet for a few seconds, and then I heard the most horrendous crash. Glass, metal, and the sound of tyres spinning out of control cut through the night air as Justin's car came to an abrupt and unintended halt. I lay on my back at the side of the road and looked up to see smoke pouring from the bonnet, twisted metal wrapped around a distant tree and no movement whatsoever coming from within. Was he dead? Surely that had not been his intention? It was me he had wanted to hurt, not himself. I clambered to my feet, a sharp pain shooting through my body as the magnitude of my fall became clear. I limped towards the car, not expecting anything much yet hoping like hell he wouldn't actually get out. I couldn't exactly see him, to begin with, but the entire front end of his car had been pushed back into the mid-section. If he had survived, he would be in a terrible way. That much I did know.

The engine continued to rev violently for a few moments before eventually dying out, leaving only the sound of a broken radiator as steaming water poured out onto the ground. I slowly and painfully limped around to the driver's side and yanked open the car door. Justin's lifeless body lay at an awkward angle in the driver's seat. His eyes were wide open. I knew then that he was dead. For the longest time, I had visualised this moment. Seeing him pay for what he had done. But standing there in the dark that night, the only thing I could feel was the numbness of my own heartbeat. How had I turned from someone who would do anything for anyone, to someone who longed for the death of an enemy?

I felt sick. My head hurt so much that I wondered for a moment if I was shortly destined to join him on the other side. How ironic would that be? I glanced back along the lane, confident that by jumping clear of the car, I'd accidentally ensured Justin's own fate. His car had been incorrectly positioned, its intended target shifted, ensuring the driver's side took the full force of the accident instead of where I had been sitting. He must have momentarily become distracted by my disappearance from the passenger seat and hadn't turned the steering wheel in time. I could not allow myself the idea of any other concept.

I realised with a jolt that I had no way of being able to find Ryan now. I had tried for days to hunt him down. Tonight had been my perfect plan to get them both together so we could finish this thing once and for all. I had been quite prepared to kill them both that night, and afterwards, I would have gladly handed myself in to the police. Even had I died in the process of destroying those bastards, it wouldn't have made a difference to me. My life was already over anyway, so it really didn't matter. Now I had no idea of how to find him and no way of getting my revenge. What the hell was I going to do?

***

I do not remember walking back into town that night or recall feeling any pain in my arm after diving out of Justin's car onto the dirt. The last thing I saw of his face was its dead stare, blood soaking his cheeks and cold eyes, blank, unseeing, already moved on to some other place. I could not believe he was actually dead. After wanting so long to hurt him and exact my ultimate revenge, I did not know how to put into thoughts the emotions that swam around my brain. I assumed his intoxicated state would simply indicate a tragic accident once his body was found within the next few hours. It had certainly not been my intention for things to end like that for him tonight, yet I was genuinely relieved he could no longer hurt another human being or breathe perfectly good air that someone else needed.

I do not recall how I managed to get back to my car, but I woke up the following morning in the middle of a field, nothing around me but cows and wildlife, the only witnesses to my existence. It was as if the previous night's numbness had worn off because pain shot through my arm, and when I removed my ripped jacket, I was met with an angry, blood-soaked wound that snaked towards my elbow. I could bend my wrist and my elbow, so I assumed I hadn't broken any bones, and as far as I was concerned, this was a brief reminder of the events of the night before. I still had the knife in my possession. I was glad of that fact, yet I didn't assume for one moment that the police would have thought anything unusual had they found it in Justin's car anyway. He was a known drug user and drug pusher, and finding weapons on those types of people were a daily occurrence to the police. Normal even.

I could not go back to the flat. One look at me would be all the girls needed to confirm that I had done something stupid, again, so I drove away from the field and tried not to look back. I had no idea where I was going. I must have driven for several hours before a lightbulb flashed up on my dashboard, telling me I was running low on fuel. I sat in a service station on the M5 motorway watching the buzz of everyday life around me and not quite able to believe that my life had changed so dramatically in such a short space of time. I purchased a Doctor Pepper, not caring that I must have looked to the assistant behind the counter as if I had been living on the streets for months. I literally had no idea where I was going. Everything I knew and loved was gone. I was nothing, a nobody, a loser who had no way of moving forward in a world he now detested.

For the following two weeks, I felt as if nothing around me was real, and I walked around in a daze, unable to comprehend any kind of reality as I struggled to get through a single day with my brain relatively intact. I had failed to telephone the girls and tell them where I was and that I was okay, and I was well aware they must have been worried out of their minds by now. Yet, at that moment, I honestly didn't care what anyone thought. I was too far gone inside my own head, my injuries a constant reminder that I would never be the same person ever again and my loss too great a pain for me to stand. I do not think I ate food, nothing held any taste to me at all, and I hardly slept, the back seats of my car now my only comfort.

My only thought at that point was that I needed to find Ryan. He had seemingly disappeared, and this was not something my brain was coping at all well with. I knew he had friends in low places and friends of friends in even lower places who would have hidden him away without question, probably because for one reason or another, they owed him. I lost track of how long I sat in my car waiting outside different locations, the likes of which I would never usually frequent. He had become a ghost, a shadow, hiding from view and always just outside my line of sight. It was all consuming. I read a noticeboard outside a newsagent about the young man found dead in his car along Millwalk Lane, and I couldn't help the smile that crept over my face.

Yet it was an empty smile because deep inside, I simply was not that type of person. Never in a million years would I ever have considered that one day I might turn so bitter and angry that the death of another human being could raise my spirits. Yet, here I was, standing in the street reading a tragic notice and feeling nothing but the satisfaction that Justin could no longer hurt anyone else ever again. It made Ryan's disappearance all the more devastating for my brain.

I vividly remember standing in the middle of some open-air market one morning, although how I got there, I simply do not know. I was making my way through a sea of bodies, soulless faces all seemingly pressing in on me at once, obscuring my path as I tried to find a space that was not already crammed with people. It was as if I had been walking around inside a thick fog, utterly oblivious to the fact that once it had lifted, I was actually surrounded by strangers I did not know. I felt panic rising in my gut. Since my accident, I had avoided crowds at all costs and finding myself in the middle of one now absolutely terrified me. It was as if a thousand voices were screaming at me all at the same time, and my head began to throb so much that I worried for a moment if it might kill me. In that very instant, something happened that I could not have comprehended in my wildest nightmares.

I had been angrily pushing my way through the crowd, yelling in the general direction of anyone who dared to get in my way, when I felt myself floating in mid-air, looking straight down at my own body lying on the ground. I could not believe what I was seeing. A group of people had gathered around me, although I couldn't tell if they were showing concern for my wellbeing or were merely trying to move me out of their way. It was the most frightening thing I had ever experienced. It's hard to explain the feeling you have when you are seconds from death. Nothing feels real, and nothing seems to make any sense. It was as if someone had pressed the mute button on a television set and blurred the picture into obscurity for effect. The shapes in front of me felt distant, as if I was looking through the eyes of an alien. I heard a muffled voice somewhere in the distance but felt nothing as I tried to blank out the people around me. It was a moment that changed everything for me, although in my mind, everything had already changed, snatched away so suddenly that it had left me spinning out of control.

It was as if, for a moment, I had fallen asleep, dreaming that I was free-falling through a cloud. And yet, I was fully awake as that same feeling enveloped me, forcing me downwards faster and faster as I plummeted towards my own body and a fate I could not see. A dense fog-like haze surrounded me, engulfing my every sensation as I hurtled helplessly towards oblivion. When the ground finally came up to meet me, I still didn't recall feeling a thing, although I know that I didn't wake up in my bed, glad to be safe and alive. I felt as if I were dead. It was finally over.

Panicking, I tried to force myself back into reality, and instantly, somehow, I shot back into my body. I lay glued to the spot for a few seconds looking up at innocent clouds floating across the sky. The sheer magnitude of what had just happened did not seem to register with my brain at all. A few people asked if I was okay, but I could not respond, and when I finally found my feet, I practically sprinted away from that place. I had no idea what day it was, and if someone had asked me my name, I seriously doubt I would have been able to tell them who I was. Somehow, I managed to find my way back to Milborough, although I cannot remember the journey and the only place I could think to go was to my mum. When she opened the front door, she looked slightly surprised to see me, and I only just made it into her kitchen before I collapsed onto the floor. The police found my car some weeks later in a ditch.

# Chapter 18

When I opened my eyes, it was in a blind panic as I realised I was connected to pipes protruding from practically every place on my body physically possible. I couldn't sit up, and something was jammed into the back of my throat that made me want to gag. It actually began to feel as if hospital beds were taking over my life, and I was starting to wonder if I was somehow cursed. When I glanced to my left and saw my mum sitting next to the bed, I actually thought I was dreaming. The first thing I noticed was the worried look on her face. It was the first time in my life I think I actually saw a flicker of emotion on her usual cold exterior.

It's funny to think back now, but I have no actual fond memories of my mother at all. It was genuinely quite upsetting to think about it. I couldn't recall her ever giving me a bath when I was young, taking me to bed and tucking me in, or doing anything at all with me that I assumed most mothers would automatically want to do with their children. I didn't know what it was like to bake cakes or read stories with her, and our mother-son relationship simply didn't exist.

I honestly couldn't understand how I was supposed to feel about her when I was a child, and I still didn't really know her as an adult, even as I lay in that hospital bed looking over towards her worried features. There had never been a connection between us, and if I'm honest, I might even go as far as to say we had always acted like the strangers I now felt we were. She did not appear to have any emotions to care about me, so I couldn't understand why she would suddenly start now.

I instinctively turned to climb out of bed only to find myself restrained by tubes and needles that stabbed into my flesh. In a panic, I began frantically grabbing at them, pulling out several at a time and not caring at all that I was leaving a trail of blood on the floor. 'What the hell is going on?' I screamed. It looked as if I was in the middle of some kind of horror scene.

Someone came running into the room. 'It's okay, Craig,' they said in a blatant attempt to calm me down that failed completely. 'It's okay.' But it was nowhere near okay. I didn't understand why I had, once again, found myself unavoidably lying in a hospital bed, and I didn't know what had happened to me. The last thing I remembered was stepping through my mum's kitchen door. Everything felt wrong. A second nurse came running in, and between them, they managed to calm me enough to prevent me from losing any more blood and passing out completely.

'What happened?' I asked my mother once I had been cleaned up and the tubes had been re-inserted.

'You collapsed in my kitchen.' Her response sounded genuinely concerned, and it took me by surprise. We had not seen each other in quite some time, my motocross and friends taking up more of my time than I had realised until today. She did not even know about my accident or the horrors I'd endured over the last few weeks.

'I'm so sorry-' I still had no explanation as to what had actually happened. I wanted to tell her that I was grateful she had stayed with me, but somehow I felt that would sound hollow and untrue. It wasn't as if I didn't want to love my mother. I simply did not know how to love her. It was not something I was exactly proud of.

'You don't have to be sorry. I was actually surprised to see you. Are you okay?' Her question sounded genuine, and I automatically nodded, yet inside, I was screaming in pain that I had no idea how to express to anyone at all. Mum looked older than I remembered her, her hair now far greyer than it used to be.

'I didn't know where else to go,' I told her as honestly as I knew how. It also happened to be true. We looked at each other for a moment, and I swear I saw something in her eyes. Guilt maybe? Remorse for a childhood lost? Whatever it was must have touched a nerve because she got to her feet and hastily patted me on the hand in response to my words. Our strained relationship seemed to melt for a moment, and she smiled at me for the first time in a very long time. I wanted to ask her if she was okay, but a doctor came into the ward and interrupted our awkward moment.

When the doctor explained the reasons for my collapse, I was shocked to discover that I had suffered a severe mental breakdown that had almost killed me. My heart, lungs, brain, and every other organ in my body had begun the process of shutting down at practically the same time. My body had technically given up on itself. It was its way of saying, *Stop, I've had enough, I'm done.* The experience I had felt at the market was the beginning of the end as my body began the process of premature death. I literally could not cope any further with what I had been through, and as a result, my body tried to block out one of the worst two weeks of my life.

It dawned on me pretty quickly that by now, I must have missed Rebecca's funeral. I had no doubt in my mind that my presence there would not have been welcomed by her parents. And yet, the thought of her being gone and no way now of being able to say goodbye was too much for me to comprehend. It felt as if there was nothing left for me to do or say that would ever make anything right again. Everything had happened way too quickly, and I had no idea how to process events that had all but destroyed everything that had meant so much to me.

As I sat in that hospital bed listening to the doctor's words, I felt my soul get up, walk out of the room and disappear. I had no idea how so much could happen to one person in such a short space of time. It was as if I could not keep up with everything that had happened, and all that was left of me now was a shell, a man who had nothing left inside him but a dull ache that I knew deep in my heart would never completely heal. I could no longer see any resemblance of the person I had been just a year earlier. I couldn't think straight. I still couldn't even hold a proper conversation. I was nothing.

*** 

My mother did her best to visit me in the hospital whenever she could to check that I was okay and, if I wasn't mistaken, probably to ease her own conscience about the previous state of our relationship. It was unfortunate for us both that her efforts were met with my constant unwillingness to participate in any type of conversation, or show her any kind of genuine attention at all. I was well aware that I was deliberately turning myself away from everything and everyone I had ever known in order to try and protect myself from whatever I felt I needed protection from. I knew deep down that it was the reason I had left things on such bad terms with the girls. It seemed to me that every single time I deluded myself that I had found happiness in my life, at some point, I knew it would eventually be snatched from me. My childhood did not hold good memories for me, and now the only person in the world who I ever really cared anything about was dead.

I began to feel extremely vulnerable at that stage. My lack of understanding of what had happened to me was overshadowed by an absence of any explanation. It seemed that no one was able to talk to me or tell me why things had changed so quickly. I felt like an obstacle, impeding every other human I came into contact with and lying in yet another hospital bed, nothing had changed. I had lost everyone who I had ever cared about, and so did everything I could to make the sorry process of disconnecting from the world as swift and painless as possible. I knew it was the wrong thing to do, but I was seriously grieving, and I had absolutely no idea how to deal with it alone. If I had a problem, it had always been Rebecca I turned to. I loved the idea that we both lived our own lives and yet came together happily in unique perfection when we needed to. I knew I would always be there for her and that she would be there for me. Now, suddenly I was faced with a lifetime stretching ahead of me without her in it, and everything felt incredibly frightening. I simply had no idea how I would be able to carry on alone.

When I was discharged from the hospital, it was once again under the strictest instructions that I could not be left alone for any reason. Because I had suffered a severe mental breakdown, my state of mind had been deemed by the hospital as fragile, and they therefore, assumed I would need round the clock supervision. They thought I might try to take my own life. I could not admit to any of them that the very thought of suicide had actually crossed my mind on more than one occasion. I genuinely did not feel I deserved to breathe good air when Rebecca would never feel the sunlight on her skin again.

Oddly, during this terrifying time, it was my mum who now began showing a constant presence in my life. We had never been close, this was no secret, but she was now showing a side of herself to me that I had never seen before. Even my stepfather, Mick, who had spent almost twenty years trying to make me feel small at every opportunity, was now acting nice and overly friendly towards me. They insisted I move in with them, seeing as I had nowhere else to go. Almost five years after I had moved out of their so-called family home, I now found myself living back under their roof, my future as uncertain as a rabbit who suddenly finds itself caught in a set of approaching headlights for the very first time.

As I dropped my belongings onto the floor of mums tiny box room, I began to cry tears that I worried might never completely dry up again. It was as if I had fallen into a deep hole and had regressed backwards. I was a child again with nowhere to go and no one around me that actually cared about me beyond a shallow display of temporary concern that had been forged only from their own guilt. I had been forced to leave everything behind, including Bella, who I adored and who I would probably never see again. Most of my friends were now long gone, dispersing after my accident and forgetting my existence when they discovered I could no longer be the person they had at one time taken for granted. It had only been Rebecca, Jade, and Grace who had remained steadfast in their support for what I had been through. Now I had succeeded in pushing Grace and Jade away too, and I had absolutely no idea if they would ever want to know me again.

I stared at the bare walls that I would now have to call home, and I wondered for a moment how everything had gone so desperately wrong. As I pulled my belongings out onto the bed, a few of Rebecca's items fell out, including several photographs of us together. It took me by surprise when I saw her face. Reaching down, I picked up those photos and crumpled them in my shaking hand. Why had she left me alone? I simply could not comprehend how this could have happened. Questions I had no place for raced across my mind, that familiar thick, hazy fog engulfing my senses as I stood on shaky legs in my mum's spare room.

Anger welled up at that moment, and before I realised what I had done, I had taken those photographs into the garden and burned every single one of them. I couldn't stand to look at her face anymore. I couldn't bear the idea of never being able to spend time with her again or hear her infectious laugh in my ears. I felt I had to either erase her from my memory forever or go completely insane. It genuinely seemed as if it was the only way to be free from the pain that was slowly destroying me from the inside. The girls tried several times to call me at the house over the next few weeks, but I refused their calls. I had pushed them so hard and for so long that eventually, they both stopped trying, and we went our separate ways.

***

Living with Mick again after all those years was not something I had ever expected to have to do, but neither had I anticipated what had happened to me over the last twelve months of my life. His guilt was evident for all to see, being nicer to me in a shorter space of time than he had my entire life. He engaged me in conversation whenever possible, made sure I had a drink or something to eat when I needed it, and ensured that mum was doing everything in her power to look after me. If I hadn't been in such a low state of mind, I probably might have laughed at the irony of the entire thing. I was prescribed a barrage of anti-depressants that I didn't take and was referred to a psychiatrist for counselling.

The strangest thing that I found about all of this was that at no point did mum or Mick actually speak to me directly about what could possibly have happened to cause my body to shut down in such a catastrophic way. They knew I had suffered a severe mental breakdown, but beyond that simple explanation, they knew nothing of what had happened to me or why. At that point, they still did not know about my accident, my brain injury, or Rebecca's death. It really showed the extent of our relationship right there. They did not know me at all, and I knew they would not understand what I had been through.

It really didn't matter to me anyway at that point. I did not want to speak to them about any of it, and I certainly did not want their pity, so I was glad. I was glad they had given me a place to stay, and I was glad I was not living on the street, but as far as I was concerned, that was where our relationship ended. I painted on a brave face and endured each day the best I could, having no one to discuss my progress with and nobody to turn to. I had never felt so alone in my entire life.

If anyone has ever been around or experienced severe depression first hand, the first noticeable thing is that every second of every day feels as if a year has gone by. Every moment forces you to endure a pain you simply cannot expel. You can glance at the clock on the wall, and seconds tick by that feel like hours. You simply do not know how you are ever going to get through each day. You can't feel anything beyond your own pain and, believe me, I had never felt pain like that in my entire life.

***

A few weeks after I moved in with them, mum bought me a cup of tea as usual and chatted about her dirty windows and the state of next doors' broken fence panels. It was as if our conversations consisted only of trivial and unimportant items, anything, it seemed, to deter any potential talk about our relationship or the state of my life. She placed a cup onto the coffee table and hesitated for a moment. She stood looking at me as if she wanted to say something and yet had no idea where to begin.

'Are you okay?' I asked casually as I leaned forward to pick up my tea.

Mum dug her hand into her apron pocket and pulled out a small, yellowing envelope. 'I wanted to give you this a long time ago,' she said, her tone saddened by something far beyond my understanding. 'But the timing never seemed quite right.' She placed the envelope next to a plate of biscuits that had been in the back of the cupboard for some time before discovering them and subsequently giving them to me. 'I'm so sorry it's late. I never meant to keep this from you for so long, Craig.' She walked quickly out of the lounge, leaving me to wonder what any of that was about.

I looked at the yellowing envelope that had a handwritten message scrawled across its front and random marks that looked as if the contents had been read many times before. *To Craig*, it read. My name had been underlined three times as if it was somehow important, so I picked it up and turned it over in my hands several times. Its paper felt aged as if it had been living in a drawer somewhere gathering decades of dust, and I wondered how long my mum had kept this in her possession. I slid out two sheets of paper that were folded together and had the same aged appearance as the envelope. The letter smelled like the back of an old sock drawer. I unfolded the pages and began to read.

*My dearest Craig.*

*I truly hope that when you read this, you might understand something about your birth that I have always found difficult to discuss with you. I hope that one day when you are old enough, I can explain this to you better, but until then, I have written it down so that you can know the truth. Craig, you were born a twin. You had a twin sister.*

Although I was genuinely shocked when I read those words, something instantly clicked into place. It suddenly all made sense as to why I had always felt so incomplete and utterly alone. It made total sense why I had always felt I needed Rebecca in my life. It had been my twin that I was missing, and yet I didn't even know she had once existed until that very moment. I continued reading.

*You were born first, but unfortunately, your umbilical cord was caught around your neck and was causing your sister to become distressed. The doctors had to push you back inside your mother and give her an emergency caesarean to save you. Your sister was successfully delivered a few minutes after you, but unfortunately, she died almost immediately through lack of oxygen. Your poor mum developed complications and passed away just a few moments later.*

I literally could not take in what I was reading. My mother was dead? Did this mean the woman who had called herself my mum for the last twenty-two years of my life and who had just given me this letter was not my actual mother at all?

*So distraught at having lost his wife and child, your father went home that very night and took his own life. His sister (your aunt) and her young daughter found him hanging at the top of the stairs in their home. I hope you can understand why I found this so very difficult to tell you and why I never told you that I was not your real mum. You were only a baby when we adopted you, and for a very long time, I wondered if it was even worth telling you the truth at all.*

*I know I haven't been a good mum to you, and I genuinely hope that you do not hate me for this terrible secret that I have kept for so long.*

*With love, Mum. xxx*

I read the letter three times so that I could properly absorb the information in front of me. There had been many questions surrounding my birth that I sadly never knew until now and many things I had been unable to directly ask anyone about. No one had ever discussed that topic directly with me. I guess as a child, they assumed I would be too young to understand and then, as I grew up, it simply became more complicated for them to explain until eventually, it became a secret they feared they might actually take to their graves.

As I sat and read that letter, several emotions swept over me. I had a family that I never knew existed and who had all died long ago, leaving me alone in a world I did not understand. The people who raised me were not my family at all. It all suddenly made sense why mum had always expressed such a profound disconnection towards me. It turned out that I didn't even belong to this family at all. But why would a person adopt a child that they didn't actually want to love? More questions began to race through my mind. Questions I was terrified to ask and even more terrified of the answers. However, it did explain why my mother had only one single photograph of me as a baby. Just one. It was an image of me sitting on a rug that I didn't recognise in a house that wasn't ours, alone with no one else in the photo. I wondered then if that was the photograph the adoption agency had taken to try and tempt a family to take me in. It turned out, that I really was alone.

# Chapter 19

The first time I walked into a group counselling session, I wanted to turn and run away from the place as fast as possible. Even as I stepped through the door of the building, I wondered what the hell was I actually doing there. I was offered a seat, and a few people attempted to make small talk with me that I didn't feel like reciprocating. I felt like a freak, standing amidst a group of people I knew nothing about and who knew nothing about me.

A once confident individual, I was now barely a shell of the person I used to be, and I found it extremely difficult to engage in any kind of conversation on any level at all. If Rebecca could have seen the man I had become, she would have been totally heartbroken. We sat down, a group of misfits with nothing in common but a mental breakdown and a mountain of pain between us. We were asked to speak, each in turn, describing our problems, and as we got to our feet to introduce ourselves, I realised how ridiculous this whole scenario actually was.

'Hi, my name is Jessica,' one girl offered, getting to her feet after the counsellor had begun our session. 'I've just split up with my partner, and I'm having trouble sleeping.' There was a brief moment of acknowledgement as the others nodded their understanding for what she had recently been through.

'Hi, I'm Tom.' Another guy stood up. 'I lost my job and turned to drink after my wife left me.'

When it came to my turn, I was unsure how to even begin. I wanted to get up off that chair and scream. There was way too much going on inside my mind for me to process a thing, and I stood uncertain in front of those strangers as every emotion and trauma raced around my brain at once. I was living with a brain injury that constantly made each day a struggle and which could literally explode at any moment and kill me. My very best friend and my unborn baby were dead, murdered by two men she actually knew well. One, a rapist bastard, who had managed to disappear like the snake he was, and the other, a coward who I had left for dead along an isolated country lane. My heart had stopped beating three times in the back of an ambulance and again at the hospital, and when I came out of a coma, I was a changed person who didn't recognise any of the people I loved. My motocross career was finished, and everything and everyone I had once cared so much about was gone. My body had literally switched off because it couldn't cope with everything that had happened to me.

How could I begin to put words to these things without any of them looking at me as if it was all totally impossible? How would they look at me then, knowing the trauma I had been through? It would make their problems look trivial. I certainly did not want their pity, and I didn't want my vulnerabilities placed on display for total strangers to see. I stood in that room with my legs resting against an uncomfortable plastic chair, utterly dumbstruck and staring at these people who looked expectantly for me to say something. Anything.

Why the hell was I even here? A couple of people offered a brief smile. *I'm Craig*, I wanted to say. *I'm already dead.* Because deep inside, I really did feel as if I was already dead. I died the day Rebecca did, and now I did not know how to cope with what was left. I would look in the mirror and hate the person staring back at me because it was ultimately my fault that she was dead. Everything that had happened to her had happened because of me. I could not hide from that fact.

If I hadn't instigated the drugs raid on that couples house after seeing Lisa off her face in that club, Rebecca might not have been attacked. If I hadn't gone after Ryan and Justin after Rebecca's attack, if I had dealt with things differently, they wouldn't have retaliated by setting up my accident, and they might not have killed her to get to me in the worst possible way they could. Although I knew I would have always worried about our future together, anything would have been better than this. It was all my fault, and I simply could not subdue the anger that burned in my chest.

I opened my mouth to speak, but nothing came out, and so, realising my discomfort, the session leader got to his feet to help out. 'It's okay. We are all friends here,' he offered with good intentions that did not reach my ears.

*Friends?* I wanted to laugh at that statement. What do any of you really know about friends? I gave him a blank smile that he incorrectly took as an acknowledgement he had said the right thing.

'I'm Craig,' I almost choked as the words escaped my throat in a strangled whisper. 'I had a mental breakdown.' I did not offer any further comment. I did not want people to hear my story. It was too painful, and it was not something I was proud of. I fully intended to keep it locked inside my mind forever.

We were openly encouraged to praise and support each other, and upon hearing my remark, the group gave a brief clap of their hands and nodded their heads. Was that it? Was that all I needed to do to gain their approval? Wow, I could not believe how shallow their attitudes were. I did not belong here, that much I knew to be accurate, and it made me feel physically sick inside. I took a deep breath and sat back down on the grey plastic chair that had provided my place here. The counsellor briefly smiled at me before returning his attention to the group. I sat listening to words I did not want to hear, hearing problems I did not care about and not once did anyone else touch upon any of the issues plaguing my existence.

I quietly shook with emotions I did not know how to cope with as I sat and listened to other people's problems that sounded so trivial and worryingly insignificant. I didn't like myself for thinking this way about these people because I knew absolutely nothing about them at all. Their problems obviously felt significant and terrible to deal with, and I certainly did not want to belittle their emotions. But inside, I was screaming. I was secretly laughing at the irony of some of the things those people deemed as traumatic. *I was kicked out of home*, I heard someone say. I was kicked out of Mick's house on two different occasions when I was younger, but it didn't mean I needed therapy because of it.

I had never really thought of myself as a strong-minded person before, but sitting in that room, I wondered why people acted so traumatised over situations that, to me, seemed incredibly trivial. I know we all have our own way of coping with specific problems in our lives that threaten our happiness. I fully understand that everyone has their own cut-off level. That poignant moment when you know you simply cannot cope anymore. But sitting listening to strangers talk about their problems that day made mine suddenly feel unbearable. If the guy sitting opposite me was having counselling because he had lost his job, and the woman to my left was seeking help because her boyfriend had left her, how the hell would any of these people cope with what I had been through? I knew I would never be able to speak to them about the things currently destroying my very existence. I was glad when the session ended, and although I returned each week for several more, I did not bother to attend the last two.

When my counsellor called to ask why I had not attended, I did not exactly have a good answer for him other than to explain that I didn't feel my needs properly fitted the group sessions. It was decided that the best cause of action for me would be to have some one-on-one counselling. It was determined they might be able to get to the root of my problems much better if I had private sessions with a psychiatrist, and because of my reluctance to talk about any of my issues, I wasn't exactly helping my own cause. The alternative was that I would need to go into a psychiatric hospital. Having seen the inside of one just a couple of years earlier, counselling was the only option I accepted. It completely summed up my life at that moment. I was a nutcase who needed to see a shrink. I slumped even lower than I could have thought possible after hearing that.

***

Although mum and Mick were trying to be as nice to me as they knew how, the only genuine thing I needed from them at that point was their support, even though, to be honest, I knew they would never really be capable of achieving that goal. Mum and I had spoken briefly about her letter, and I had pretended that it was okay and that I was grateful for her honesty. But in reality, it had only aided in adding to my disconnection from the woman I called mum. During my first appointment with a new psychiatrist, I was asked if I would like my mum to sit in with me during the sessions. When I told him I didn't, he genuinely looked surprised. It is usual for patients to receive some kind of support from friends and family, and when explaining that I had neither, he gave me a look that stayed with me for a very long time.

We talked a lot, but nothing was ever said that actually touched on any of the fundamental issues that were slowly destroying me inside. He took me back to my childhood, and although events that had happened to me during that time often shocked him, he did not understand that my current issues had nothing to do with my past. The fact that I did not feel close enough to mum to share my problems with her had indeed added to my swift decline, but she had not factored in my life for quite some time, and I had learned to get on well enough without her help. I still had no idea what I should even feel about the woman I called mum. After all, she had never really been a very good one to me. I had spent way too many nights recently wishing that she had not adopted me at all, and I didn't like myself for feeling that way.

The counsellor and I spoke about how my life and childhood had contributed to the possible causes for my depression, but at no time was I able to offer the real reasons behind my state of mind. I did not see the point in going over things I had no control over. Would talking about any of it help anyway? Would holding a conversation with this stranger find the evidence I needed to convict Ryan for Rebecca's murder? Would it be able to bring her back to me? Would it be able to find a cure for my progressive brain injury? It was far easier for me to keep things locked inside my head, and I had no intention of speaking the words of what had happened aloud to anyone.

I did not want people looking at me with that same uneasy look spread across their faces that I had seen on so many occasions from my so-called friends shortly after my accident. Neither did I want these people offering sympathies they could not sustain. My problems were mine and mine alone, and as far as I was concerned, they would remain that way forever. The guilt I was feeling about Rebecca's death was snowballing, and in my own mind, I felt that if anyone should ever find out what I had done to cause her death, the shame it would cause would be too much for me to cope with.

We would talk for the duration of my hourly session each week, with the shrink offering a textbook script he had obviously learned from some college. I would sit on the opposite side of his desk, knowing that this guy understood nothing of what was going on in my head. How could he? Unless he had been in the same situation as me, of course, and, if that were the case, he would probably need counselling himself.

'Tell me about your family?' he would begin in the same way, always assuming my problems somehow stemmed from my childhood.

'What family?' I answered sarcastically during a session where I was feeling exceptionally verbal.

'Mmmm,' he nodded his head, sounding almost patronising. 'I sense some animosity in this subject. How is your relationship with your mum?' What did it matter that I had suffered a childhood that was less than ideal? It didn't actually matter now that I had no real feelings for my mum. How could you love someone you barely knew? I didn't know what it was like to have a mum. So what? I had moved on from those early years quite some time ago and had got on with my own life the best I knew how. Not having parents there for me when I was growing up made me strong and forced me to stand on my own two feet from a very early age.

The sad truth was that this had nothing to do with my mum. It was what had happened to me as an adult that had caused the real pain, although ironically, if our relationship had been better, I probably wouldn't have sunk as low as I did. In the end, the psychiatrist concluded that it was my head injury that was causing the depression, and I had no strength left inside me to argue.

***

Around two months after Rebecca's death, I had hit an all-time low and tried an attempt on my own life when it seemed there was no possible way of moving forward. I couldn't bear the thought of continuing with my life, knowing that I had no one around me who cared what happened to me, and because the pain inside my head was getting worse every day, my body screamed at me to give up. I just couldn't do this anymore. I wanted out. I wanted the world to swallow me up and end this unbearable pain once and for all. I just wanted a one-way ticket off the face of this Earth and feel some peace that I didn't believe I deserved.

I had not spoken about my head injury, my emotions, or how Rebecca's death had affected me to anyone, least of all to the counsellors that were being paid to help me. To make matters worse, no one around me now even knew what had actually happened. I began accepting regular prescriptions of sleeping pills from the doctor and storing them in my sock drawer, ready for my planned escape. They were my way out of this life I now hated, my way to be with Rebecca again and free from the pain that plagued my head daily. It was a weak moment, but at the time, my depression had left me utterly unrecognisable from the person I had once been. After swallowing as many of the pills as I dared, I lay down on my bed, fully expecting mum to find me dead the following morning. I assumed that it would not affect her too much. After all, we barely knew each other. I was simply desperate for everything to go away.

There must have been someone looking over me that day because the only thing that happened was that I slept soundly for around four hours before being rushed into hospital to have my stomach pumped. Mum had popped her head around my door when I had not answered her calls, finding empty bottles and un-swallowed pills scattered across the floor. The most ironic part about the whole thing was that even after seeing me at my utmost lowest point, she still did not have the voice inside her to ask any questions. She didn't ask me once why I felt so low, and she didn't ask me if I was okay. It was as if we both existed in a world of denial that either of us could cope with or be able to sustain indefinitely.

I kept myself to myself most of the time now, doing little more each day than going to work, coming home, cooking myself some dinner, and spending my evenings isolated in my room. The only thing I had left in my life was my car that I spent most of my Saturdays out on mum's driveway cleaning. I had nothing else, and I practically went out of my way to keep people as far away from me as possible. I used to have many friends, good friends, and now they were gone, the last thing I needed were new ones. I did keep in touch with Andy and John, although we saw each other rarely, and they were simply more people from my past who didn't really understand what I was going through or why. Although they had known Rebecca well, they believed as everyone else had that she had committed suicide, and because we could not prove otherwise, the whole situation had been left hanging in mid-air. As I was the last person to see her alive, it was evident to them that I must have had something to do with it, and although they never actually said so, I could see it in their eyes whenever we met.

To make matters worse, I had still not managed to locate the whereabouts of Ryan. He had disappeared into thin air, and I no longer had any contact with the people who could tell me differently. I had to get on with each day, knowing he was out there somewhere, getting on with his life and oblivious to the pain he had caused. I hated that I may never now be able to find justice for what had happened to Rebecca, and living with that fact almost destroyed me.

I began hating everyone around me, mistrusting everything they did, and questioning every word that came out of their mouths. Strangers in the street were not immune from my anger, and I learned not to trust people at all. I continued to search for Ryan whenever I had the strength in me to do so, my evenings either spent tearing my hair out alone or driving around with hatred inside me that consumed my every waking moment. After every failed attempt, I would return to mum's house exhausted, angry and bitter to the point where I felt I might never be able to recover.

*** 

People say that time heals all and that the pain we feel when we lose someone slowly fades. That is not true. The pain remains as vivid as it ever was, but it gets easier to live with the longer you are without that person in your life. You can trick your brain into thinking about something else other than them for a few moments each day until eventually, one day, you find yourself able to think of other things for several hours at a time without feeling as if your world is collapsing around you. After those first few months had passed and the anti-depressants that I had been prescribed were firmly in my bloodstream, I slowly found myself able to venture outside without a panic attack stopping me in my tracks. I was not happy that I had taught myself to hate everyone around me, and so in an attempt to cast off the life I had now been given, I tried to force myself to get on with things the best I could.

I had attempted to banish every memory I had of Rebecca, including ridding myself of everything that reminded me of her, but each night I went to bed with vivid visions of her racing through my mind in addition to the slide show that plagued my every moment. It was unbearable. I had attempted to block out my entire life by burying my memories as deeply as I possibly could get them to go, and yet frustratingly, nothing seemed to work. No matter what I did, I simply could not close the hole that I could feel growing deep in the pit of my stomach, and neither could I retrieve the feeling of exhilaration I had felt during those now somewhat distant motocross days. It was as if a volcano had erupted inside me, and I literally did not know how to settle it down.

After the initial shock of her death had rocked my entire world, a new emotion took its place. Denial. I felt that if I didn't think about it, it meant it hadn't happened at all, and this denial slowly began closing off my once caring nature. No longer could I openly laugh and chat with people on an equal level. I saw everyone I came into contact with as a threat who could not be trusted under any circumstances. I was hollow inside. I was nothing. I felt nothing, and I wanted nothing to do with a single human being.

As my depression grew steadily worse, I began to develop obsessive, compulsive disorders. They came slowly at first, and I barely even noticed, but by the end of that summer, I was washing my hands at least three to four times an hour, and simple tasks such as switching off lights and locking my car door could keep my mind paralysed in a loop for several minutes at a time. Because my short-term memory had taken a severe battering after my accident, I was already more forgetful than I once was. So even though it would often take me fifteen minutes or more to leave the house, I still managed to convince myself that my actions were completely normal. After my hands became sore and angry blotches started to appear due to the skin being scrubbed from my palms, I knew something was seriously wrong. Yet, at no point did I tell a soul about what I was dealing with. It was as if I was hell-bent on punishing myself for a history I believed I could have prevented.

Time flew by quickly, and I settled into a pattern of ups and downs, slumping into a routine of anxiety and low self-esteem. I was still attending my counselling sessions, but they had become part of the pattern that kept me in a steady decline, and I was struggling to lift myself out of the slump I had accidentally disappeared into. I had not stepped foot inside a gym since my accident, and because of that and my breakdown, I had lost a lot of weight.

To add insult to my significant injury, I could no longer be bothered to cook healthy meals and lived on whatever I could summon the energy to prepare. My diet was now a mixture of beans on toast, biscuits, and cheaply made ready meals that I could pop into the microwave and forget about. I was told after my accident that I needed to eat well for my brain to heal correctly, so my new lifestyle did not help my health much at all.

However, throughout this entire time, the one thing I did not do was turn to drink or drugs. It could have been so easy to lose myself at the bottom of a bottle or float away into oblivion, but I did none of these things, determined that no matter how desperate things became, I was still strong enough to remain lucid in both body and mind. My problems would still be there when I sobered up anyway, and I would have to face my suffering all over again in addition to new issues that would have been caused by drink and drugs. I did not understand the point in putting myself through any of that. I was suffering enough.

***

As with everything else plaguing my life at that point, I kept my depression and OCDs to myself, convinced that if I ignored them long enough, they would go away on their own. Of course, they did not subside. Rebecca was still dead, and even if, by some miracle, the police did start an investigation and Ryan actually got life in prison, he would still be breathing, and he would be out and free at some point in the future. I tried not to overthink this, but as 1991 drifted by in a complete blur and with Jade and Grace now also a distant memory, my old life seemed a dream that had never happened at all.

I tried searching for them again after the pain of those first few months had subsided, realising that by pushing them both away, all I had done was lose two of my dearest friends. But Rebecca's flat had now been sold, and I had no idea where Grace had moved. I attempted to get on with life as best I could, but it really did feel as if I had lost everything.

Although it was the last thing I genuinely wanted to do at that stage, I knew if I was ever going to get any kind of existence back again, I needed at least to try to force myself to get as far back to normality as I was able. I realised that giving up was not an option for me and, in the long term, would do me no good whatsoever. I never used to be the type of person to let external circumstances affect me for long, and although Rebecca's death had brought me completely to my knees, I knew I could never let them win.

If Ryan or Justin could see what I had become over the last few months, they would have found the entire situation amusing. It was a thought that nagged at my brain and one that I could no longer allow. They had attempted to destroy everything I stood for, and seemingly, judging from the way I had been acting recently, they were actually succeeding in their mission. I simply could not let that happen. I owed the girls that much, at least. I dumped the last of my anti-depressants into the bin and vowed that from that day forward, I would try and see things in the way that Rebecca always did.

# Chapter 20

I had been busy cleaning my car, as usual on a random Saturday afternoon, oblivious to my surroundings and not wishing under any circumstances to be disturbed when Andy walked up mum's drive towards me. I nodded my head towards him, placing my sponge into the bucket of cold water next to my leg.

'Can I speak to you for a minute, Craig?' Andy's tone was flat as if he had something to tell me and he wasn't entirely confident how I'd react.

Although I was slightly surprised to see him, it didn't register in my mind that he should be here with any actual important information. 'Hey, Andy. You okay?' I asked him casually as I wiped my wet hands on my jeans.

'I know where Ryan is.' I wasn't expecting his reply, and I swear I felt my legs wobble.

I stood on my mother's driveway with my mouth wide open as if someone had stuffed something painful inside it. Had I heard him correctly? 'Are you actually serious?'

Andy nodded. 'He's in Spain.'

Jesus Christ. Why had I failed to figure this out myself? 'Spain? Seriously? Oh my God, don't tell me he's been at his dad's villa this whole time?' It all made sense. Of course, he would be in Spain. Where else would he be? He would be hiding out and waiting for the dust to settle before daring to step foot in England again. The bastard's dad had lied to my face when he told me he didn't know where his son was. Yet, of course, he did. Who was I even kidding?

Andy nodded. 'I only found out this morning. There was talk at the club, and I made sure I was close enough to overhear what was being said.'

I had to take a step back, to lean against my half-cleaned car and absorb the enormity of what I was hearing.

'You have to help me.' It wasn't a request.

'How can I help?'

'You can get me over there.' I was deadly serious.

'You don't need me-'

'I don't have a passport, Andy. I can't just hop on a plane. You know where the villa is, and you happen to have a boat. You can help me.'

Andy hovered for a moment. I knew he was considering my request, and I could only assume he was contemplating what might happen if he said no. 'Well, my dad was due to go to Calais in a few days to pick up some duty-free. Maybe-'

'Yes. Please, Andy, I need you.' I didn't care if I sounded as if I was begging. The truth was, I genuinely did need him. I clasped my hands together in an automatic prayer position. 'Please. I'll pay you. I won't expect you to do this for free.' My heart was pounding. It genuinely felt as if it was going to explode.

'Okay.' Andy hesitated for a moment before adding, 'I'll pick you up tomorrow morning at six. Be ready.'

I wanted to shout *yes* as loudly as my lungs could muster the energy, but I simply nodded a calm thank you towards him as he winked at me and walked back to his car.

\*\*\*

I abandoned my car cleaning, throwing the remainder of cold

water over its paintwork in a hurry and wiping it down with a damp leather cloth so as not to arouse suspicion of why I'd not meticulously polished and buffed it as I usually would. I raced into the house, not even caring that I had left a trail of water across mum's hallway carpet. At that moment, the only thing in my mind was getting a few belongings together that I would need for the journey and withdrawing as much money as I could from the nearest cashpoint. I sat in my room for hours watching the clock, and by the time it was actually bedtime, sleep did not come easily.

'Sleep well?' Andy asked sarcastically as I climbed into his car the following morning and seeing the tired look on my face.

'Funny,' I replied, my nerves in tatters, the anticipation of what lay ahead infused with thoughts of revenge I had almost given up hope of ever finding. There was much to discuss, many aspects of this journey that needed verification. 'I do appreciate this, Andy. I hope you know that.' Andy offered a simple nod as he pulled away from mum's house, everyone still asleep and unaware of my sudden disappearance or reasons behind it. I promised myself that I would call mum from Portland Harbour before we got on the boat, yet my mind was elsewhere and unable to confirm such a weak idea. I concluded it would be easy to come up with some excuse that I need to take a short break for a few days. Mum knew I had been struggling, so would have thought nothing of it. 'So, what's the plan?'

'The fact that you don't have a passport actually goes in your favour.' Andy was turning onto the M6.

'It does?' I wondered for a moment how that could possibly be a good thing.

Andy nodded. 'I don't know what you plan to do to Ryan when you get to him, and if I'm completely honest, I really don't want to know. I won't ask questions, and I won't expect you to give me any details. But because you don't have a passport, no one will suspect you actually had any involvement with-' he paused, obviously looking for the right words. 'With whatever it is you're planning on doing.' Andy was right, of course. I could comfortably dissipate any involvement because I was unable to travel outside the U.K, my lack of passport confirmation that I could have had nothing to do with his sudden demise. Andy's parents' boat was moored in Dorset, and we would be taking a diverted route to Calais for the French coastguard to verify Andy's intentions before setting off towards the Spanish coastline. 'We need to be clever about this, though, Craig. No one must know you're even on board.'

He was absolutely right. I was about to be smuggled out of the country, my plans something no one in their right mind would want to acknowledge, least of all Andy. I didn't know where Ryan's dad's villa was, and so it was lucky for me that Andy did, his cousin having stayed there two summers previous. Andy's parents were keen boaters, trips to Calais and beyond in their luxury forty-foot cabin cruiser was something they regularly did. We were heading for Castro La Playa on the North West Coast of Spain. Our mission, to head to Calais whereby Andy's cruiser would be recorded as landing in France, his parent's knowing nothing of his plans thereafter and suspecting little more than the planned duty-free collection he'd offered to complete on their behalf. Andy's plan was pure genius, and by the time we had set course for Dorset, even I was somewhat overwhelmed. Three hours later, we arrived at Portland Marina, my entire body shaking with anticipation and anxiety, the likes of which I'd never known.

'No one will check the boat at this end,' Andy offered as we unloaded our supplies from the car. 'But when we get near Calais, you're going to need to swim out to sea whilst I head into port to get the boat's paperwork checked.' He was deadly serious. Suddenly I was grateful for the fact I was a strong swimmer. 'Stay about a mile offshore. I'll head around and pick you up once the coastguard is satisfied.' He did not smile or make any jokes about what we were planning on doing. The seriousness of the situation wasn't lost on either of us.

*\*\**

Andy's parent's boat was a luxurious and comfortably designed, fully specked cabin cruiser with a high-powered engine. I'd seen it once, a few years ago in a photograph, and we had joked about spending a weekend away in it at some point, yet never had I imagined taking a journey with him under such harrowing circumstances.

'Don't get comfortable,' Andy added firmly as we descended the steps to the galley. 'I'll let you know when we're ready.' His usual calm and chatty persona had been replaced by the tone of someone with too much on his mind. I nodded and dropped my hastily packed bag onto the floor. I couldn't speak, not even had I wanted to thank him for what he was risking on my behalf. I unscrewed a bottle of water that I'd taken from mum's fridge and took a well-needed swig. I couldn't believe this was actually happening. 'We leave in fifteen minutes,' Andy called back as he went up on deck to do his checks and ready the boat for our departure.

I sat down for a moment on the seating area that curved along the back of the boat in a kind of semi U-shape. I was terrified of being caught by the coastguard, yet more terrified of travelling all that way only to discover that Ryan had already escaped my grasp, again. I wasn't concerned by the idea of being in the sea or having to swim some distance to evade unwanted capture. I couldn't think too much about actually getting to Ryan either because I knew I would know exactly what to do when I saw the look on his face. Every second felt like an hour had passed. I just wanted this whole thing over and done with as quickly as possible. Spain suddenly felt as if it might have been on the other side of the world.

I helped Andy throw off the ropes whilst he started the engine, ready for our departure. A large boat, The Sun Lady, would have usually been crewed by Andy's parents and whichever friends joined them at any given time. The fact that it was just Andy and myself on board must have made him nervous, yet he showed nothing of his concerns as we manoeuvred out of the marina, careful to avoid colliding with other boats in the process. The open ocean awaited us, as did my vengeance and quiet resolve. At no point did I allow myself the possibility that Ryan would escape my wrath again. I couldn't think that way. He had been hiding in Spain for several months already. I assumed he would have by now considered himself in the clear and free from any potential justice that might be heading his way. He was also arrogant, vein, and so completely in love with the idea of his own image that he would never have assumed I might actually at some point find him and confront him face to face. Different country or not.

\*\*\*

I usually loved the sea. The mere idea of the ocean, vast and wild, capable of so much more than anyone could imagine and stretching beyond constraints of landlocked dwellings and the people who lived there. The fresh smell of sea salt and abundant marine life in my nostrils would normally feel good. With the light breeze against my cheeks, the sun on my face, I could think of nothing better. There was nothing more beautiful or alive than the ocean. Yet today, my senses were awash with nerves, the motion of the boat in the swell enough to bring bile rising to the back of my throat.

'How long until we get to Calais?' I asked Andy, more to take my own mind of my pending nausea than anything else.

'About two hours give and take,' he replied, his focus on the course he'd set, his mind concentrating dead ahead, nothing but vast ocean in front of us and a thin line of land some way off in the distance. He turned to look at me then, probably for the first time since we had left my mum's driveway. 'You okay?' It was a genuine question, and I knew it came from a good place.

I nodded. 'I will be.' For the first time in months, I had something important to focus on. It was a good feeling despite leaving me trembling as if my insides had been ripped into shreds.

***

Andy saw the shores of France long before I had registered we were anywhere near. 'Craig,' he called as I absently stared out across the English Channel. I looked up and got to my feet, my legs once again shaking with anticipation. 'You'd better get ready.' I nodded my acknowledgement and quickly went below deck to put on the wet suit that Andy had readied for me. I pulled on a life jacket and flippers and climbed onto the boat's ledge, sitting calmly for further instructions. Andy turned and nodded towards me, and without hesitation, I jumped off the boat and into the freezing ocean below. I was grateful that Andy's wet suit was a good quality one, yet the volume of water that engulfed me took me by surprise all the same. I bobbed in the water for a moment like a plastic bottle, watching The Sun Lady disappear ahead before I began my swim.

The first thing that hit me was the silence. The only

sounds now were that of waves crashing against my tiny body and birds some distance above me as I projected myself through the vast salty water. I was wearing a bright yellow lifejacket, easy to spot upon Andy's return, I hoped. No one would have expected to see a random swimmer in the middle of the ocean, so I could happily stay out of the way of any potential passing boats. I had no idea how long Andy would even be, hoping the French coastguard would simply need to stamp his passport, a full boat inspection unrequired.

It must have been adrenaline that kept me going because I swam some distance before I actually realised I could no longer see Andy's boat at all. I wondered for a moment that should I somehow drown right then, would anyone ever be able to find my body again? I assumed not, yet the idea of that thought didn't seem to bother me too much at all. I had never been able to float, my inability to allow water to hold my weight something Rebecca had once found unequivocally amusing. So I was glad of the lifejacket that kept me upright, treading water, the vastness of the ocean below me something I tried not to think too long about. I had no idea how long I remained like that, my body completely at the mercy of whichever direction the current was trying to take me, but when I saw The Sun Lady making its way towards me, I felt relief like never before.

'Sorry, it took longer than expected. Bloody French.' Andy stopped the boat alongside me, and I grabbed onto the ladder as it floated gently past, pulling myself out of the water and grateful for the lifejacket that had obviously made me stand out nicely.

'Everything okay?' I asked, sounding more out of breath than I actually was and wondering if the strange tone in my voice was more to do with my nerves than anything else.

'Yeah, all good. I had to grab some duty-free booze for dad so he wouldn't get suspicious, of course, though.' He pointed towards three crates of beer and a box of white wine that he had piled next to the cabin door. 'My passport is stamped, so we should be able to head round to Spain now without much hassle.' I removed the lifejacket and wet suit and towel-dried my hair. It would be a while until I could relax, this journey every bit as terrifying as the look in Andy's eyes.

We sat together on that boat for several hours, feeling every bit the smugglers we actually now were. I felt terrible for asking Andy to do this for me, yet grateful this journey had even been possible, my own desperate needs far outweighing that of anything else. Every time a boat came into sight, Andy flinched, wondering if the coastguards were about to stop him, to check that his intentions were good and that his paperwork was in order. I was on constant alert, ready to jump overboard at any given moment. Luckily, no one interfered with our journey; Castro La Playa was now well within reaching distance, the call of the Mediterranean looming.

'Are you sure you know where you're going?' I asked absently as we stood at the helm, nothing but ocean stretching ahead of us.

'Relax,' he replied with a snigger. 'What do you think navigation systems are for?' He pointed to the extensive equipment adorning the helm in front of him. 'Why don't you try and get some rest,' he added. 'It's going to be a long journey.' I nodded and headed below deck. I did need some rest. My head was pounding.

***

I don't recall falling asleep, but I awoke to the sensation that I was in an earthquake. The boat was rocking violently from side to side, waves crashing aggressively against the side of the hull. I clambered to my feet to see Andy calmly playing a game of cards with himself at the table. 'A storm came in,' he offered as he got unsteadily to his feet and picked up a kettle from the stovetop.

'Where are we?' My thoughts were as foggy as my head.

'In a small cove just off the western coast of France. I think.' Andy laughed at the uncertain look I gave him when he added 'I think' to his sentence. 'Relax, Craig, jeez mate, you really need to take a breath.' He laughed again. 'Don't worry, I know where we are. I could see a storm coming in, so I thought it best we spend the night tucked away out of sight.' It was probably a good plan, to be honest. Navigating to Spain in a cabin cruiser wasn't like driving along the M1. There were no signposts or service stations to make stops at. You needed your wits about you. The ocean was perfectly capable of veering you off course before you even notice.

'I guess I am a bit tense.' I ran my hand through my hair and leaned a hand against one of the portholes. 'I just want this over with.'

Andy looked at me then, something behind his eyes telling me he didn't want to know my thoughts on the subject. 'Cuppa?' He held up the kettle he'd filled moments earlier.

I nodded. 'Cheers.' I glanced out of the window. It was getting dark. The only thing I could see was a thick sheet of rain hitting the glass, the sound of the wind tipping the boat in violent aggression, and beyond that, jagged rocks that disappeared out of sight and into the distance. 'Are you sure we will be safe here?'

'Yep. Nobody will see us tucked away down here.' He turned on the gas and waited for the water to boil. He knew as well as I did that I had too much time now to sit and think. To ponder my next moves and consider exactly how to deal with Ryan when eventually I found him. Andy looked at me for a moment. 'How are you doing?' It was an honest question. A genuine question.

I shrugged absently. 'I'll let you know.'

*\*\**

By early dawn, the storm had passed, and the sun was once again trying to dissipate my darkening mood. It couldn't have been more different from the night before. We set off at just after five o'clock in the morning, neither of us wanting this journey to take longer than it had to. Andy had cooked eggs and bacon, yet I wasn't hungry, my belly aching for peace that would only come with seeing the look in Ryan's eyes when he saw my approach. For hours, my head swam with images and visions I could have told no one about, my heart yearning for an end I didn't know how to perceive. Hours seemed to pass slowly, my mind having nothing to focus on but dark images that plagued my every breath. By the time we saw land again, I was unsure it was real at all.

'There,' Andy pointed towards some distant shoreline that his GPS system directed the boat towards. My heart skipped a beat. In fact, it missed several entirely. I could see a sandy beach dotted with dunes and coves wrapped around a gentle coastline on the horizon. Spain. I swallowed hard, forcing my thoughts deep into my gut. Andy changed direction slightly, aiming his vessel towards a thin jetty that lined a neighbouring cove. 'I'll have to get the boat safely around the corner. The fewer people who see us, the better.' I stared at Andy for a moment, wondering if he was having second thoughts about any of this. As we neared the shore, I jumped onto the jetty and pulled the ropes around the cleats, tying them off safely and glad my own boating experience would now serve me well.

Satisfied that the boat was in a good position, Andy turned off the engine. 'Okay,' he jumped onto the jetty and stood next to me, close enough for me to believe he didn't want anyone else overhearing what he was about to say. 'Ryan's dad's villa is about five hundred meters or so from the beach, just back around that cove.' He pointed to the corner we had just driven around. 'We need to stay well out of sight for now. We don't want to accidentally tip him off before you're ready for him.' I literally could not have said that better myself. 'I'll lock up the boat, and then I can show you where the villa is.'

***

My mouth was already feeling quite dry as we ventured into the sand dunes and through a small clearing that opened up to a single row of bars and restaurants lining the beachfront. It was a beautiful location, one the girls would have loved. I held my breath, unwilling to dwell on things I could no longer change. In silence, we casually walked away from the beach, keeping a constant eye out for any sign of the enemy.

'You see that white building by those old Cypress trees?' Andy pointed towards a villa that seemed to be perched overlooking a cliff edge. I nodded. 'Ryan's dad's villa is the one just behind that.' I couldn't help sucking in air that stuck in the back of my throat. Andy noticed. 'Come on.' He headed up a hill, keeping close to the bushes in case we needed to take an unexpected dive into them at any moment. I followed in nervous anticipation.

Ryan's dad's villa was a single-story, traditional Spanish property that looked as if it had seen better days, yet still more than I could have imagined owning. Andy pulled me roughly behind a tree and crouched down. Ryan would no doubt be in there right now, unaware of my presence a mere fifty feet away.

'We should probably lay low for a day or so, watch his

229

comings and goings, see where he goes and when.' I knew Andy was right, of course, but I didn't want to wait any longer than I had to. I wanted to walk up to that place right then and break the door down while I had the chance.

I took a breath for a moment. It was cool under this tree, a welcome shade against the heat of the sun and a complete contrast to my thoughts. Never having visited any foreign country before, this was not how I had anticipated any potential travel arrangements, yet it had suited me well enough, it seemed. It didn't take long before a door opened, and Ryan walked outside, shirt undone, his cheap, tacky jewellery glinting in the bright sunlight and that usual smug look on his face that I wanted to smash. I flinched for a moment, considering racing out from behind my hiding place and running straight up to him, but Andy noticed and grabbed my arm.

'Don't be a twat,' he spat. 'Wait.'

I waited, yet it went against every emotion I was experiencing. I had wanted for so long to catch up with him, and here he was, standing just feet away from me, no idea I was even watching him at all and no clue as to the thoughts racing through my mind.

'Tonight,' I whispered, knowing Andy could hear me yet caring nothing of how my tone sounded. I lifted my hand and made a gun shape with my fingers, pointing it directly at his head in my line of vision. 'Bang,' I said calmly under the shade of the tree. 'Bang.'

# Chapter 21

We spent the next three hours closely watching Ryan's movements, walking sneakily behind him as he ventured down to the shops and back, chatting up passing girls that made me want to vomit in the process. At one point, we even got close enough to hear him speak, his arrogant tone and attitude towards girls still as disgusting as ever. When two young women walked past him, he turned and vocalised his liking for the way they were dressed, bronzed bikini bodies, sarongs tied around their waists, just tourists having fun.

The girls said a fond 'hi' back to him and giggled, a potential holiday romance, something they had probably waited all year to experience. Ryan gave them both a longing look, eyeing them up and down and having thoughts that should have made those girls run a mile.

'Until later then, ladies,' I heard him call after them, and I wanted to throttle him there and then.

It was at that moment I had a thought. It was devious, calculated, but it might actually work perfectly in my favour. The girls had continued their journey towards the beachfront, Ryan's attention being something they were still chatting to each other about. I walked up to them and casually tapped one on the shoulder. She turned and smiled at me, an innocent smile that I felt guilty about.

'Hey girls,' I said, trying to sound as calm and friendly as

I was able to. 'Sorry to ask you a random question out of nowhere, but you girls might just be able to do me a massive favour.'

One of the girls smiled. 'Oh yeah?' she asked, flicking hair out of her eyes and adjusting her sunglasses.

'Are you staying around here at all?'

'Yep,' she pointed to a large building situated at the bottom of the hill. 'Just there at the Playa Casa Hotel.' She looked at me and winked. 'Why, are you guys looking for fun?'

I laughed, my friendships with girls allowing me a relaxed mannerism I knew didn't come naturally to most males. 'How do you fancy earning some quick cash?' I held my hands up in a defensive manner, realising how that might have sounded. 'Not like that, in case you were wondering,' I laughed, keeping the conversation as casual as I could. 'But I do need you to bring someone down to the beach for me tonight. There's two hundred quid in it for you if you're up for it. No questions asked.'

The girls looked at each other for a moment, their interest piqued at the idea of such a large sum of money. 'Who's the someone?'

'That guy you were chatting to a minute ago.' I pointed towards where Ryan had only moments earlier walked back up the hill towards his villa, oblivious to my presence at all.

'Oh him?' one of the girls laughed. 'Yeah, he's been trying to chat us up all week, actually.'

Perfect. 'Then this should be the easiest two hundred quid you've ever made,' I added.

They looked at each other and then at me. 'When do we get paid?'

I pulled my wallet from of my pocket and out dug several twenty-pound notes, showing the girls that I was deadly serious and had the cash to back up my words. 'I'll give you a hundred now and the other hundred when you have bought him down to the beach later tonight.' I held a hand towards the girls, five twenty-pound notes fluttering in the breeze.

'Why not,' she offered. 'We're going home tomorrow anyway, and this will give us the best last night of our holiday ever.' They both laughed, and I handed them the cash.

'Do you know what time he usually gets down to the bar?' I didn't have to enquire as to 'if' he actually frequented those bars. I knew Ryan well. He would spend every night down there if he could.

'We usually see him around nine in the Coral Reef,' she said, gesturing towards the row of bars along the beachfront.

I nodded. 'Make sure you girls are hanging around here when he leaves his villa. And make sure he sees you watching him. Dress nice.' I knew it wouldn't take much to pique Ryan's interest. Two attractive females showing him some attention. He would love every moment of it.

'Oh, don't worry about us,' she answered coyly. 'We know how to handle guys like that.'

'And no one is to know we had this conversation,' I added with a serious after tone that threatened to bring up my breakfast. The last thing I needed was Ryan being tipped off ahead of schedule.

'Understood.' The girls giggled, thanked me for the cash, and walked off down the hill towards the beach, my money now tucked in their hands like sweets given to a child at Christmas.

'That was a bit risky, wasn't it?' Andy asked after they had left.

'Worth every penny,' I replied—worth every, single, penny.

***

I watched the clock until I could have practically predicted every second that ticked by. Nothing appeased me, and nothing helped take my mind off the forthcoming evening and events yet to unfold. Andy offered me food I wasn't interested in eating and made me drinks I left untouched.

'Calm down,' he said eventually after watching me almost lose it several times in a single hour.

'I can't mate,' I sighed as I paced the boat, threatening to wear the wooden boards under my feet out completely. 'I don't know how much more of this waiting I can stand.'

Andy knew I had wanted this moment for so long. We hadn't spoken a word about what was obviously going to happen. He knew I wanted to hurt Ryan, yet I wondered if he knew what was really going through my head. No matter how hard I had tried to move on with my life, nothing made a shred of difference. Rebecca was still dead. My baby was still dead. There would never be anything I could do about that now. I had spent so many nights longing for revenge. For Rebecca and the baby. Now it was actually a possibility, I was shocked to discover I felt empty by the concept, desolate even.

It was as if something inside me had died, and I simply did not know what to do about it. I wondered how I would actually be able to move forward from all of this. Ryan and Justin had literally become the very reason I forced myself to get up in the morning. They had been the reason for my mental breakdown too, but I wasn't going to dwell on that.

*****

I have no idea how long I sat on the beach in the darkness with the sound of the ocean in the background, nothing surrounding me feeling real at all and the events of the last couple of days a blurry haze that I knew would soon end in the exact way I had dreamed for a very long time. It had taken just a few moments for my entire life to come crashing down around me, every day since then consisting of a desperate need for revenge that now, suddenly and without warning, I had no place for. A single moment in history had shattered every dream I ever harboured and every ambition I strove to achieve.

It was ironic to think how quickly everything I held so dear to my heart had changed in a millisecond, and the things I once took for granted now felt a million miles away. My life had quite literally performed a one hundred and eighty-degree turn, and in the time it had taken to blink, I had found myself lost, standing in a world I no longer understood. I closed my eyes for a moment, wishing the world would stop, just for a second. I could hear seagulls in the background, and yet initially, I wasn't even listening, my head in too much pain for me to seriously understand the importance of what I was actually doing here.

I casually watched people coming and going, getting on with their evening as if nothing in the world could touch them. I wished for a moment that life really could be that simple. My life used to feel that simple. Spain had become Ryan's secret hideout, yet he thought I didn't know it, my misspent evenings looking for him now something that had seemingly paid off, eventually. I shivered as I sat in the darkness of the beach, the sand cool against my legs and between my fingers as I ran my hand over the tiny particles, observing the lives of people I knew nothing about. I would like to say that I didn't know what I was going to do when I saw him, but that would be a complete lie. I knew exactly what I was going to do. There was only one thing left for me to do now. Only one thing left that made any sense in my mind.

Sitting on that beach, I wished I could hide away and happily become as invisible as I already felt. I watched as holidaymakers squeezed their way through a growing crowd of people, the distant music hitting my senses against the hot, sticky air. In all the years I had enjoyed nights out in clubs and bars, socialising until all hours and driving to work the following day without even having gone to bed, I was surprised now at how badly my body reacted to an environment that had become so alien to me.

Although I had tried on many occasions to overthrow this new feeling that overtook my senses every time I stepped into a crowded room, nothing helped, and tonight was no different. I was waiting for Ryan to show up here tonight, any moment appearing ahead of me like the demonic freak he appeared in my mind. My recent pursuit of him was something I could not easily forget, and my earlier payment for his appearance sat uncomfortably in my gut. I considered turning around and getting out of there. To abandon my quest. But I forced myself to remain calm, my mind focused only on what it needed to achieve.

If life is, indeed, made up of events that deliver us abjectly to where we are at any given point; an unparalleled journey that enforces lessons in strength where strength cannot be found, to understand others when others turn their backs, and to believe in truth when the truth is only a distant fantasy, then that night should have taught me something fundamentally important. I often hear that everything happens for a reason, and although that may be true, the memories of my life had become so jumbled, confused, and downright unforgiving that I had nothing left inside of me, of the man I always believed I was. I wanted to believe that it was entirely down to Ryan that I was standing here with thoughts going through my brain that threatened to disembowel me entirely. But the truth was, I was here because of what my own actions had allowed me, and only my actions would now release me from the pain that tormented my every waking moment.

I was searching faces around me for confirmation I wasn't going completely out of my mind. I would like to believe I might have reasoned with myself that I could have actually allowed the police to do their job. They would obviously catch up with Ryan at some point. It would only be a matter of time, and I didn't for one moment allow myself to think anything differently. He was a scumbag. People like him always got what they deserved, eventually. Yet I knew in my mind that he was also a cockroach, and cockroaches needed squashing.

I have no idea how long I stood with the sea at my back and warm air against my skin, waiting for confirmation that my instincts had been right to trust two complete strangers with my fate. My head was throbbing, the noise of the music too loud and the heat from bodies nearby, too much for me to deal with. Yet nothing I could have endured was bad enough to force me back to the boat right then. I must have had a look on my face that unnerved people because every now and then, I noticed strangers giving me sideways glances as they stepped as far away from me as possible. I might not have looked so menacing had I been standing there with a machete in my hand and covered in blood. Ryan's blood. I could all but dream, I guess.

When I saw one of the girls I'd paid a hundred pounds to only hours earlier, my heart lunged. Ryan appeared behind her, his arms wrapped around the other girl's waist and standing a mere twenty feet away from me. I couldn't quite believe my own eyes. I swallowed, wondering if he was actually standing in front of me like the evil vision I'd wished for, or if I was merely hoping. He was talking into the left ear of my poor honey trap victim, seemingly having a detailed and insidious conversation with her that I dared not imagine the contents of. I motioned forward slightly, my legs unstable yet my focus clearer than it had been in quite some time.

When both females moved slightly to one side, and I saw Ryan lean in and ask for a kiss, it was as if the whole world had stopped completely. Nothing seemed real at that point. I couldn't understand the thoughts that swam like ghosts through my mind. I stepped forward, allowing my feet to carry me where I needed to go. One step closer, then another, as I edged myself towards Ryan as if there were no other people in the world apart from the two of us. I wanted him to see me, yet I knew I needed to remain unnoticed until I was close enough for him to be unable to escape. This was it. This was really it. The moment I had waited so long to experience yet felt it might never actually come.

I would like to say that I didn't exactly know my intentions at that point, but I would be lying because I knew exactly how everything was going to play out, in the tiniest of minute detail. Ryan did not even see me as I walked up and stood right behind him. I must have been mere feet from his back for a good few seconds, the stench of his sweat strong enough to make me feel as if I had fallen into a pit of excrement. It was unbearable. The girl by his side noticed me only when I was literally inches from Ryan's head, and she nodded a confirmation that she had done her job well. I smiled and passed the remaining one hundred pounds to her that she took from me with a simple 'thank you' before removing herself from Ryan's unwanted grasp.

'He's all yours,' she said as she cupped her arms around her friends, and together they scurried back along the beach, giggling, unaware of why he had been summoned at all. Ryan spun around too fast, seeing me only at the very last minute. I lunged forward, punching him as hard as I could in the gut to take him by surprise.

'Jesus Christ,' he spat as the realisation that I was actually standing in front of him caught up with him swiftly. I caught the shocked look in his eyes, the fear that hid in secret.

'Sorry, but he's not going to help you,' I taunted as I grabbed him and dragged him by the head roughly along the beach, away from noticing eyes and into the darkness of the shoreline. I threw him to the sand, watching his body roll twice, his would-be candid mannerisms disappearing with the violence of my presence.

'What the fuck are you doing here?' he screamed, scrambling to his feet; the sound of his jewellery and the stench of his aftershave more than I could stand.

'I've been looking for you,' I taunted back. 'Surprised to see me?'

I didn't notice the knife at first, but when I saw a flash of metal coming towards me, I instinctively grabbed his arm. Ryan had intended on stabbing me. His eyes were colder than anyone I had ever had the misfortune to encounter. It was as if he was already dead somewhere inside, and I wondered for a moment what could have possibly happened to this guy for him to do the calculated things he did to others with no remorse whatsoever.

We grappled for a few moments, no one behind us even seemingly noticing the fight that had broken out on the beach in the dark. The buzz of the bars that lined the shorefront continued in a haze as I brought my knee up high and kicked him between the legs, forcing him to release the knife that landed in the sand.    Without thinking, I lunged forward and grabbed it. My fist wrapped around its wooden handle with an intent that, to be quite honest, actually frightened me. Ryan lunged at me from behind, and I swung around and plunged the knife deep into his belly before I had the chance to change my mind. I did not even hesitate. For a moment, he looked shocked, staring at me as if he didn't quite believe what I had done. I could feel warm blood running across my hand as I held my fist firmly against his body, forcing the knife deeper into his gut as slowly and painfully as I could.

He looked confused, as if the pain had not yet registered but knew something was wrong. I pulled the knife out of his flesh and stood waiting for him to drop to the ground. Instead, he staggered sideways and retreated away from me as fast as he could, further along the beach in a desperate attempt to escape my wrath. I followed, no one around us aware of what had just happened at all. I knew I had gone too far, yet in my mind, this was perfectly acceptable to me because, as far as I was concerned, it was either him or me. It had been purely self-defence. The knife was his, not mine, and he had intended to use it on me with no qualms whatsoever.

Ryan staggered into the water's edge, the cool night air and gentle breeze a contrast to the poison that engulfed my mind, his grunts and groans something I could not stand to experience inside the cavities of my ears. I followed, allowing the sounds of revellers behind me to grow ever quieter.

'Get away from me,' Ryan's words were desperate, fearful. He knew I was coming for him, and he knew there wasn't a damned thing he could do about it. I grabbed him by the throat and dragged him to the sand, bearing my full weight down on top of him with everything I had left inside me. There was so much I wanted to say to him, so much pain inside me that I needed to release.

Being here with him right then, I couldn't have possibly imagined how I would actually feel. And yet here we were, finally together, finally able to express all the emotions I had struggled to deal with since the night of Rebecca's attack and subsequent death. I could never have imagined that things would ever go as far as this. I hated him, but I would have gladly lived my life without ever having to deal with him or think about him at all. Now, because of what he had done, he had turned me into something else. Something bitter. Something twisted.

'What are you going to do?' Ryan screamed as he lay on

the beach at my mercy, my knees pressed into his chest as if they wanted to penetrate his ribcage.

'I want you to see my face when you breathe your last breath.' I had no idea how I could sound so menacing. So devious, so cold-hearted and full of hatred.

'Please,' Ryan was begging, and it was disgusting to witness. 'Don't kill me. I can go. You will never have to see me again.'

'But that's just the problem,' I pressed the knife against his throat, the sight of fresh blood still dripping from its blade making me gag. 'You took everything I ever loved from me. You killed my baby, you bastard.' I couldn't help it when a tear rolled onto my cheek, and my emotions got the better of me. 'I can't let you keep getting away with the shit you do.'

'I'm sorry, I'm sorry. I didn't mean to.' He was actually crying. It was the most pathetic thing I had ever seen. I felt something warm against my leg and wondered for a moment if he had actually wet himself.

'I'm not,' I answered coldly as I plunged the knife deep into the side of his neck without any hesitation whatsoever. I sat on top of him, watching as he choked and gagged. Every emotion I had ever experienced seemed to flash through my mind in that single moment. He looked up at me from the flat of his back, the life literally draining from his eyes as blood pumped out of his neck and along my arm as if taking with it every agony he had forced me to endure. I dared not let go of the knife, even for a moment. I was terrified that if I did, he would somehow escape, yet again, creeping into the night like the cockroach he was and taking my pain with him.

Instead, I sat and watched as he slowly died in front of me on the sand, staring coldly into his eyes and desperate for him to know that the very last thing he would ever see on this earth was my face as I took his life in the same way as he had already taken mine. Even when I saw no further movement from him and his eyes were staring cold and dead, I kept my hand around his throat for a lingering moment, the knife welded to my hand as if it might actually take a crowbar to prise it away from my clenched fist. Blood soaked into the sand below us, and I felt my jeans mopping up what was left of his life force. Only when I was completely satisfied that he was actually one hundred per cent dead, did I dare get to my feet again.

# Chapter 22

I could not believe it. It was a moment I had dreamt about, pondered over, created detailed events in my mind as to how I would eventually kill him and how he would actually die. I visualised his cold, lifeless eyes in my mind every night when I went to bed and every morning when I woke up. And now he actually was dead, lying on the cool sand in front of me, nothing but a slab of meat I could have happily kicked to death as if it were nothing more than an overstuffed rag doll.

I leaned over and vomited, the realisation of what I had done and the smell of Ryan's blood suddenly slamming my senses like a gun to the chest. I was covered in blood, sand, and a mixture of sweat and tears that I felt might never wash off. I even had blood in my hair, and although I couldn't see my own face, I could feel something hot and sticky running along my cheek.

As I stood alone on that stretch of beach in a strange country, I felt something shift inside me. A weight that I had been carrying around for three years felt as if it had been removed, leaving me standing in the dark on wobbling legs that I couldn't actually get to work correctly. It reminded me of how I had felt when I had learned to walk again after my accident. I was not a murderer, and yet Ryan had turned me into something I could never have imagined. The worst part of it all was that I did not even feel a single shred of remorse whatsoever. I was not sorry. He was finally dead and would no longer be able to haunt me or hurt a single human being ever again.

I stared down at his pathetic, lifeless body. The only sounds I could now hear were that of the sea behind me, upbeat music some distance away and unacquainted laugher of strangers. Methodically, I swiftly relieved Ryan of his watch, money, and jewellery and left him lying on the sand as if his death had been nothing more than a mugging that, for him, had gone horribly wrong. I retreated back across the sand dunes in the darkness, around the cove and back to the boat. I had nothing left to prove and literally nothing left inside me that I could make any sense out of anyway. I stepped onto The Sun Lady at twenty past eleven that night, covered in someone else's blood and still carrying the knife I had used to commit the offence. I did not want to cover up what I had done or hide the reasons for my crime from Andy.

I casually told my poor unsuspecting friend that we could now go home. I did not dare look at his face. I was fully aware that I was still clutching the knife I'd used to kill my archenemy with. I felt that if I wasn't careful, it might actually become a part of my hand at some point, literally unable to release the feelings that had built up inside me for so long. I was actually quite glad when Andy managed to grapple it away from me because now, it was finally, one hundred per cent, over.

***

I sat on the back of the boat, trembling quietly to myself, whilst Andy busied himself for our swift departure. I was not at all concerned by the fact that I had left a dead body on the beach behind me, although what Andy might think of such matters, I could not predict. He gave me a knowing look, almost as if to silently ask if the job was done. Yet I knew he already knew the answer to that question by the state of me.

I had unwittingly become embroiled with the life of a psychopath, setting in motion a trail of disasters that none of us could have ever imagined possible. It had bought me to this somewhat isolated place tonight, forcing my hand until there was nothing left for me to do but commit murder. I should have known there was always only ever going to be one conclusion, one single outcome, in the end. There was really no other way to end the torture and suffering of the last three years, and no way my mind would ever have accepted anything less.

A prison sentence for either Ryan or Justin would not have sat well in my mind anyway. At some point, they would have been free, and I knew I wouldn't have been able to live with that fact. As we set out into the ocean, around the cove, and away from the shore, I turned around only once, witness to the tiny lights that signalled the beach's location behind us. Its bars and restaurants awash with holidaymakers and locals alike, none of whom knew at that moment of the body that lay cold in the darkness of the beach, a mere three feet or so from the water's edge.

I got to my feet, surprised at how shaky they felt and knowing it had nothing to do with the motion of the boat. It was as if my mind had silenced. Every thought I had ever experienced was now gone, as if my soul had disappeared the very moment Ryan's heart stopped beating. Andy had taken the boat out into the ocean, full throttle giving way only to the breakwaters that violently lifted the vessel above the waves. I knew he wanted to get us as far away from shore as possible, the knife and Ryan's belongings still in our possession, telling of a vital deed complete. I stared at my hands, blood-stained and trembling. My own clothing a stark reminder of the night's terrifying events.

My mind was in a daze as I picked up the knife and pulled Ryan's belongings from my pocket, turning them over in my hands as if I couldn't quite get my brain to register what they were holding. It was over. It was really over. I looked skyward for a moment, allowing the stars to engulf me.

'Better get rid of those,' Andy called towards me as he turned around to see me standing in the middle of the boat like the madman I truly felt, clutching items I had no business holding.

I picked up a discarded plastic bag still onboard from an earlier takeout lunch and stuffed the items inside. I loaded the bag with pebbles I'd taken from the dunes only hours earlier, a strange little habit I'd formed through my years of friendship with the girls. Ensuring the load was heavy enough, I tied a knot at the handles and lowered it over the side of the boat, watching as it hit the water. It floated for a few seconds before sinking below the surface, leaving only bubbles behind and disappearing into the void below. I didn't expect anyone would find it down there. Items washed out to sea every day, never to be seen again.

I had been through some of the worst times anyone could ever imagine having to endure, and yet standing on the deck of Andy's boat that night, I felt truly and utterly unrestrained, probably for the first time in my entire life. I finally felt as if I had been released from the pain that had engulfed me for so long, poisoning the very heart of who I was. I sat down on the seating at the back of the boat and considered the idea of handing myself in to the police. It was something I always maintained I would have no issues with, always assuming I would not be overly concerned by what the girls would feel when they discovered what I had done. But the truth was, I was absolutely terrified. I had constantly told myself that I would be completely happy to accept my punishment, go to jail if needed, the only thing at that time driving me forward being pure and evil revenge. And yet now, after it was all actually over, the very idea of my friends knowing what I had done and spending decades in prison because of it, was more than I could bear.

How would the girls look at me now? How would they actually feel, knowing what I had become? I had pushed them away because of my grief. Now I wondered if they would ever see me in the same light again. I genuinely thought that by killing Ryan, I would secure them a world that would finally ensure their safety. They would be able to live their lives free from the torment of looking over their shoulder just in case something else terrible happened at the hands of that crazed bastard. Ryan would no longer be able to hurt them, and that thought alone should have been enough to keep me going through whatever impending prison sentence I might have had to endure.

But had any of it been really worth it? In the end? I sat on the seat of a boat that didn't belong to me, thinking thoughts that had no place in my head. Rebecca was still dead; as was the unborn child I would never now know. It had been my own inability to let things go that had bought me to this ultimate conclusion. I had no one else to blame for any of this but myself. I closed my eyes, allowing the sound of the waves and the roar of the boat engine to swallow my thoughts. I knew that Andy would never be able to look at me in the same way again. The look on his face tonight had verified that. And if I was candid with myself, a prison cell wasn't something I would probably be able to cope with either. My head injury would make damned sure of that.

So there would be no hero's ending for me, no confirmed sense of justice, or pat on the back because I could never tell a single soul what I had done tonight. In the overwhelming madness that had become my life, I had lost everything I ever cared about, myself included. I was now a murderer. A killer, cold and calculated, and I knew I would now never be able to fully get past that notion. I was no better than Ryan or Justin, my own actions taking me along a dark path I could never have predicted. I loved the girls with everything I had, and I would have done anything for them, my best friends, my true friends. In the end, I guess, I committed the ultimate act of love, the ultimate sacrifice.

I knew without a shadow of a doubt that it was love that had taken me to that desolate place in the end. It had always been love that drove me forward in life and kept me going when I could see no light ahead of me. I stared at the stars, wondering if there was actually anything out there that could see me now. See what I had become. I closed my eyes. I knew that whatever happened after this night, and despite everything that had happened, I still had love in my heart and, therefore, would always have the girls with me. The love I had for them and the love I had for Rebecca was a love few people in life get to experience. I was proud of our friendship, and I knew that no matter what happened to me now, I would always have that gratitude.

'I might go and have a lie-down,' I called to Andy as he set the GPS's course for Calais.

Andy nodded and made a tiny grunting gesture, not really turning towards me at all, his attention set now only on getting home, safe, and probably as far away from me as possible, I had no doubt. I looked at the back of his head for a moment, grateful for the friendship he'd shown me over the last twenty-four hours that, without which, would not have had such a satisfying conclusion. Life often throws challenges our way that we are neither expecting nor prepared for, but it was only after I killed Ryan that I fully understood that it is how we choose to deal with situations that truly make us who we are. Andy had unwittingly accompanied my journey to hell, and I wondered if he was now in his own personal one as well.

I headed below deck, ensuring Andy heard the clarity of my footsteps. I needed him to believe I was safely below deck, asleep, oblivious to the night's events and the thoughts he was undoubtedly having. I wrote Andy a detailed note, folded it in half and held it in my hand for a few moments, contemplating my next move. I sighed. Maybe there really was no going back to my everyday life again after tonight. As quietly as I could, I headed back up on deck and tucked Andy's note firmly into the flap of his rucksack that was resting next to his dad's cheap beer crates. I wondered for a moment if it might blow away but confirmed I was overthinking that concept and stepped gingerly onto the back of The Sun Lady.

I tiptoed along the edge of the boat and sat at the stern, my back to Andy, allowing my sand-covered shoes to dangle over the edge as I watched the propeller churn saltwater to foam as it thrust The Sun Lady forward in the darkness. I wondered for a moment that if I were to simply slip into the water, how long would it be before Andy noticed my absence. It could be hours, my body long gone, no one able to correctly pinpoint the exact moment I entered the water or my subsequent whereabouts.

I looked towards the helm, tiny lights in a black sky the only thing showing Andy the way home, the back of his head telling nothing of his mood, his emotions or his needs. I dangled my hand into the water, its cool liquid feeling somewhat refreshing against the heat of my palm. It would take less than a second. No longer than that. I smiled, whispered a fond farewell to my friend just several feet away from me, and slipped silently into the water with a single splash.

For a moment, I allowed my body to absorb the expanse of the water, the black ocean below me pulling gently at my soul, calling my name to a place I longed to find. Without the continued support of the girls I loved dearly, I would have probably given up a while ago, allowing my injuries to take my life long before now. Life is short, and time is precious, and yet I did not fully understand this concept until I watched The Sun Lady sail away into the night without me. I was fully prepared for what I had started, yet it had turned me into something I couldn't have imagined. I had to follow my path to the end now until it was completely over for me. I literally had nothing left to give.

I thought about the note I'd left Andy and hoped he would understand why I had to do what I did in the end. The lights on the boat were fading fast, Andy's speed maintaining its pursuit of freedom. 'Thank you, Andy,' I whispered into the darkness around me before allowing my body to slip quietly below the surface of the ocean forever.

Andy,

If you are reading this note, please know that my decision to leave this world wasn't something I made lightly, and you made it possible for me to find closure I might never have otherwise known. I want you to know how grateful I am to you for what you did for me, and thank you from the bottom of my heart for allowing me to reach my ultimate destination.

My actions took me to a place that meant I lost everything and everyone I loved and cared about along the way, including the very person I thought I was. I spent so long wishing for the death of an enemy, that I lost my soul along the way. I genuinely hope you never find yourself in a situation where vengeance seems your only hope because vengeance is not an answer at all in the end. It only escalates and spirals out of control until there is nothing left but ash and embers where your life once existed. I promise you, it's not worth what's left when the dust has settled.

I guess this was always the way things were destined to pan out for me. But please know that I am free now, at last, finally able to release the pain I've carried with me for so long.

Life will go on without us now, friends who loved life once. Everything I did, I did for my friends, yet it took until I actually killed a man for me to realise that no matter how bad life seems, you can always do things differently, be the better person and walk away from bitterness and anger. I didn't walk away. I allowed my pain to escalate until there was literally nothing left. Please don't ever be *like me. Don't allow revenge and despair to fuel your desires. It doesn't have a happy ending, of that I can promise you.*

*My own end now is fitting of a life I no longer wish to live. I am so tired, Andy. So exhausted by pain. I feel that I leave this world grateful in the knowledge that Ryan Miller can no longer hurt another female ever again. Of that certainty, I am thankful. Things that happen in your life define who you are, so please ensure you define your life by the good you do and the people you love. When all's said and done, I was fully prepared to take things to the bitter end and accept the consequence of my actions.*

*Thank you, my friend. Thank you so very much.*

*Craig*

# Acknowledgements

*Thank you to my incredible husband for supporting my writing journey and putting up with random plot ideas that popped into my head at the most inopportune moments. Thank you for offering your thoughts and making the ending of this book a truly emotional journey.*

*Thank you also to SRL Publishing for believing in my abilities and helping my author journey begin in earnest.*